O...
WAY or
Another

ALSO BY COLLEEN COLEMAN

Don't Stop Me Now
I'm Still Standing

One WAY or Another

COLLEEN COLEMAN

bookouture

Published by Bookouture in 2018

An imprint of StoryFire Ltd.

Carmelite House
50 Victoria Embankment
London EC4Y 0DZ
www.bookouture.com

ISBN: 978-1-78681-407-4
eBook ISBN: 978-1-78681-406-7

To Julian.
You are the love of my life and my best friend.
You asked me to surprise you, hope I have. Thank you for
making my life all that it is. Cx

CHAPTER ONE

'So there you are, Katie Kelly! Up to your bloody cheffy she-nanigans again.' My boss, Bernie, slams down her clipboard on the stainless-steel countertop and points at the door. 'Into my office, NOW.'

I go to open my mouth. A reasonable 'What have I done?' stuck in my throat, hovering over my tongue. But Mel and Zoe furrow their eyebrows at me, simultaneously, raising blue, plastic-gloved fingers to their lips. It's our code for keep your mouth shut and keep your job. This one little gesture of solidarity means we know batshit Bernie is no mere catering supervisor: no, she's a complete despotic maniac. So best just agree with whatever she says and remember, it's only a job, it's not worth losing my cool. Or my weekly salary. Or my self- respect just because the boss hates my guts.

I get it.

They're right.

I shut my mouth and loop my hairnet over both ears. Like it's a hard hat with the power to protect me from the verbal ambush that no doubt awaits me on the other side of Bernie's office door.

Mel starts to hum a tune. Cheery and upbeat and completely escapist, an effort to boost me up mentally, help me to remember the bigger picture.

The small picture being that I'm a hen-pecked catering assistant pulping beige mush in a retirement home eight hours a day.

I hum too, summoning perspective, trying to zoom out of this career-low scene, which is way too close-up for my liking.

Zoe must be able to read my thoughts because she calls out after me, 'Be the bigger person, Katie. Remember what we talked about… *rise above it.*'

I turn back to give her a weak smile and nod. This job is low but it's not rock bottom. Since my restaurant folded, it is pretty much the only thing between me and rock bottom. And like my friends keep telling me, it's just for a little while. It's just until I get back on my feet, just until something else comes along. I'll suck it up because there isn't any other option out there for me right now. I had my chance at being my own boss and I ballsed it up.

So here I am. Here I am at Parklands Senior Residence. Chief potato peeler. Executive pot-wash. Master blender of incongruous gloop into less lumpy incongruous gloop. But the silver lining is that it's full-time, five days a week, it pays okay, it's walking distance from the flat and it's what I'm qualified to do.

*Over*qualified to do… but hey, beggars can't be choosers. Like Bernie told me in my interview, a cook is a cook is a cook. Throw the food in the pot, serve it out on time and under budget, end of story.

So I take a deep breath and follow Bernie from the kitchen prep area to her office, biting the inside of my mouth with every step. Once I'm in, she slams the door behind me.

'Are you actually trying to kill our residents?' she screams at me.

I have absolutely no idea what she is talking about.

Bernie takes an oversized ziplock plastic bag out of her pocket and throws it on the table between us.

'*Contraband substances* is what I'm talking about!' She points to the small pouches of dried herbs. 'Parsley, eh? Oregano? Rosemary. Thyme. Nothing gets past me, let me tell you. I found these stashed behind the cans of soup. I've had my suspicions about you right from the get-go, Katie, and looks like I've been right all along.' She folds her arms and curls her whiskery top lip at me. 'So come on, let's hear it, Katie. I can hardly wait to see you try and worm your way out of this one.' She leans back on her table, smiling smugly.

'Fine. They're mine. I brought them in and put in a sprinkle to flavour the soup, so it would have, you know… some flavour.'

Bernie pushes her tongue hard into her cheek and snatches back the ziplock bag, unsealing it and sniffing the leaf like a customs officer. 'How many times, Katie? That's not how we do things around here. Herbs and spices and other fancy-pants stuff are not included on the recipe cards. And your job is to follow the recipe cards TO THE LETTER. Which you are clearly still not doing. And you're spending far too long on service chatting to the residents. Your role is to cook and serve the food the way we like it – that's it – not involve yourself in rambling conversations about the minutiae of their days. Which brings me to my second point, what about Mrs Rosenblatt's pudding?'

'I can explain that.'

Bernie pushes away from her desk and claps her hands together. 'I knew it! I knew it would be down to you, Katie, you and your so-called haute cuisine! Do you know what you did to her? She was on the toilet for three hours this morning. Three hours! The nurse thought she might have a gastric bug and wanted her hospitalised. But the old girl refused, said it was your pudding that caused it.'

'Excellent!' A smile breaks my lips. 'Mrs Rosenblatt told me she was constipated, she asked for my help. I knew a little prune and spiced pear crumble would get things going.'

Bernie makes a tight fist. 'You can't keep doing this. Breaking the rules, switching up the menus, creating your own meals for residents… it is *not* the way we do things around here.'

'So you just want me to clock in, throw the food in the pot and leave my brain and my heart at home.'

'Exactly.'

'Sorry, Bernie, not going to happen.'

She is kind of quaking right now. And growling. And turning a funny colour. I'd call it mottled meatball.

She leans towards me, jabbing her finger into the air in front of my face. 'I am so sick of you. I've told the Catering Manager straight that I'm not happy with you on my team. I told him everything – the constant changes you make, the way you don't listen to me, the way you backchat, the time you waste jabbering on to the residents during service. He agreed that as soon as anyone even half-qualified walks through those doors, you are gone from here. You don't fit in, you won't fit in, and I, for one, can never see a day that you *will* fit in. The only reason you are still tolerated around here is because we're so stuck.' Bernie clenches her jaw and narrows her angry eyes to slits.

I know she's saying this to try and hurt me, or frighten me, or bully me into doing things her way. But, actually, I echo everything she's said. I don't ever want to fit in here. And the only reason I'm here is because I'm stuck too.

I close my eyes and I think of my mother. I picture her in a supermarket car park years ago. Some crazed driver approached her and started yelling. The whole time she just smiled. When it all blew over, I asked her why she did that. Shouldn't she have yelled back? Shouldn't she have stood up for herself, scared him off? She said no. Sometimes it's best to smile at those who want to overpower you. It confuses the hell out of them.

So I open my eyes and give Bernie the biggest, brightest smile I can muster.

And I feel like my mum would be proud of me. And for that I smile even more.

Bernie shakes her head and sucks her teeth at me. 'Get out and take that great big stupid grin of yours with you.'

She throws open the door and I am free to leave.

'Bring Mrs Rosenblatt a soft cheese sandwich up to her room – *a plain soft cheese sandwich* – would you? It's the least you can do after all the upset you caused her.'

I give Bernie a thumbs up as I walk out her office door.

But there's no way I'm bringing Mrs Rosenblatt a plain soft cheese sandwich.

Because I like her way too much for that.

CHAPTER TWO

'Hey Mrs Rosenblatt! Heard the prune pud caused a bit of a stir – in more ways than one!'

Mrs Rosenblatt peers over her broadsheet paper at me, a giggle in her eyes. 'I feel a million dollars thanks to you.'

She is immaculately dressed, hair coiffed in her signature Elizabeth Taylor curls, her blue-kohled eyes smiling at me. Her room in the home is quite unlike any other; I imagine it's what a magpie's nest is like. Full of jewelled sparkliness in an array of shapes and colours, everything reflecting the light and catching your eye. Although Mrs Rosenblatt never leaves here, she still makes up her face each day with rouge and lipstick as if she's just about to go for pre-theatre drinks.

She shuffles up in her bed, the neckline of her dusky pink nightdress beautifully embroidered with sequinned peacocks. I love coming in here to see her. Every time I walk into her room, there's something that reminds me of walking into Santa's grotto, like there's still kindness and magic and possibility in the world and all I've got to do is be good and try my best and all will work out just fine. I've noticed that just being here makes my heart stop beating a thousand anxious raps a second. The moment I step in and smell the mingling scents of floral perfume and talc, it soothes me. It makes me feel like time has stopped and there's nothing to worry about, that everything will be all right if she tells me so in her ever-reassuring, dulcet voice.

I place the poached eggs and smoked salmon on a tray table by her bed.

'Lots of omega-3 in that,' I tell her. 'Good for brains, hearts and immune systems. So eat it all up.'

Mrs Rosenblatt holds out her hand. 'Come over here and give me a cuddle. You've made an old lady very happy indeed. It is small acts of kindness that make all the difference in a place like this. So enough of this Mrs Rosenblatt business. Martha. Call me Martha. Friends ought to refer to each other by their first names.'

I do as Martha asks and let her envelop me in a warm soft embrace. There is no comfort like it in the world. She smells like fresh linen and strawberry jam all at once.

Just before she tucks into her breakfast, I open her window and tear off a little peppermint from the small herb garden she has growing in her window box.

'Good for digestion, a little in hot water with a slice of lemon,' I explain.

Martha takes it from me and inhales the fresh, sweet smell. 'Oh that's joyous. Reminds me of Morocco. Oskar and I loved to roam the souks and feast on all their spicy wonders. Heaven. Yes, peppermint tea, that would be a real treat. Thank you, Katie, you do spoil me.' She points over to a heavy bound photo album which has morphed into more of a scrapbook, with invitations, concert tickets, postcards and personal letters stuffed between the pages. 'Pass that over if you would, so I can show you something.'

I fetch it from the small bookshelf by her wardrobe and hand it over to her.

My shift is finished now so I take a seat and she chats through her memories with me. All of her photographs are carefully glued to the thick card pages, each of them dated with captions in her elegant cursive handwriting. Such a life Martha had!

She flicks through to the middle and strokes her hand over a very small photo with a frilled border, its colours muted with age. It shows a much younger Martha, her hair pressed in perfect waves, and a man with a Poirot moustache grinning broadly into the camera whilst leading a camel in the desert.

'Cairo, that was our honeymoon. Oskar said that we should start our married life with an adventure and so we did. I was against it at first, too lavish. I protested, but Oskar would have none of it. He told me to *take the trip, buy the shoes, eat the cake*! This was his motto, and by golly did he live by it! So we took the trip. I arrived in Egypt a new bride and I left there an expectant mother. Adventure indeed. Oskar Rosenblatt, you sure knew how to show a girl a good time.'

She gently closes her album and I put it back in its special place. While she then leafs through her newspaper, we chat about films and books and holidays, about work and house prices and airline strikes and everything else in between. I prune the window box for her, water the herbs, and take a few leaves for myself. I'm not in a hurry. There isn't anything I need to do, nowhere I need to be. This is one huge difference I've found since I had to shut my own little restaurant, the relentless amount of time I've got. For the first time in my life, I have huge swathes of time. And I know that most people would think that this is enviable. But, actually, I hate it. I realise now that I was married to my role as restaurateur – so it feels like I've been dumped and deserted by an unrequited love. Because god knows I loved that restaurant; I gave it everything. I gave up everything else to focus on it completely, to give it my all. For me it really was till death do us part – although it was more like till *debt* do us part in the end…

All this endless, aimless time has been one of the worst, and most unforeseen, results of going near bankrupt and losing my job and business. I no longer use my time productively, which makes me frustrated with myself even more. I use it to spend too long reading labels in little delis that I can't afford to shop in and flicking through food channels and browsing cakes on Pinterest and Instagram and dragging my feet along the long walk home, which brings me past my locked-up restaurant. The curtains drawn, a 'For Lease' sign in the window. Being time-rich and cash-poor is zero fun. I need to be busy, to have a structure, a purpose, a goal. Before, I ate drank, ate, slept, bathed and burped my restaurant-baby. It consumed every waking moment. There were not enough minutes in the hour, not enough hours in the day. No time for myself, or my family, or my boyfriend, Ben. Well, that's what he told me just before he left to chase his big break abroad. And now that everything is all over, with Ben and with my restaurant, I'm at a complete loss as to what I'm supposed to be doing with myself.

So at first, to put a silver lining on things, I thought, well, I'll have oodles of time now to do all the stuff I couldn't because I was working so damn long and hard. I can get fit, go on some dates, take up a new, life-enhancing hobby.

But the truth is I'm no good with all this time on my hands. I don't want to lift dumb-bells or sit in a pub with a stranger or learn how to paint in watercolour.

All I want to do is chef. I doubt that's ever going to change. And now that I can't, well, killing time is killing me. What I had before was a very brief chance at heaven. I had a boyfriend I loved and a career that made me tingle with excitement. Every. Single. Day. Losing them has been hell. So I guess I'm stuck washing spuds in this purgatory until something else comes along for me.

I stick on the kettle and make us both another peppermint tea.

'Katie, I'm puzzled,' says Martha, holding up her newspaper. 'I need to ask you, what on earth is a "snowflake"?'

'Snowflake?' I repeat and shrug. Martha was a top city banker and she certainly hasn't lost her marbles so I know it must something beyond the obvious. 'What's the context?' I ask her.

She holds out the newspaper to me. 'Go to the back page, you'll recognise that vile man. Jean-Michel Marchand. Complete narcissist if I ever saw one… He's taken a full-page ad out. Shameless exhibitionist. I met him, once: tiny man, gigantic ego.'

I turn to the back page. And sure enough, there he is. Jean-Michel, the most famous chef in the country, has taken out a full-page ad featuring his life-size face, so close up it's as if he is really staring right back at me. In big bold letters across the top of the page reads, 'Do YOU have what it takes to be Jean-Michel's next Grand Chef?'

I take a seat on the soft corner of Martha's bed.

Martha sits up and points to the small print under his chin. 'See there at the bottom, it says "No home chefs or snowflakes need apply." What on earth does he mean by that?'

Wow. Jean-Michel is looking for a chef. Not any old chef. A Grand Chef.

'Do you know what he means, Katie?'

I turn to answer her, peeling my eyes away from a face I've studied in recipe books and on television since the moment I knew that food was my future. 'I can't be sure, Martha, but I think it's kind of a derogatory label for my generation. Some say that we can't handle real life and we take offence to everything. So they call us "snowflakes" because they say that we think we're special and unique and have an inflated sense of entitlement but don't know what hard work is, so we melt easily under pressure.'

Martha taps her finger on the paper and shakes her head. 'I wouldn't expect anything less than sensational nonsense from such a brute.'

'He may be a brute. But he's also a culinary god.'

She considers me a moment then slides her glasses up her nose. 'You should go for this, Katie. Throughout my entire life, I have been wined and dined and eaten the most wonderful meals by the most esteemed chefs and I can tell that you have that in you too. That passion, that work ethic.'

Yep. I know this spiel. It's sweet, but it can really lead you in the wrong direction if you take it seriously. Make you believe anything is possible, yada yada.

'Thanks, Martha, but it takes more than that. I already had my shot. All that "*go for it, you can do it, if you can dream it, you can achieve it*". I bought into that, hook, line and sinker. And both me and my debt manager can tell you, it's not true. It's a very expensive and painful delusion that passion and hard work is enough to succeed.'

Martha purses her lips and narrows her eyes at me. 'Are you a home chef?'

I shake my head. 'Um, no! I passed my four-year program at Le Cordon Bleu in London. I'm a fully qualified French cuisine chef.'

'Are you a snowflake?'

I laugh. 'Do you seriously think that any person with an inflated sense of entitlement would work here? With Bernie?'

Martha taps her finger on the paper and meets my gaze. 'Well then. You've got what it takes. Applications cut off at midnight tonight, so I suggest you pull your finger out, chef.'

I blink my gratitude for the well-intended compliment, however misguided. It is really nice that she wants to big me up, give me a dream to chase. But Jean-Michel is a shark. He'd chew me up and spit me out. It was already impossible to get a decent cheffing gig after my grand failure, so a bad word from Jean-Michel would finish me off in the fine dining world altogether.

'I appreciate the confidence, Martha, but as you rightly say, the man is a brute. He expects, he *demands*, perfection at every point. I'm good, but I'm not good enough for him. This is a whole different level. Every serious chef in the country would want to be in a kitchen with Jean-Michel; the competition would be outrageous. And cut-throat. So even if I got through, he'd throw me out in the first stages of selection. The smart thing to do would be to save myself the time and trouble.'

Martha takes both my hands in hers. 'You know, being old isn't as bad as you may think. It brings with it great wisdom, it means you see things differently. And, Katie, I see you here, every day, struggling. So I'm going to tell you this plain and simple. You think you are saving time and trouble staying put? Wrong. Because, sweetheart, whether we are twenty-nine or eighty-nine years old, none of us can take our futures for granted. None of us have time or chances to waste. Your time is *now*, honey; take it or somebody else will.'

And in that instant something sparks, deep inside me. It feels hot and urgent like anger and ambition and outrage and passion and it's burning up in my chest.

The crippling overheads and soaring rent took my restaurant from me, the promise of promotion and adventure took my boyfriend from me, cruel and ruthless illness took my mother from me. Bernie's even taken my herbs from me for crying out loud.

I can't let anything else be taken.

Nothing else is up for grabs.

I look back at the photograph of Jean-Michel. This phenomenal chance to work with one of the greatest living chefs is up for grabs. I take in the anger and ambition and outrage creased in his brow, the manic intensity in his eyes, the tightness in his jaw, and the defiant rise of his chin. He wouldn't stay put. He wouldn't settle for anything less than perfect.

What would Jean-Michel do if he were here, right now, in my current position? Fresh from another robust bollocking with the biggest opportunity in the culinary world staring him in the face? He'd take it. He'd grab it. One way or another, he'd fight his way out, claw his way back and rise above everything else that got in his way.

I study his lips, his fingers, the deep lines burrowed across his forehead like old battle scars. Who are you, *really*, Jean-Michel? How did you build your empire? How did you get to where you are today? What makes you tick? What's your secret?

I shake my head in confusion and fascination. One thing's for sure: if there's a teacher out there worth learning from, it's him.

Martha reaches out and gives my elbow a gentle squeeze. 'Katie, with the greatest respect, what have you got to lose?'

We both know the answer to that.

CHAPTER THREE

'What the…?'

Alice, my best friend and, luckily, home-owner and provider of emergency accommodation when I could no longer afford my rent, stands in the doorway with her mouth open and the palms of her hands pressed to her cheeks.

'I will tidy everything up. I promise… Those pots are just soaking.'

Alice kicks off her work heels and unhooks her bra, sliding it out the sleeve of her blouse and throwing it over the armchair. This is the moment Alice waits for all day long, the moment of freedom as she steps into the privacy of her own flat where she can exhale and get comfy and she doesn't have to be uptight-Alice-the-meticulous-employment-lawyer any more.

'Oh that feels good. And *wow*, does that smell good.' She wriggles out of her black pencil skirt and throws on a pair of shorts.

I look away from the steak I'm cooking and around at the kitchen space that I have completely taken over. On every ring of the hob there's a pan, every inch of counter space is over-run with the contents of the fridge and the cupboards… Ingredients, knives, chopping boards, weighing scales, hand whisks, wine, whisky… For stocks and sauces, obviously.

'Sorry, Alice, I know it's like a bomb has hit. I got a bit carried away. Surprise, surprise.'

She sidles over, wrapping one arm around my shoulder. 'No, I don't care. You're cooking again! That's GREAT!' She dips her baby finger in to the creamy cognac sauce I've just taken off the heat. 'Holy shit, Katie. This is insane. I need that sauce in my life.' She grabs the wine bottle and pours herself a glass. 'Tell me I'm eating that tonight and it will nearly erase the last eight hours from my consciousness.'

I ladle a small bowlful out for her and hand her a chunk of bread. 'Did you eat today?'

She shakes her head. 'No time.' She begins dunking into the sauce.

'Are you okay?' Poor Alice, she's always been the brainy one, and right now, it feels like she's being punished for it. Every time she feels it's time to leave, they dangle a new carrot in front of her or guilt her into taking on just one more client and then the cycle starts again with them making promises that they don't keep.

Alice shrugs. 'I will be. It's nothing. Just the same old work stuff. Doesn't matter now; I'm home and you're here, and this sauce is making me want to have its babies, so… Forget it, it's all good now. Everything wrong has now been put right.' She dunks another warm crusty hunk into her bowl and starts to foodgasm.

Just as well she doesn't dine out very often.

She shudders and hits a really high note. 'This is too good, as in *The Best Yet*. I need it on prescription. Actually, no, I need to step away now. Cut ties, knock it on the head.'

Alice is my best critic. She adores food but has no idea what goes together and has been caught dipping vegetable crudités into Nutella. Poor colour choices drive her mad – wear a lipstick that's more ketchup than siren red and Alice will disown you – but will she feed herself a dinner of curry Pot Noodle on a bed of blue cheese? Oh yes, she will.

Alice mops up the last of the sauce, kissing it before she throws it back into her mouth. 'Is there an AA for carbs?'

When she finally stops whimpering and sighing and opens her eyes again, she's back to being Alice. Her eyes are wide and clear and full of excitement. There's colour back in her cheeks and her entire body has relaxed. She looks at me. 'What's brought this on? Has something happened? I thought you were done with all this.'

I point to the fridge, where Jean-Michel's intense glare is now staring from the door, the full newspaper page pinned with alphabet magnets.

She squints to read the heading. 'Do YOU have what it takes to be Jean-Michel's next Grand Chef?' Her fingers fly to her mouth, her eyes blinking. 'Are you serious?'

'Deadly serious,' I tell her.

'But he is *psychotic*. Haven't you seen the documentary they made about him? We actually watched part of it as a training course in rights and responsibilities, because the way he treats his staff, the language, the culture of fear and intimidation… It's illegal! I can't believe he hasn't been sued yet. Why would you want to do this to yourself, Katie? You've been through enough. Give yourself a break.' She pulls a face.

I shake my head. 'I hear you. But I've had a break and I'm ready. I know it sounds crazy but I miss it. I miss the crazy.'

At this Alice balls her fists and gently pounds either side of her head. 'You know that *is* crazy, right? I put up with a lot at work. I have a sneery boss breathing down my neck and looking down my top. I get to the office in the dark and go home in the dark – I spend no more than the eight minutes a day I take for lunch in the sunlight. I have more conversations with screens than with people. But go work in a high-stress environment with an infamously erratic chef as my boss? Um, even I don't want that much crazy, thank you very much.'

'That's different. You've got a proper career, you've got a mortgage. Even if nobody likes you at work, at least they respect you.'

Alice flashes me her middle finger. 'Fine. But actually it's me who doesn't like *them*. And they don't like each other either. And nobody feels happy and supported. We are all equally miserable.'

I carve up the steak that's been resting on a plate and hand her a nice juicy strip on a fork. 'Remember how we thought we were going to take London by storm? Great jobs, great social scene, great friends?'

Alice nods enthusiastically. 'Yes. Public me: total London baby, doing so much better than all our classmates who settled down in small rural towns. Actual me: I spend most of my waking hours filled with a blind rage at strangers online and if my Facebook Year in Review video were honest, it'd just be quick cuts of me screaming and using the word "fuck" as various parts of speech. Where'd it all go so wrong?'

I nudge her in the elbow. 'We got the *great friends* bit right.'

She smiles at this. 'Yeah. And I'm having a great night: come home to a gourmet meal by your own live-in private chef, what more could you ask for, right? Now all I need is a massage and sixteen million pounds. We're in a rut, but yeah, as far as ruts go, this ain't the worst. So, that just leaves the shitty jobs. Crack that and we'll have it made.'

And then I hold up my secret weapon, my one-hundred-year-old cast-iron skillet pan and place it on the stove top.

Alice understands immediately. She knows what bringing out the pan means. She bites down on her bottom lip and smiles. 'Right. Well, crack on. Grand Chef it is then. So this is the final part of the puzzle! Clearly you have to have someone to act as chief taster. Where do we start?'

I tell her all about the selection process: first an online application, and then a shortlist will be invited to Jean-Michel's kitchen to prepare their signature dish in less than fifteen minutes in front of a judging panel. After that, a series of tasks will whittle down the final candidates and then they'll have to fight it out until the Grand Chef is chosen.

I fill both our glasses and we raise them in the air.

'Whatever doesn't kill you makes you stronger right?'

Alice tilts her head. 'You do know it was Nietzsche who said that. While he was dying of syphilis.'

'Okay then, smart-arse.' I slosh more wine into the glass I've already emptied and break off another chunk of bread. 'How about *whatever doesn't kill you leaves you with a lot of unhealthy coping mechanisms and a dark sense of humour?*'

'Weirdly biographical.'

We clink glasses again and Alice breaks in to a giggle as she licks her fingers 'At least there's this.' She holds the bread up in front of her. 'This is literally the only sensory experience left. Sometimes, I just think that I might as well fully embrace a life of celibacy and then go live in a big country house in the middle of somewhere gorgeous, drink wine, eat cheese, stop waxing and just let myself go completely.'

I grin at her. 'Don't stop believing.'

She pretends she can't hear me and changes the subject. 'So when will you find out if you are shortlisted?' she asks.

'Closing date for applications is midnight tonight. I sent mine through already, so I guess I'll hear in the next week or so. But I want to start practising now, just in case I get the call. You can't over-prepare for Jean-Michel.'

I finish making my signature steak Diane, we drink a bottle of red each, we crack open the crisps cupboard, and we draw cartoons of Alice's workmates and make up limericks about them. We imagine we are on death row and think of all the amazing things we'd order as our last meal... No issue of cost or calories. Finally, I bid Alice goodnight as she slopes off to her bedroom and I pull up the sleeping bag onto her sofa. This has been my nightly routine for nearly two years now whilst I've been repaying my debts and then trying to scrimp and save enough for a deposit of my own.

I know I've done the right thing. It's out of my hands now; I've sent my application, all I can do is wait. The waiting will be the hardest part. Not knowing how or when or if I'll hear back. A flicker of the possibility that I don't make it, that I don't get through and I don't get called flits across my mind. And that makes me feel sick, even more than the huge quantities of cheesy Wotsits Alice and I have munched through.

And in that instant, I understand how important this is to me. How much this means. My last venture was an epic failure so I've got an awful lot to prove. To everyone, but especially all the Bernies of the world who think I'm just a jumped-up pain in the arse. I need to show *myself* that I'm more than a jumped-up pain in the arse wasting time, that I'm pursuing something that's actually going to lead somewhere, someday. Prove to my dad that moving away from my family in Ireland was worth it all in the first place, prove to my sister, Rachel, that I am happy and getting on despite the failed restaurant, prove to my brothers that I'm a survivor, strong enough to handle whatever comes my way and prove to myself that I made the right choice choosing my career over Ben.

My phone starts to ring. I presume it's a wrong number or a butt dial. No one would ring me at this time of night, unless it's family…

It's an unknown number but, half-drunk and unable to reason, I decide to answer it, just in case.

'Hello? Who is this?' I ask, panicked at the thought that it is my dad and something has happened to him.

'Is this Katie Kelly?' The voice is low, deep, gravelly. The line is terrible, but this person doesn't sound English or Irish. I can't place the accent. My heart starts to pound in my chest as my mind races.

'Yes, who wants to know?' I am kneeling up on the sofa now, my hand quivering.

'*I* want to know. Jean-Michel Marchand.'

I scramble forward to standing. Is this a prank? I clap my hand over my mouth. I want to scream down the phone that calling at this time has scared the living shit out of me. Who the hell rings at this time of night! I swallow hard. Good God, Jean-Michel, you really are a bastard.

'You have made the cut. Be at the Rembrandt Hotel, Chelsea tomorrow at 4 p.m., wear chef whites. Bring your own ingredients. You must prepare a dish in less than fifteen minutes for the pre-selection panel.'

'Are you joking? How did you—?'

'Instinct. The first mark of any leader is exceptional instinct. Without instinct, you are a follower, not a leader.'

And the line goes dead.

I guess that's Jean-Michel's way of saying congratulations.

But to be honest I don't care how he says it. Everyone in my family is safe and I've just got off the phone with *Jean-Michel Marchand*.

I made the cut. My name has been shortlisted. He knew my name. He called my phone.

And tomorrow has just become the biggest day of my life.

I've passed the first stage.

I'm cooking tomorrow.

For Jean-Michel. The crazy, erratic, angry, genius bastard that he is.

I grab my pen and paper and start scribbling down my ingredients list and then I set my alarm for three hours from now.

Because I know exactly where and when the best cuts of steak can be found, and that means being at Smithfield Market at 4 a.m. I've been dealing with this particular butcher forever. He always does a little deal for me as a loyal customer, throws in a little something extra: a second fillet, a few chops or stewing steak. So I imagine whatever happens, myself and Alice will be feasting again tonight.

I pull the blankets up to my chin and try to force myself asleep. Sleep. As if.

Maybe I *am* crazy.

But I do know that whether I force myself to sleep or not, the alarm will sound and I will throw everything I've got at Jean-Michel.

One way or another.

CHAPTER FOUR

I arrive at the interview with everything I need in the basket of my bike. It seems quiet; perhaps I'm the only one? Is Jean-Michel's instinct that selective?

I enter through the front doors of the ultra-plush Rembrandt Hotel and am met with a typed sign: 'Grand Chef Pre-Interview Auditions, please enter through kitchen entrance at right-hand side of building.'

I step out and turn the corner, where I am met with a sight that makes my heart stop. There are at least thirty chefs in a snake-like queue, looking as terrified as I feel.

This is my competition. Clearly Jean-Michel's instinct is more scattergun than sharp-shooter.

I step up to the administrator seated by the door.

'Name?' he asks.

'Katie Kelly.'

He hands me a sticky label with number 48. 'Ingredients?'

I hand him my bag. He sticks a 48 on that also.

'Name of dish?'

'Steak Diane.'

He looks up at me. 'Are you serious?'

I nod.

He shrugs and writes 'Steak' on the sheet. Then he looks back up at me. 'Is that a frying pan in your hand?'

'A skillet.'

'You're going to cook in a fully equipped kitchen. There is no reason to bring your own pan.'

'Yes, there is,' I tell him.

He sighs. 'Of course. You're a chef. I'm sure it makes perfect sense to you in your own head. As sensible as serving steak to Jean-Michel.' He raises an eyebrow and laughs dryly. 'Now, that is going to be memorable. Should he expect a McFlurry for dessert?'

I tighten my grip on my skillet pan and look back at the queue. There are people of all ages: some very senior, experienced-looking chefs with manicured silver moustaches, some young, slick guys in their early twenties, exuding confidence and poise. There are a handful of women, though not very many, which is typical in this industry; some put it down to the brutality and violence of the kitchen environment, the institutional sexism, whereas others say it's because the hours are so long and family-unfriendly that we lose our best female talent early on. Either way, male or female, young or old, experienced or fresh out of training, we are all here for one thing: the opportunity to work with the god that is Jean-Michel, to stretch and challenge ourselves, to reach the zenith of culinary excellence, to work alongside the best and, perhaps, even *become* the best…

The admin guy clicks his tongue and hands me a questionnaire and a pen. 'You can fill this in while you are waiting. You're in the last call. So far we're on schedule. Four candidates will be called each round to prepare and serve their dishes to Jean-Michel and his panel. We've had one or two drop out already – nerves got the better of them – so keep your ears open for your number in case we call you early. Otherwise, join the back of the line and good luck.'

I thank him, press my sticky label to my chest and join the back of the queue, taking the chance to read through the single-page questionnaire. I check the back page too but it appears there are only two questions. How hard can it be?

Question One: What are your top ten professional rules?

Easy! I start to scribble down my answers. I know them like the back of my hand; they used to be laminated on the tiled wall of my own little restaurant.

1 – My KNIVES are my KNIVES – HANDS OFF!

If you are looking for a sure-fire way to bring a cook to insanity – try picking up his or her knives to use without asking.

2 – DON'T be LATE – On TIME is AT LEAST 15 MINUTES EARLY.
3 – I MAY YELL AT TIMES TO GET A POINT ACROSS – DON'T TAKE IT PERSONALLY.

Some may view this as the creation of a hostile work environment and it can certainly be seen as just that, but when used sparingly it can be effective.

4 – WORK CLEAN – ALWAYS!
5 – SWEAT the DETAILS – It's ALL in the DETAILS.
6 – NEVER SACRIFICE QUALITY for SPEED, NEVER SACRIFICE SPEED for QUALITY, be PREPARED for BOTH.
7 – You START it – You OWN it.

Put a pan on the stove, turn on the flame, add a bit of oil, and walk away assuming that someone else will keep an eye on it for you? I think not.

8 – A HANGOVER is not an EXCUSE. (Drunk is not an excuse either btw.)
9 – In THE HEAT of SERVICE – ALL for ONE and ONE for ALL.

10 – STAY PROFESSIONAL – DON'T be a DICKHEAD.

There is no room in a professional kitchen for renegades who think that all of this is a joke. This is serious business and your cooperation is essential. If you want to be a rebel and come across as an arse, then I would encourage you to look for work elsewhere before the crew decides to straighten you out.

These are my top ten rules for professional life, which I stick to religiously. In light of my closed-down restaurant, I should probably add: 'Get someone who knows their arse from their elbow when it comes to the business side of things and hire someone reputable to do the books.' But this is a pure cheffing gig; I won't have to concern myself with pricing or quantities or tax or budgets. All I get to do is dream and create and cook. Sounds like heaven from where I'm standing.

Question Two: What is your one personal rule for life?

Hmm. I re-read the question to make sure I've understood correctly. Who on earth cares about this? Why isn't there another question on food or experience or technique or future possibilities? I have never known a chef to even *talk* about their personal life never mind sit and contemplate rules… Maybe Jean-Michel is certifiably insane. Already, this is turning out to be the strangest and most unpredictable job interview I've ever gone for. Midnight phone calls, queuing with a motley crew of candidates in an alley, philosophical questions on a questionnaire… It's all bizarre, completely out of the ordinary. But I guess that's because the prize is extra-ordinary.

I glance back down at the question and try to come up with something, anything, that makes me sound like a deep and thoughtful person whose personal life is completely under control. I feel a flutter of panic as my mind draws a complete blank. I hate this feeling; it reminds me of being in school; not knowing what is expected of me, exposing myself to looking really stupid.

I take a deep breath and tell myself to get a grip. This is the last bit of paperwork I need to fill out and then I can get into the kitchen and back into my stride.

One personal rule for life. It's tricky as I've never thought about rules for my personal life; it's never crossed my mind. *On my honour, I promise to serve God and my country, to help people at all times and live by the Girl Scout Law.* Right, I think the last line's a bit of a giveaway, so it's going to be hard to claim that as my own.

What's the use in having a personal rule for life anyway? It implies that there is some kind of rulebook, and a set of rules that are actually implemented, that are adhered to by one and all. But life doesn't work like that. Rules are broken, ignored and discarded *all the time*. Drivers cut up cyclists at junctions. People like Bernie get to be in charge. There's a Big Mac sold every twenty seconds and my little restaurant didn't see its first birthday. Young families are forced to grow up without their beautiful loving mothers.

A rule for life? I'm seriously struggling here.

What I want to write is 'don't waste your time answering ridiculous questions'. But I know from my own school exams that it is less than impressive to upset the examiners.

I look up and down the snaking queue of fellow hopefuls. Some are also filling out their questionnaires, and look like they're struggling too, especially a portly chef fiddling with the gelled tips of his carefully groomed moustache. And then I know exactly what I'm going to write. Courtesy of Mr Poirot-moustache himself, Oskar Rosenblatt, I write down in my neatest handwriting: 'Life is short. Take the Trip, Buy the Shoes, Eat the Cake.' Done.

I'm more than satisfied with my questionnaire, and just as I finish handing it back to the administrator, I hear the bolt of a metal door clang and see four chefs straggle out. They are all shaking their heads. One is holding her clenched fist to her nose and is sobbing uncontrollably.

Nobody in the queue budges forward to help her, but everyone turns to take a look.

This must be the first group. I'm judging by their ghostly pallor that none of them were successful, but they don't look like they've just come from a kitchen. They look like they've been spewed out of a house of horrors.

The crying girl whips off her chef hat and opens her eyes.

I lean forward to take a closer look. She looks very familiar. In fact, she looks exactly like Georgia Jacobs, a girl I trained with. A girl that I didn't exactly get too friendly with as she never stopped flirting and throwing herself at Ben the entire four years we were all in the same class.

She takes a huge gulp of air and starts crying even harder.

The admin guy stands from his chair and places his hand on the small of her back rather roughly. 'Okay, hard luck. But please move on now. We need to keep the passage to the doors clear.'

Georgia is rooted to the spot, her nose starting to stream. This is very hard to watch.

I reach in to my pocket for a tissue and call out to her. 'Georgia?'

She turns in my direction and finds my face immediately, a wave of relieved recognition washing over her features.

I leave my place in the line-up and wrap my arm around her shoulder, gently taking her out of the way of the queue and all the gawping faces making her misery even worse. 'Come on over here, give yourself a bit of space.'

Georgia walks with me and we lean against the wall. 'Oh my god, Katie. You're here too! Don't do it. It was awful. He is a pig. He is an absolute vile, evil, arrogant, bastardy pig.'

I give her another tissue. She blows her nose and wipes her eyes before raising them to meet mine.

'He took one look at my dish and said, "You really do surprise me, that you can be so well trained and serve something so crap". He cut through my venison and said it looked like dehydrated turd.'

'Wow, venison, that was brave. Especially because I remember that desserts were your thing. Seriously, Georgia, your petits fours were always mind-blowing.'

Georgia nods and takes a deep breath, but her eyes are starting to pool again. 'And then he tasted my jus and said it was bland, tasteless piss and that his grandmother could do better... and she's dead.'

Holy shit. I bite down on my lip. Jean-Michel is clearly not holding back in there. If anything, he sounds even more scathing than I imagined. Maybe the admin guy was right, maybe my steak will be utterly underwhelming... Shit, what can I do? I've sent my ingredients in, there is no time to change now...

'And then he stood up, and he said, "What if this muck was served up to a critic? What if *The Times Review* judged me on this? You know what that would do to me? To my career?" Then he took my plate and threw the whole thing in the bin.'

Oh my god. I put my hand on Georgia's shoulder. Even though I wasn't her biggest fan at college, I certainly don't like seeing her so upset.

'He said, "That is rubbish and so are you".'

My own heart is beating at a thousand beats a second and I feel a cold sweat coming on. I'm scared. I'm properly terrified now about what's going to happen, what he's going to say to me.

'Oh Georgia, that's awful. Don't take it to heart...'

I'm struggling to know what to say. It's on the tip of my tongue to add 'what does he know?' But it's Jean-Michel, he knows everything. If anyone knows venison from dehydrated turd, it's him.

I try to change the subject, to distract her. 'Where are you working now?'

'At The Buckingham, I'm pastry chef.' A flash of a smile passes over her lips.

'The Buckingham! That's fantastic, Georgia. I've heard such good things. So forget Jean-Michel, you've got a great kitchen, and as a pastry chef, well, you are already way up the ladder, right?' If she knew my situation, she'd really appreciate how far ahead she is. The Buckingham is a world away from my kitchen at Parklands.

She nods and wipes her eyes with the sleeve of her chef jacket. 'I heard about your restaurant. Sorry it didn't work out.'

I nod and try to paste on a smile. 'Yeah, me too. But we all get setbacks, right? Guess we just got to dust ourselves off and fight another day.'

This time Georgia nods, appearing to take some comfort in my failure. 'And how's Ben?'

Bloody hell, Georgia, I thought I was the one trying to cheer you up.

I shrug. 'We're not together any more.'

Back at college Georgia would have pounced all over Ben's single status, but now she just bites down on her bottom lip. 'That's a real shame. You two were like the perfect couple.'

That's sweet. *Bittersweet.*

'Well, turns out we both wanted different things. He was desperate to see the world so he took a job on a luxury cruise ship and I stayed put to open the restaurant.'

'Wow, and how does he like it?'

I shrug. 'Good, I guess. I mean, he didn't come back, so I can only assume he's really happy and loves it. We're not in touch now. It's been a couple of years.'

And then, without warning, we hear the bolt of the metal doors crack open once more. Another shell-shocked foursome are dispatched.

But this time it's the men who are all crying.

CHAPTER FIVE

Number 48.

I walk into the open-plan kitchen and I see *Number 48, Katie Kelly* written on a Post-it note on the corner station.

I turn to my left and there are three other chefs also standing by, our ingredients laid out in front of us.

I check out my area; everything is spotlessly clean and perfectly set out. So far so good. I've got fifteen minutes to make or break this.

The main kitchen door swings open and three judges file into the service area – in full view of everyone and everything.

I feel like I'm about to have a heart attack.

A maître d' leads each to their high stool and stands tall beside them. Martha was right, Jean-Michel is a small man. Much shorter and skinnier than I imagined – but I guess I've never been this close before to anyone I've only seen on the screen or in print. Especially someone as legendary as Jean-Michel – and yet here he is in the flesh, just as remarkably short as Martha mentioned but every bit as enigmatic as I'd imagined. He's a man who is used to walking into a room and commanding it. The judges finish settling into their seats. The maître d' rings the bell for our attention. My heart can't possibly beat any faster than it is right now.

'Thank you for your patience. In a moment we will begin. I introduce to you our judging panel, award-winning chef Jean-Michel Marchand, renowned sommelier and food critic Pip Taylor and global hotelier of The Rembrandt group, Octavia Timmins.

Today they shall observe your basic technical skills, the quality of your palate and assess your suitability for this highly sought-after position. I have no need to tell you that being selected to work for the world's most famous chef is truly a once-in-a-lifetime opportunity. The education you will receive from this culinary savant is beyond extraordinary. Jean-Michel has made a mark by being the youngest chef to have received three Michelin stars, at the age of thirty-three.'

Jean-Michel lightly strokes his own chest as he listens to this glowing accolade of all his achievements. He remains silent, head bowed, eyes closed.

'He is not just the king of culinary but also a kingmaker of sorts, for he has trained his students to become top chefs around the world. Today is your day to have your name pass the lips of these three extraordinary leaders. *Bonne chance*. Your time starts now.' He hits the timer. I light the gas.

I have fifteen minutes to change my life. Every millisecond counts.

Pip walks over to my station, inspecting my knives, my ingredients and finally, my face.

'Katie. Talk me through what you are offering us today.'

I pause my prep and raise my gaze to answer him even though all I want to do is power through. 'Classic steak Diane. Filet mignon takes well to sautéing in a simple pan sauce of shallots, butter, mustard and cream that's laced with brandy and set aflame – that cooks off the alcohol and contributes rich caramel notes to the dish.'

'Steak is a pretty safe choice.' He sniggers, hunching his shoulders. 'You really think it's going to be enough to get you through?'

'Absolutely, sir. This cut was bought from the best butcher in Smithfield market this morning. I've brought my own skillet pan to finish. It's nearly one hundred years old and has never seen soap or water. Passed down the generations from my great-grandmother to my nana to my mother and then to me.'

Pip looks amused. 'You believe this makes a difference?'

'All the difference, sir.' I tell him without looking away.

He keeps eye contact with me a moment longer, appearing to search for some kind of code or clue to my character, then taps his forefinger against his lips. 'Too elaborate is risky but too simple can be risky too. I hope you can pull it off, Katie.'

So do I.

I lose myself in my preparations whilst the judges circulate the room until I notice Octavia approaching my station, observing every move I make. She stands like a statue. It's impossible to read her from her face or body movements, or indeed her icy silence. Finally, she crosses both hands across her chest and finds my gaze.

'How long have you been cooking?' asks Octavia.

'Since I was thirteen years old,' I tell her as I tilt my pan, watching the golden butter bubble and froth. 'I come from a big family and I took over the family kitchen and cooked every night for them from a young age.'

'What's the food dream, Katie?'

I can't stop to answer; I just have to keep talking as I pivot from one counter to the other, my priority being to plate this up on time. 'To create something special, something memorable. I want to bring people together,' I tell her over the steam and sizzle. 'To give them something to remember and a place to make those memories.'

Octavia nods and gives me a very curt smile. This could mean that she understands exactly what I mean. Or that she thinks I'm a babbling idiot.

I turn up the gas. I need the pan smoking hot. The clock is ticking; I need to get my sauce off and my steak on.

Octavia leaves my side and moves on to another chef. Jean-Michel has not said one word to me. He's paced by me a few times but not even made eye contact. Maybe the admin guy was right; maybe my steak is too simple, maybe Jean-Michel has already dismissed me as someone plain and dull and below average.

My hand starts to quiver and then the real shakes take over. I get it sometimes with nerves. Always during exams, my pen would quiver like a jaunty polygraph across the page, spilling the truth of my anxiety. Once I got to catering college, I thought I'd have more control over it as I'd be moving away from Maths and English and into my comfort zone of food, but it appears any time I feel under scrutiny, any time I feel like I'm being judged, the trembling and shaking returns, near impossible to control and even harder to hide. Far from ideal when I've only got this one shot to cook something extraordinary to secure my future.

I have no idea where I am here; I can't work out what they are thinking, what it is they are looking for. Am I in first place? Last place? Token laughing stock? In the bin with Georgia's venison? Oh dear God, what if Jean-Michel rips me to shreds in here in front of all these people just like he did to Georgia? My hand is now quaking so much it looks like I'm holding an invisible vibrating wand. I have no choice but to stop, lay down my knife and breathe in deeply and slowly, try and steady myself before I lose any more precious time.

'Five minutes remaining,' calls the maître d'.

Great. No pressure then.

My plate is warm and ready, my garnish is set, my steak is now cooked beautifully, the right side of rare, and will be rested to perfection for service, my Alice-approved brandy sauce is silken. I taste it with my pinkie… Seasoning spot on, texture just right. I grab the handle of my skillet pan and raise it off the heat; I've just got to get it on the plate and I'm done. I'm proud. It's good, I know it is. I get what Pip is talking about, but I've selected the finest ingredients and I've done them justice. He's right that too simple is risky, because if I don't get this perfect there is nowhere to hide; my technical ability is thoroughly transparent here. If I get steak wrong, then I don't belong here – and it's back to Bernie and her gravy granules with Pedigree Chum.

I've got this. I can feel it. I've just got to let my hand know so it stops shaking.

Hang on… It can't be. It can't be him.

Out of the corner of my eye, I see a man who looks exactly like my ex-boyfriend Ben walk through the swinging kitchen doors and straight up to the maître d', and for a split second I do a double take. The heat, the pressure, the sleeplessness, the desperation: it's all clearly getting to me. From my trembling fingertips to my visions of Ben's gobsmacked face, this process is already pushing me to the edge. Because this can't be right… I *can't* be seeing this properly; it just can't be, because the person I think I see in front of me is sailing around the world. This doesn't make any sense… There is no way that *Ben Cole* has just walked through those doors. *My* Ben. *Those* doors. Well, my ex-Ben. But still *those* doors.

I blink my eyes shut and when I reopen them it's even worse. Because it is, without a doubt: the same soft black hair, same olive skin, same beautiful full lips always resting in a side-smile. It's the same Ben all right, right here, right now, smack bang in this very kitchen. And he is staring straight back at me, a stunned, disbelieving look in his eyes too. I take a deep breath, grab the tongs and lift my steak over to the plate and then, from nowhere, my hand jolts upward of its own accord. Then the steak isn't there any more. It is not in the tongs, it is not on the plate.

It is on the *floor*.

I dropped my steak. I dropped my freaking perfectly cooked filet mignon on to the floor.

This is all it takes for everything to change. For my world to stop dead. For it all to be over. Just a split-second flickering lapse in concentration, an unexpected vision and a quivering hand and my absolute worst nightmare has occurred.

This cannot be happening. Oh, too late. It already has.

I look up to the sky, choking on the curses in my throat, and then down to the floor again just to make sure this isn't a stress-induced hallucinatory nightmare. Then I dart a glance over to Jean-Michel. Maybe he didn't see? Maybe I can just start again and he'll never know?

But I hear him snort from right behind me. Oh, he's looking at me now all right. And I can read very clearly by his sneer that there's no extra time for accidents or mishaps or excuses in this kitchen.

I spin on my heel, but where this brings me is even worse. Because now I'm facing Ben head-on, and he is staring at me, a stunned, worried look in his eyes. I shut my eyes tight and raise my hands to my temples. What the hell have I done? Blown it! And this is always the problem, this is always what happens to me… My dad calls it Icarus Syndrome: wanting to go too far, too fast, too soon and then fireballing. What I can actually do falls short of what I want and what I think I can do. Every. Single. Time.

My breath starts to quicken and I can feel a hot panic creep up my neck as I turn back to my smoking skillet pan. It's over. I came close, so close, but that's the story of my life. Always just falling short, always prioritising the wrong thing, running when I should stand still, standing still when I should be running, always just missing the mark and falling flat.

Whatever happens with Jean-Michel now, which I imagine will be a torturous public tongue-lashing, I can't let Ben see this happening to me. He hasn't seen me in nearly three years, I *can't* let this be the impression he has of me. Flustered, flailing, failing. I need to fix this.

My trusty skillet is still smoking hot. I've got four and a half minutes left. So I need to claw this back right this second and sear this steak to perfection. It's not over yet; I'm still in with a sliver of a chance. I look at both Ben and Jean-Michel and give them an Academy-award-winning *I know exactly what I'm doing* smile as, courtesy of my lovely butcher, I throw my second steak onto the red-hot skillet with an extra heavy splash of brandy and watch it flame while I speed-chop my onions and mushrooms to make a brand new sauce.

Under intense scrutiny, I tilt my pan and dress my sizzling filet in hot, golden butter, working at an astonishing speed, spoon after spoon, like a cartoon on fast-forward – anything to keep me from having to look up. I just focus everything I have on what's in front of me, until the rest of the world fades into insignificance. Just like always when I cook. Just the way I like it.

Can a brand new express take of a classic French preparation be executed in less than four minutes?

I'm about to find out.

CHAPTER SIX

'Five, four, three, two, time's up! Hands in the air. Please bring your dishes down to the front for inspection.'

It is what it is.

I step around my station, Ben just visible out of the corner of my eye. I can't stop to figure out why he's here, whether he's part of the panel or a candidate like the rest of us. My time is now and I need to gather every ounce of focus. Taking my plate, I join the other three chefs who are tentatively walking towards the service bench, ready for the judges' inspection.

They begin with the tall, bearded chef on my far left.

'Sebastian, talk me though the dish, please,' says Pip.

'Saffron risotto with scallops wrapped in burdock root.'

Shit. That sounds incredible. Skilled, ambitious, delicious, inventive. How on earth did he manage to cook and plate up a perfect risotto in just fifteen minutes? This dish does make my steak sound like a Big Mac.

Jean-Michel presses his fingers to his temples. 'Visually, if you can still see the centre of that bright grain of rice, what does that mean?'

'That it is perhaps undercooked.' I watch as he blinks rapidly, almost batting away the confrontation. 'But considering the time restraint—'

'Perhaps... *PERHAPS* undercooked?' Jean-Michel grabs his fork and stabs the scallop, holding it under Sebastian's nose. 'It's not "perhaps undercooked", it is all definitely *RAW*. You should know that it is impossible to cook this dish to my exacting standards in such little time. You have no grasp on basics. You have wasted everyone's attention and, worse still, wasted ingredients. It is not time that restrained you, it is your own idiocy…'

Pip sighs heavily. 'I mean, do you understand why we are even here? What we are looking for? Instinct. Expertise. Invention. Excellence. Do you know how many applications we had? Over a thousand. So don't you dare come here and patronise us. This is not a game. We're not fooling around.' He flings down the fork and moves on, dismissing the second chef even more quickly.

Octavia moves on to the next chef, a short red-haired chef a little younger than me. I recognise her from a *Good Food* article about exciting rising stars. I used to be one of them. Before my star crashed and burnt.

'Elle, talk me though your dish,' says Octavia to the smiling redhead.

'I've got lamb ravioli with bell pepper and jalapeno salsa spiced with a little cumin.'

Lamb ravioli, great choice; in the tight time frame too, that's smart. Super smart. It's going to be hard to top this. All my steak salvaging may have been in vain based on the standard of this competition.

Octavia slides her knife and fork into a ravioli pillow and tastes, taking a moment to chew, then licking her top lip, squinting slightly and placing her fork back down on the table.

'Cumin is not a spice that is used often in pasta. And for good reason. All I'm getting here is a mouthful of peppers with a really nasty, bitter aftertaste… This doesn't work. This doesn't work at all.'

So clearly Octavia isn't the nice one like I imagined.

From where I'm standing, I can see Elle squeezing her fists. She doesn't agree and I can tell that she is itching to tell them.

This isn't the kind of forum for open dialogue; I think of Zoe and Mel, *just keep your mouth shut and suck it up.*

Pip steps forward and takes a bite. He grabs a napkin and spits it straight out again.

'Classics are classics for a reason. They are appreciated time and time again, through centuries, across generations. There are universal food laws. If you don't understand them, if you don't respect them, then you have no place in the kitchen. Certainly not this kitchen.'

Elle juts out her chin and shakes her head, eyes blinking in outrage. 'I'm sorry but that's not true... You said you want inventive, but then when you are served something bold, something daring and fresh and original, something truly different, you slam it for not being classic.'

A heavy stillness descends as Jean-Michel raises his gaze to her. I see her shrink back. Her bottom lip starts to tremble as he approaches her.

'Whoever you are. Whatever you think you are. You are exactly what I don't want. You are here, making your own vulgar additions to classics without any regard for provenance or craft, just to show us how cutesy and clever you are. Well, congratulations, you have just got yourself a one-way ticket to wherever you came from. And so now you can go back to your cutesy friends and the six people who told you that you were talented. You are not fit to peel potatoes. You know the only thing worse than a cook with no taste buds is a narcissistic little snowflake like you. You will never learn because you refuse to listen. Thank you for nothing.' Jean-Michel takes her plate and throws it in the bin. 'Next.'

Oh sweet Jesus. That's me. I am next.

Octavia does not ask me a single question. She takes her knife and cuts straight through the middle of the fillet. She raises it to her lips. Puts it in her mouth, closes her eyes.

And she smiles. An actual upward-turning smile.

'This is cooked exactly as I like it. It's as much a chef's skill to know when to stop, when to stand back and let the food speak for itself, not to overcomplicate or overwork something. It's simple, it's elegant, it's high-quality, it's well-presented. The risk paid off, Katie, well done.' She turns to Pip and Jean. 'This is the best I've had all day.'

Now both the other judges step up and try my steak. Both nod as they eat, dissecting and inspecting every morsel on my plate. So far no faces are being pulled, there are no choking sounds, no crashing porcelain.

Pip sighs. 'I agree with Octavia. It is good, very good, excellent even. But, for me, I can't excuse the clumsiness. I mean dropping food on the floor. Seriously? At this stage of your professionalism, we should not be seeing this. To me, it's messy, it's careless, it's dangerous, and it's expensive… Next time, at a critical moment, in a high-pressured kitchen, it may not be so easy to turn it around. For me, it's a no.'

I nod graciously even though my cheeks are burning red. I take my hands behind my back to try to conceal my returning shakes. So far, I have one yes, one no. My future hangs in the balance. I can't call which way it's going to go.

Jean-Michel considers me carefully, looking from my face right down to my shoes. Right now, I really wish I had better shoes, not these cheap, work-worn black pumps. It is up to him now. It depends on whatever potential he sees or doesn't see in me. He turns to Ben who has been standing quietly by the door all this time.

'My wife recommended you. She dined at your table and called me from somewhere in the middle of the Mediterranean. "I have found him!" she told me, "I have found your Grand Chef."'

Ben bows his head modestly.

'So, by the way my wife has raved about you, I can take it that you can cook. But still, your suitability? That is yet to be revealed.' Jean-Michel hands Ben a knife and fork. 'Try the steak.'

Ben does as he is told, approaching my plate. I wait. He tastes the food and nods his head. 'Delicious.'

Jean-Michel looks back to Octavia. 'According to my wife, I should appoint Ben as Grand Chef immediately. Perhaps Pip has a point and that's exactly what I should do? We could cancel the rest of the competition now. Do we really want to waste more time and effort wiping up after inferior applicants? We need people at the top of their game, not dropping high-quality ingredients on the floor.'

Octavia looks at me and back to Jean-Michel. 'We have seen over forty chefs today already. Most were nervous, most made a mistake. Most served substandard dishes. Katie is different. Something went wrong but she adapted and recovered. We asked her to produce a high-quality dish within fifteen minutes, and she did. She came up with the goods. The success of this dish began before she even entered the kitchen. Her steak choice is very smart. It demonstrates that this chef understands food and the industry very well; I think she's come here well prepared and working to her strengths. She plates ingredients that show well. And I admire that. But what I admire even more is that she hit an obstacle and instinctively adapted. This shows strength and resilience and determination. With a new restaurant, there will be challenges and obstacles and we need a chef that has proven capacity in overcoming them. So, do I think she deserves a shot? Yes. I do.'

Jean-Michel raises his fingers to his mouth, and then takes a deep breath.

'Okay, I am executive chef; I will make an executive decision. I don't love it what you did. But I hate it less than the others. You have a lot to prove based on today. Do you think you have what it takes?'

'Yes, chef.'

'You are ready to sacrifice everything I ask of you and give me your all?'

'Yes, chef.'

'You understand that this will not be easy, that if you want easy you should leave the process now?'

'Yes, chef.'

'You are through. Not because what you did was perfect. But I think, with time, it could be.'

'Thank you, chef.' I wring my cold, clammy, quivering hands behind my back. *I am through.*

'*D'accord.* Buy yourself some good grip gloves because you drop one more thing, Katie, and I drop you, *tu comprends?*'

'Yes, chef.' I bow my thanks to Jean-Michel Marchand. And notice that now we are the only two left in the room. Octavia and Pip have already turned out through the swing doors and all the other candidates, including Ben, thankfully, have been ushered out the back entrance.

I bow my gratitude a second time and he nods to indicate that I am dismissed.

And all I can think of as I untie my apron and gather my things is that Martha was absolutely right. Jean-Michel is such a small man, for a giant.

CHAPTER SEVEN

'Hi Dad! You won't believe this; I have *the* most amazing news.'

Once he answers the phone I hop off my bike and duck into a high-street doorway, cupping my hand over my other ear so that I can hear him over the crackling line.

'You've won the lottery so you are coming home for good to keep your ol' man company.'

'Oh much better that that!' I tell him, still breathless from the adrenalin of the process and all the uphill pedalling I've done cycling home from The Rembrandt. 'I've got an interview with Jean-Michel!'

'Jean- who?'

'The famous French chef? Only the one I've been obsessed with since forever,' I tell him.

'I thought you were always obsessed with a woman chef, what's her face, Celia Someone?'

'Yes, well, I do love Celia Sanderson and always will, but this is completely different, this isn't hotpots and fairy cakes. This is *fine dining*, Dad. This is like the premier division; the highest level chefs can go. If I get this, it's like being signed by one of the top managers in the country – in the world. This is my big, *big* chance.'

'Right, I see, if you say so.' He exhales into the mouthpiece. 'It's hard to keep up with you, Katie. We went through all this with the restaurant, now here we go again and it's gung-ho about something else entirely…'

'Oh, this is something else all right. Jean-Michel's opening a new restaurant in London and he wants a whole new fleet. And I've got through the pre-selection! I'm into the next stage.'

A sigh on the phone. 'But it's still a cheffing job? In London?'

'*The* cheffing job in London, Dad, a million chefs would kill for this chance.'

'Yes, I'm sure they would. Kill themselves working around the clock in a thankless job, no doubt. No holidays, no pension, no sick cover or insurance. Remember when you burnt your hand with scalding water? They slapped some antiseptic and a bandage on it and you were back the next day. It's not right, Katie. Worse conditions than a sweatshop.'

'That was my choice, Dad, it looked worse than it was. It healed pretty quickly anyway.'

'It did not. Sure, didn't we all see it at your sister's wedding? Wearing a lovely bridesmaid's dress with a glove like Michael Jackson trying to hide it from us. You should have let us know, let us help you. So why on earth would you want to involve yourself in all that all over again? We've been through this before. You gave it a shot, your very *best* shot. It's time to let it lie. Cut your losses, and move on to something else.'

I can hear the frustration mounting in his voice. I called him because I thought it'd make him happy, proud even. The last thing I wanted to do was distress him.

'But that's exactly what I'm doing, I'm moving on. And hopefully, moving up.'

'So tell me this: are you still staying at Alice's?'

'Yes.'

'On the floor.'

'Well, yes. Just temporarily.'

I can hear him inhaling heavily through his nose. Not a good sign.

'And are you still working for next to nothing at that old folks' home?'

'Yes. That's why I need this—'

He cuts in to my attempt at an explanation, his voice an octave lower. 'I'm sorry to be the one to say this to you, Katie, but coming up thirty years of age, you are too old to be staying on mates' floors, surviving, if you can call it that, on less than living wage. Your mother and I didn't bring you up to be struggling this way. There's utterly no point living in one of the most expensive cities in the world to do a job that won't even cover your rent—'

'Dad, that's totally unfair.' Now *I* cut in before he goes any further. I hate when he brings my mother into things. As if she was still here. As if she was standing beside him nodding her head in agreement. 'What choice do I have?' My voice is reaching a pitch now. I take a deep breath and study the melted skin that the scald left on my right hand. It's only a scar. It's not like it hurts.

'Plenty of choices, sweetheart! Ah, Katie, I'm not trying to upset you. I'm so proud of how hard you tried, but for your own good, now may be a sensible time to step away for a bit. To try something else. You have the world at your feet, you're hard-working and you have plenty of solid, respectable choices at your disposal. Why not just consider looking at other careers, retraining, going back to college and setting yourself up in something a bit—'

'Something a bit what?'

'Something a bit less gladiatorial.'

Now it's me that's sighing.

'Rachel said you sounded very tired on the phone the last time she spoke to you,' he says.

'But I haven't spoken to Rachel in ages!'

'Yes, she said that too.'

It's hard to come back on that one. It's true I've not answered my little sister's calls in ages. Or Skype or Facetime. Everything is going so well for her; she's settled in Australia with a great husband, a baby on the way. I can't compete with that. Not that she sees it that way, but I don't want her to worry about me. Because I feel fine, as in I function okay, when it's just me by myself, or it's just me and Alice. But if I stop and look at myself through my little sister's eyes, seeing me as I must present to her, I feel like such a let-down, a disappointment – not the big sister she so admired when we were growing up, that's for sure. I know what Rachel will be looking out for, what she's trying to find – signs of happiness, of energy, of hope and excitement. And I also know that my skinny frame, pale skin and dark hollowed-out eyes wouldn't exactly send that message to her sunny veranda in Melbourne.

'Okay, I'll definitely call her. Soon, I promise,' I tell him, surprising myself with how convincing I sound.

'That's great, Katie. She'd appreciate a nice long chat with her big sister. With the baby on the way, I think she's a little homesick, you know? Your brothers are great, but it's you she can open up to, I guess. She misses you, that's all. Hold the line, I just have to let the dog in. Back in a tick.'

I swallow. How I miss her too. I miss them all. And ironically, sometimes I feel much, much *worse* for speaking with them. I miss them more acutely remembering how far away they all are. My brothers are complete nutters so they both joined the Irish Navy, Adam as a medic and Conor as an engineer. When my brothers are not at sea, they spend their time diving to explore wreckages or climbing mountains and sleeping in caves. For fun, clearly. They're survivalists, so they like to live off-grid and push themselves to mad extremes of cold and hunger and remoteness. We don't share that gene. Rachel and I like custard and fluffy socks, so we've always just let them off to do their own thing. So mostly they are in far-flung corners of the earth or in the middle of the deep, blue sea. Or indeed, under the sea. Which is what they've both wanted to do since they were ruddy-faced lads, knee-deep in mud. And as bad and as mad as it sounds, I hate hearing their voices because it feels like a punch to the heart. Then there's hearing them laugh, and all too soon it's time to say goodbye and to hang up. Oh my god, how I hate hanging up, cutting off the beautiful, soothing homely comfort of their voices telling me they love me and promising a time when we can all get together again. It's more than I can bear, this vision of us all in one place, in touching distance, so close that I could reach out my hands and pull them tight to my chest. Speaking to them on the phone is a fleeting joy that leaves me aching, surrounded by their absence. So that's why I don't answer and I don't call back. Not because I don't miss them. But because I really, *really* do.

Like seeing Ben today. Even fleetingly. It was mercifully brief, but it still shot something through my heart that I knew as longing. And heartache and regret. So I did what I always do and busied myself with something else. Distracted myself with something that demanded every ounce of my attention. And it worked. Sort of.

I hear my dad back on the phone which is a welcome interruption to my thoughts of Ben and what might have been. 'You know, it just struck me there, why don't you think about doing law? You were just as smart as Alice in school, she could give you a foot in the door of her firm and you could work together. Look at how well she's doing for herself!'

Oh yeah, if he saw her crying whilst eating ice cream in her knickers he'd know *exactly* how well she's doing…

'I'll think about it, Dad. I need to go,' I tell him, even though I don't. I was expecting this phone call to go differently, for him to be excited for me. To wish me luck, not to scrunch up my big chance and toss it back like a piece of scrap paper, reminding me of all the holes and heartache in my life.

'Don't be like that, Katie. I just want you to be happy. I know what's pushing all this, and it's time to let it go. You have nothing to prove; you are free to live your own life now. It's what I want for you. It's what we *all* want for you, just to be happy.'

'Sure, thanks. I do really need to go though; I've got to make arrangements for the next round of selections tomorrow.'

'Ah, well, speaking of arrangements, I am making some myself as we speak.'

There is a stilting quality to his voice; I can picture him with his fingers pinching his lips, almost daring himself to let the words pass across the line. He always does this with bad news. I brace myself.

'I've been offered early retirement and I've decided to take it.'

'Wow. That's great, right?'

'Yes, I'm excited. There's more to life than just work. I fancy a bit of time off, a change of scene. I might go travelling, visit some places I've always wanted to see – maybe even go to Australia to help your sister with the new baby.'

'Dad, that's great! Maybe you can come to London and visit me sometime. We could grab a bite to eat, check out the sights—'

He cuts me off. 'And in order to do this, Katie, I'll need to downsize. It means selling the house.'

Aha. I knew there was going to be bad news. Amazing how you can live thousands of miles away from someone yet still read them like a book, be completely fluent in their cues and quirks. I bet he's pinching his lips till they are blue now.

'But we can't sell our house, Dad,' I tell him.

'It's time, Katie. It's not practical with just me at home on my own now. I'm rattling around in it. I'm afraid I've made my decision; I want to move on, release some equity and live my life to the fullest. Your brothers and sister can see it from my point of view and they support it one hundred per cent.'

'So you've told them all except me…'

'I've tried to call you many a time but you never seem to pick up.'

I blink back tears of anger. I can't believe everyone knows except me. I'm the last one who should be on the very outside of the family… even if it is my own doing.

'Katie? Please, love, say something. It's nothing personal, it's just been so busy and with everything you've been going through, it's been hard to find the right time.'

I blurt out the words before I even feel like I've processed them. 'You *cannot* sell the house. It's where we grew up. It's where all our memories of mum are.'

I can't find any more words. I shouldn't need any more words.

'I thought you'd feel that way, but you can't stay in the past, Katie, you can't hang on to something that is gone, never to return. Maybe you should think about that too. Maybe it's time you took stock and considered doing something else altogether. Something that lets you have a life. That lets you get *on* with life. Look at Conor and Adam, building great careers, careers for life! And how about Rachel, she's happy, married, starting a family, she's got the balance right, able to keep a relationship.'

Ouch.

'Maybe this time you could meet somebody who wasn't a chef. That might be the key.'

I open my mouth to speak, to scream. But I'm actually too upset. If I start shouting back my protestations, I'm going to get hysterical and that's not something I want to do here in broad daylight on the high street.

'I can't keep the house on as a storage unit, Katie. You'll have to find some time to collect your things and some place to put them before I start the viewings.'

'Fine. Do what you like. I need to get ready for tomorrow.' So much for the best day of my life so far. So much for the congratulatory call home.

'Okay, but just remember: the definition of insanity is doing the same thing over and over but expecting different results.'

And at this, I hang up the phone. Insanity? Well, if I am insane, it must be genetic. Selling our family home? I am appalled. This is the worst idea I have ever, *ever* heard of in my twenty-nine years.

As a family, we were broken by grief and now we are scattered through circumstance. The only thing that binds us together is our family home. And Dad wants to sell it? To move on? No way.

My dad is wrong. He is so wrong about me and so wrong about the house. It's not being a chef that's holding me back; I just need my big break. Last time was different. I took on too much, and I was naive, inexperienced. I put all my focus on the food and completely ignored the finances. I put too much trust in staff I hardly knew. I didn't plan for a rainy day. Or cancellations. Or unforeseen expenses in the form of a blocked toilet or a leaky roof or customers who stole the silverware. I never even opened an Excel spreadsheet. I never read my bank statements, I didn't check my cash flow, I didn't secure my rent and I didn't have insurance when the water mains blew. All this eventually totalled my profit, so I paid suppliers on my credit card and before I knew it, I was in the red. Severe red. Bright, flashing, danger-sign, bloodbath red.

Then it became clear that my staff were being extremely liberal with the float and what I can only call tipping themselves. I was called in to the bank, dark suits behind a table, managers, solicitors, debt advisors… Everything was presented to me in very clear, numerical terms… and we came to an agreement. The only way I could manage the debt that I had accrued was to cap my arrears and stem my losses. And that meant unplugging the fridge, closing my beautiful bright blue door and turning the key for the final time on my perfect little restaurant and having no choice but to walk away.

So what else could I do but take the first job that paid weekly? To rely on the kindness of friends? To pack up my knives and my chef whites and fall into line with the rest of the broken and near-bankrupt?

So, yeah, Dad has some valid points, but that does not make him *right*.

Because as bad as it was, I learnt a lot. I own all the mistakes I made. But not everything I did was a mistake. There was a lot of good in there too. My menus were original, exciting, appealing and, most importantly, delicious. The reviews were positive, the footfall increasing; I was getting busier, I was growing professionally, creatively, skilfully. I was trying new things and often, they were working. I was getting faster, more assured, more daring.

And it was just about then that I got the bank call, and everything unravelled. I had to look to myself and accept that it was my entire fault, because the buck stopped with me. So, when I had finally faced the music and looked deep inside myself, I learnt that I could go through something like that, start right back from the bottom and, with Alice's help, survive. I remember her telling me that very first night, when I was still very tender and wary of what lay ahead, that a mistake that makes me humble is better than an achievement that makes me arrogant. That all the arrogant lawyers she works with have never failed because they've never tried anything new and, as a result, they don't have a lot to draw on. They can't empathise. They don't really know themselves or anyone else.

So, what did I learn about myself? I learnt that if all I could do was crawl, then I'd start crawling. I crawled to Alice for a place to stay and I crawled to the catering agency for a job that started the next day. I know first-hand that it's not about life getting easier or more forgiving. It's about me getting stronger and more resilient and taking all those mistakes and turning them into lessons for the future.

My future. The one I want to be excited about, not afraid of.

I want to ring my dad back and tell him, you know what? I'm not insane. I'm not doing the same thing over and over and expecting the same results. I learn, I adapt, I change. I dropped the steak. I cooked a new one. So maybe the most important thing that's happened to me is not falling but rising up all over again.

But I'm spent, and too tired to try and convince him of something he's already made up his mind about, so I decide to text him instead.

Do whatever you think is best. And don't worry about me. Because I'll find a way. I always do.

And then I wait a split second and send another text because I can't stay mad at him, for all his good intentions and law-oriented suggestions, he's the only parent I've got left.

And I'll ring Rachel soon. I promise, Kxx

CHAPTER EIGHT

'Why are you here? It's your day off!' says Mel, as I walk into Parklands kitchen at the end of her shift.

'I know, I came in to see you guys.' I open up the newspaper and show them Jean-Michel's advert. 'I went for this and I got in!'

They start to jump up and down, hugging me in between high fives, and winding their waists and hips in a celebratory dance.

'You can do it! You can go all the way, girl!' shouts Mel, pumping her arms either side of her chest as if there is some very happy music playing that only she can hear.

'You better not forget us when you are cooking Bombay duck with oysters and champagne for all those high-class millionaires,' laughs Zoe

'No, that's just it. I haven't got it *yet*. I'm just through to the selections round, which could last a couple of weeks. Or it could be all over tomorrow. Jean-Michel is pretty unpredictable. So I need to ask a favour.'

Zoe folds her arms across her chest and pouts out her bottom lip. 'What exactly is it that you need?' she asks, her eyes tight with mock suspicion.

'I need to swap shifts. I'll need to do the late-evening shift so that I'm free in the daytime to attend the selections.' This is something I have been dreading. Not because of the long hours or the workload, but because it means coming to and from work in the dark. And I hate the dark. A shiver travels down my neck and I wring my hands behind my back. It's not for long, I try to remind myself, I can suck it up and do it for Jean-Michel, I can do it for a better future… 'What do you think? Do you think Bernie will be okay with that?'

Both Mel and Zoe shake their heads in time.

'Mmm, mmm. *No* way. She will hit the roof and do everything in her power so you don't get what you want. Under no circumstances can she know about this. If she does, she'll ruin it for you, believe me,' says Mel, folding and unfolding her arms in agitation.

'But this is what she wants, to see me out of here. Surely it serves her to help me get another job?'

Zoe points a sharply tapered, long turquoise fingernail in the air. 'Ah. That's where you're wrong. This ain't just any other job. She wants you to move on out of *here*, that's for sure, but she doesn't want you to move on to something better! Nope, if it means so much to you to work for this French guy that you are willing to work two shifts back to back, then you can't afford for her to find out about any of this. She will see to it that you do not get your chance.'

I sink back on the steel bench. How on earth am I going to do this? I can't give up work because I have absolutely no money. I'm already taking more than I'm comfortable with taking in terms of floor space from Alice. I can't ask anybody else for handouts and I can't live off nothing either.

I run my fingers through my hair. I can't give up this shitty job! But I cannot possibly ring up Jean-Michel and say I'm withdrawing from the selection because I need to clock in to Bernie. This the most depressing catch-22 I have ever got stuck in.

This cannot be happening. This feels so wrong. I press my hands into my eyes, but I refuse to cry. However, I might vomit. This is worse than not getting selected at all. Having a chance but having to throw it away.

Zoe claps her hands together. 'Mel, are you on rota this week?'

'Yeah, why?'

'Right, I think I've got it. Good job I know you guys hate Bernie as much as I do and have absolutely no moral issues with us lying through our teeth.'

'No moral issues at all,' I confirm. Mel nods along too. We're unanimous in our deceit.

'I'll tell Bernie that Katie has to work the late shift to help me with childcare this week because Tash's dad isn't able to help out. That way, she'll think that we've solved the problem between us and saved her a headache. That's our best chance, what do you think?'

Mel frowns in confusion. 'I don't know, guys. It's risky, I mean this is Bernie we're dealing with. If she gets even the slightest sniff of us doing something behind her back, she'll really go for us. I heard her screaming at the cleaner yesterday. Believe me, I was scared!' Mel bites down on her lip and rubs her neck. 'Why doesn't Katie just take time off? That'll sort it and it's a lot safer than trying to mess around with the shifts.'

Zoe shoots Mel a look. 'Because I imagine that Katie here can't afford to, right?'

I nod. 'I need every single penny.'

Mel nods her understanding; we're all in the same boat on these wages. 'I know what you mean.'

Zoe nudges her in the elbow. 'We never got caught when we covered for each other before. We can pull this off.'

'But that was only the odd shift. This is over a whole week, right?'

I shake my head. 'You're right. Thanks but I can't ask you two to do this. It's too much. It is too risky.' I'm going to have to think of something else. This is my chance and I'm going to have to find a way to make it work. On my own.

Mel takes a deep breath, looks around the kitchen and then blinks her eyes, as if waking up from a trance. 'No. We're going to do this. What am I even thinking? We're not doing anything wrong. We're just helping each other out. The job will still get done. What are we afraid of, right? Ignore what I said before. All you got to do is come in for the late shift and Zoe and I will sort out all the rota stuff, okay? You leave all that to us. Bernie's no match for us, right, Zoe?' They wink at each other and bump hips.

'That's my girl,' says Zoe. 'You had me worried there for a sec!'

The hairs stand up at the back of my neck. Zoe and Mel would do this for me? They'd put their own necks on the line to help me out? I actually do think I'm going to cry now; tears are pricking my eyes. Zoe and Mel, what have I done to deserve such great girls behind me?

I'm going to the selection. I'm going to make it. *And* keep my job at the same time.

I nod my head and my eyes well up. 'What would I do without you guys?'

Zoe shrugs. 'You'd do the same for us. Hell, you *have* done the same for us. You covered me when I had to take my driving test and Bernie wouldn't let me go.'

Mel chimes in, 'And you baked that unicorn cake for Tash's sixth birthday. She still talks about that cake. Friends do that. And friends don't forget that stuff.' We wrap our arms around each other's shoulders in a playful group hug.

'Hey, when you work in a home like this for as long as we have, you realise the importance of friendship, right?' Zoe nods affirmatively. 'The healthy residents are the happy residents, and you know what? The happy ones are those that know that someone cares about them, that someone has their back. Those are the ones who enjoy their days. The ones without that? Well, the day can feel very long. So, you go out there and do your best, girl, and remember your friends are behind you – every step of the way.'

I squeeze them both one last time and then Mel whips me with the tea cloth.

'Right, now get out of sight before Bernie gets here and starts smelling a rat. But before you go, up you go and see Martha, she's been asking after you.'

I pop my head around Martha's door. She's awake. Propped up on two pillows, newspaper in her hand, lipstick on and hair set.

'You're looking rather lovely this evening, Martha.'

She glances up at me, a smile breaking across her face.

'What's the special occasion?' I ask.

'New doctor. Very handsome. Bloods.'

I laugh. Only Martha would go to such lengths to get a needle in her arm.

'It's very important to look your best at all times. You know, when I worked in finance I knew many a colleague that made investments based on a client's choice of tailor, rather than the sum of their balance sheet. But I don't have to tell you that, you know that people eat with their eyes.'

I smile at her and put on the kettle. 'How are you?'

She waves her hand in front of her face. 'I'm fine. Never mind me, how are you?! I've been thinking of you all day. Any news on the Jean-Michel front?'

I perch on the side of her bed and I tell her everything. I explain about seeing Ben and just freezing, panicking, which, along with my nerves, caused me to drop the steak. I tell her about Octavia sticking up for me. I tell her about my dad thinking it was the wrong move, that I'm about to make the same mistakes all over again.

'And this Ben? He must have meant a lot to you once upon a time to startle you like that?'

I nod.

'How did you meet?' asks Martha. 'I'm an old romantic; indulge me.'

'I met him at chef school. I'd just arrived from Ireland on a scholarship and Ben, a born and bred South Londoner, offered to show me around, help me get my bearings. There was this idiot called Ozzy in the class who kept mimicking my accent and saying that I didn't deserve a scholarship, I should have to pay like everyone else. Ben told him where to go and he didn't bother me again after that. That was day two, and by the end of the first week, we were inseparable. We spent four glorious years that way; we moved into a studio apartment on top of a café in Clapham and everything was perfect. Then college finished and we had to start thinking about the real world: getting jobs, juggling shifts to be together.'

'And how did that go?'

'Fine at first… We both worked in the industry so we knew what to expect. Long hours, no holidays… But then Ben was headhunted as a chef for a luxury cruise company. Everyone told him it was career suicide, and even I felt that he was taking himself out of the game, that he'd find it hard to get back into a high-end kitchen afterwards. But he was so excited, I could see him light up every time he talked about it. The offer had planted a seed, lit a spark in him and I could tell he just had to go. Explore, discover, get it out of his system – whatever you want to call it. He had wanderlust and I didn't want to be the one to stand in his way. So I pushed him, I told him to go for it. I told him that he needed to do what he needed to do and so did I. And that was that, we had to follow our own paths and see where they led us.'

'And he was okay with that?'

'Not at first. He wanted us to do it together. To sail around the world, to travel together, to launch this big adventure. But that was his dream, not mine. All I ever wanted was to have my own restaurant and eventually earn a Michelin star. One way or another, we'd have to make a choice. Either to compromise and stay together, or to pursue our goals and go it alone. So I convinced him that neither of us had time for a relationship at that stage. That we had to pursue our own goals first because if we didn't, one of us would end up losing out and being resentful and that was no way to move forward.'

"'If you love somebody, let them go, for if they return, they were always yours. If they don't, they never were,'" says Martha gently with a smile.

'Yes, well, Ben didn't return. Until now that is. And he's returned for Jean-Michel, not for me.' I feel a sting in my eyes at the thought of this. I let him go. And it may have been partly out of love, but it was mostly out of stupidity.

Martha reaches over to her bedside locker for a tissue and hands it to me. 'What happened next?' she asks.

'The café below the apartment came up for lease and I invested everything I had into it. My dream had come true, I was opening my own little place. I thought everything was working out how it was meant to but then I lost that too.'

'And maybe it *is* working out the way it is meant to. Maybe you and Ben were supposed to meet again.'

I shrug. 'I doubt it. It's been almost three years. That ship has definitely sailed. He could be married with four kids by now for all I know.'

Martha places her hand on mine. 'Well, let's not speculate just yet on the ifs, buts and maybes. Stick to what we do know: the facts. Will you see him tomorrow at the selection?'

I nod again. 'Yes, he was talent-spotted by Jean-Michel's wife so he's already tipped to win. And he deserves to, he's an amazing chef. To be honest, I don't think I can beat him.'

She nudges me. 'Enough of that. Tomorrow, show up, head held high, knowing that you have every right to be there and are as good, if not better, than everyone else.'

The whole time I've been talking, Martha has rested her hand on mine and listened with every fibre of her gentle self. It feels so good to talk to her like this that I've ended up saying much more than I intended, much more than I ever realised I felt in the first place.

'I may not be around as much this week, with all this going on,' I tell her.

Her face falls a little. And she nods a soft, resigned kind of smile. And immediately, I am back to being thirteen years of age. Back to when I had that conversation with my mum, all those years ago, perched on the side of a starched hospital bed just like this one. Her soft, tissue-paper-skin hand in mine telling me that it might be time that we started thinking about a future without her. That even though this wasn't what she wanted, we'd have to be strong, be positive, make the best of it, put a smile on our face even if inside we were breaking. Until that moment, I'd believed that she'd beat it. But I knew then, from her eyes, from her sad smile, that she was telling me to place my belief somewhere else. To believe that we'd be okay without her, believe that we'd make it, that, eventually, we'd smile again for real. Not that we could ever imagine that we would. She told me to look out for the youngest, Rachel, that the boys had each other but I was the only sister Rachel had. I promised I would. Of course, I'd have promised anything.

It was soon after that conversation that she died, and I went home and realised the hole that had already been left in the middle of my family. My younger brothers and sister were eating dry cereal directly from the box. My dad was spreading greasy yellow margarine and spongey luncheon roll on day-old bread and stacking up sandwiches nobody wanted to eat. Alice was with me, and I gave her a shopping list, and with full understanding she went to hunt and gather while I set the table one place less. I lifted down my mother's skillet from its hook beside the Aga, and I started cooking.

I cooked every night after that: hot, healthy meals. I insisted we all sat together, ate together, and looked each other in the eyes again. And slowly, the hole receded. Slowly, our broken circle healed. Slowly, just as Mum had promised we would, we started to feel closer to full again.

'I'll miss you but I'll be fine. You concentrate on this new exciting adventure, that's what's important,' Martha tells me, handing me the entire tissue box so I can dab my welling eyes.

'I'll pop in, okay? I promise you. I'm not sure what the hours are going to be, but I'll definitely be in. I'll need my daily Martha fix, you can count on me.'

I'll miss Martha. Without her, I wouldn't even be going for this. I think of what Zoe and Mel said, about how the day can be so long all by yourself, without a friend popping in for a chat and a laugh. I know Martha doesn't have visitors; her only son transferred offices to the USA a few months ago, and that's why she's here and not living with him.

'And I'll ask Mel and Zoe to keep a special eye on you too, in case you need anything. Just let me know and I'll sort it, okay?'

Martha smiles at me. 'Go home, get ready, put your best foot forward and let them know you are a professional and you mean business.'

I cycle the shortcut home, not my usual meandering journey to kill time and snoop around where I used to live. This has got to be a positive. I haven't got time now for circling old sites and relics of the past, because I'm going places, and my time is valuable again and I've not got any urge to look back. But as I go, I spot myself in the mirror of a shop window and it makes me stop. My jacket does look a bit grubby. It's slightly frayed around the buttons and it doesn't fit quite right any more. Probably because when I got this chef jacket, just before my restaurant opened, I was broader. I was stronger and healthier and weighed about two stone more than I do now. A lot of that was down to Ben.

I couldn't resist his food. I adored him and I adored the way he fed me. Then in the space of a few months, when it sunk in how much I missed him and the joy of eating together, I kind of lost my appetite too.

I pull at my loose neckline, the result of being on the sleepless-night, caffeine-and-fear diet that I was on involuntarily for the best part of the following year. These clothes don't fit me now. And tomorrow, I really want to look my best, look like a pro, look like I know who I am and what I'm doing. That I mean business. Just like Martha says, presentation means a lot.

I need new whites. But I'm going to have to sell something to pay for them. What's left that I can do without?

I need my knives, that's non-negotiable. Without those babies I'd never have been able to recover like I did, chopping like a speed demon during the pre-selection. No, they're my tools, my weapons, part of my arm. They've got to stay.

I need my bike. Otherwise I'm never going to get across town to be at all the places I need to be at once. Also, it means I can move faster through the city, not have to wait on trains or buses. And ultimately, it saves me money because unless I get a flat tyre, this bike runs on fresh air and pedal power. So no, the bike needs to stay.

My phone? It's risky. After all, it's the only way Jean-Michel can contact me, and with all we're doing to keep Bernie in the dark, I need to keep communication lines clear and open with Mel and Zoe too, just in case we do get rumbled. And my dad would be even more disappointed in me if I came off the radar altogether. So nope, phone needs to stay too.

I check my watch. I better make up my mind quickly if I'm going to go through with this. I need to get sorted before it gets too late, too dark and the shops close.

And that's when I realise – *aha*! I've got the time all right. I've got a timeless little timepiece ticking away happily on my wrist. A birthday present from Ben that he picked up in Paris for me during his final-year placement. He snuck it out from under the pillow the morning I turned twenty-six. I woke up to see him leaning on his elbow, watching me sleep, waiting for me to wake up. It was a Sunday, our usual day for lazing and eating after a crazy Saturday night service. He handed it to me in a little red bag tied with gold streamers. Even in my sleepy half-consciousness, I knew it wouldn't be a ring. We were so in tune with each other, there just wasn't any chance that he could carry around an intention like marriage without me picking up on it. I'd nearly expect him to ask me if he should ask me to marry him, if that was the case. I thought we were so different to everyone else; I thought we were so similar to each other that we'd stay together. Turns out it was the opposite. We were so similar to each other that we had to go our separate ways.

I held up the dainty little watch, the rose gold strap catching the late morning light.

'Do you love it?' he asked.

I nodded. 'Almost as much as I love you,' I told him without flinching.

He smiled and pointed to the tiny clock face. 'There's a second hand on it, if you notice. That should solve the little problem of your split hollandaise.'

'Cheeky bugger,' I laughed. 'My eggs Benedict are the best far and wide, and you know it.' And we dived back under the covers, making the most of our rare days off together.

I stroke the rounded pink dome. I really do love this watch. It fits me perfectly, it keeps time perfectly, and it's waterproof so I never have to take it off.

But I ask myself aloud, 'What is it really time for?' I don't need to *read* the time, I've got to *seize* the time. I need to look smoking hot tomorrow. To send a strong, powerful message to Jean-Michel and the panel, to all my competition… and to Ben. A message that says: I'm back, I'm ready and I'm going to kick ass.

I unfasten the strap and stick it in my pocket. *Time to move on.* Maybe Dad isn't the only one who's clearing out the old to make room for the new. I pull out the watch again and glance at it once more. This is an investment. If I pull this off, I'll be in a position to buy it back. Along with all the rest of my stuff that's in bags and boxes at the back of an East London shop.

I take out my phone and call a contact that I had hoped I was finished with.

'Hello, Paul's Pawns, what can I do you for?'

'Hi, it's me. What's your best offer on a La Roche rose gold and marble watch, high-quality French design, one careful owner?'

'Katie, come on down and I'll take a look, see what I can do for you.'

I thank him and start my cycle in his direction, knowing already that as long as he offers me enough for a smart, tailor-fitted, gleaming new white chef's jacket, I'll be going home with a bare wrist for the first time in years.

CHAPTER NINE

When I get back to the flat it's almost dark, so I lock up my bike and carry my brown-paper-wrapped, new-cotton-smelling parcels up the poorly lit stairwell with extreme care. I've been dealing with Paul for long enough to know how to strike a good deal, but even I was flabbergasted at how much he coughed up for my watch. It made me realise how much Ben must have spent on it for me in the first place. I had no idea it was so valuable. Paul's given me four weeks to buy it back, so if all goes well and Jean-Michel takes me on, it's one of the first things I'm going to reinvest in.

Because I loved that watch and I can't help but still be a little bit fond of all it represents.

So, with nearly three times as much cash as I was expecting in my pocket, I went shopping. Not that it took me very long; I saw exactly what I wanted in the window and, like a bride at a bridal fitting, the second I slid this baby over my head, I knew it was the one. The sales assistant knew it too, and within fifteen minutes, the little starched white number had gone from the store mannequin to my bike basket. But something was still not quite right. My scruffy trainers looked even more grubby against the gleaming brightness of my new uniform. I decided for the second time today to take Oskar Rosenblatt's advice and 'Buy the shoes'. So, new ensemble complete with a new pair of non-slip, sparkling white chef clogs thrown in, I can now put my best foot forward.

Alice is away with a work conference, so I batch-bake banana bread with cinnamon butter so she can feast on that whenever she gets back I shuffle around the living room, knowing that I should try to get an early night. But with all the excitement and nerves, I know I still won't sleep, so I figure the best thing I can do is spend the rest of the evening swotting up on everything I can find out about Jean-Michel, Pip, Octavia, and this brand new world that I'll be crashing into tomorrow.

I begin my cyber-stalk with Pip Taylor because a) I don't know much about him and b) he's the one who didn't want me so I'm going to have to try extra hard to get him onside. I start with his professional biography.

Pip Taylor *is a renowned American winemaker, restaurateur, author and entrepreneur. Along with his business partners, he owns thirty restaurants worldwide, including Loca in Las Vegas which was recently awarded one Michelin star. Taylor has co-authored two award-winning books on French and Italian wine, and his memoir, Wino, became a New York Times bestseller within a week of its release.*

Okay. Pip Taylor. Now that I know who you are, I'm even more embarrassed that I dropped the steak. This guy is big time. I take a deep breath and wonder if I should read any more. This is getting very real and overwhelming. I got flustered when I didn't even know Pip was a big deal, so what will I be like the next time, with thoughts of his Michelin-star restaurant sending tremors through my fingers?

I move on to Octavia. She's my favourite. She backed me. I type in her name and another flurry of results appear. I click on a video that shows an interview with a young and glamorous Octavia, looking like a blonde Joan Collins. The brown-suited, flat-haired interviewer is visibly nervous, somewhat overawed by her beauty, her confidence, her wealth and, no doubt, her shoulder pads. 'What is the secret to your unparalleled success as an international hotelier?' he asks her.

She dips her chin, scarcely smiling and widens her pale blue eyes. 'If it's simple and done well, people will get it. You don't have to hit them over the head with marble and gold. And frankly, if you do, it means you are hiding something. I only worry about quality and execution. And then I don't need to worry about anything else.'

I watch a few more videos of Octavia. I think I'm a bit in love with her. I watch the way she keeps her poise, her posture, the deliberate way she listens and considers her answers. I straighten my back. I slow down my breath. I try to channel my inner Octavia. I repeat the words 'simple', 'done well'. I can do that. I can do simple and I can do it well.

I scroll down. Lots of glamorous pictures across the decades of Octavia in backless dresses and sweeping gowns at banquets, charity balls, meetings, events with presidents and prime ministers, sheiks, big-screen royalty – even actual royalty. Then I see a single thumbnail photo of her in black lace dress, long-sleeved, high-neck, veiled face and large dark sunglasses on a grassy verge. The funeral of her husband and 'soulmate' three years ago.

And that's the most recent result the search engine offers up. Despite my best cyber-stalking efforts, I can't find a single photo or interview or mention of Octavia Timmons since.

I make some tea and slather up a hot slice of banana bread, licking the oozy golden cinnamon butter from the back of my hand. I have a feeling I should steel myself and bite into some carby-courage before I google Jean-Michel Marchand. I go to take a second warm, sweet bite and type in his name. And in 0.69 seconds, with my mouth still open, I'm presented with 50,900,000 results. Over *fifty million* returns.

Is that normal?

I type in 'Ireland'. 896,000 (0.74 seconds)

Jean-Michel is bigger, more famous, than an entire European country. I swallow my hot mouthful and try to get my head around this.

I type in 'Bananas'. 176,000 (0.76 seconds)

Jean-Michel is more widely searched and documented than food itself.

I type in 'Christmas'. 1,940,000,000 (0.51 seconds)

Oh, thank god for that. I fling my head back and blow out my cheeks.

But still, with over fifty million starting points, where do I begin? How am I supposed to sniff out the crucial truffle of insight that I need to know in order to win this position? What does he love? Hate? Value? Regret? What drives him? What fuels his passion? What's his stance on dried mushrooms?

I want to know it all. But I don't want to spend the entire night chiselling through this data trove to find it.

I type in 'New restaurant Jean-Michel London'.

A single article appears in *La Revue*. It is in French, but between my own fairly competent grasp of the language from school and recipe books and a little help from Google Translate, I should be able to work it out.

Opening this year, the restaurant is to include a fine-dining room with only twelve tables, a bar area that can accommodate seventy for dinner, and three flamboyantly large banquet rooms. Forecasters predict the start-up will cost eight million pounds.

Marchand is clearly experienced at this sort of venture – the restaurant, which will be called Marchand at The Rembrandt, will be the fourth business he has named after himself, joining a Marchand in Tokyo, New York and Paris.

Plain sailing? Not exactly.

This will be his first restaurant in a decade.

This will be his first restaurant in London.

This will be his first restaurant since his public disgrace late last year when he was captured on camera very drunk, mid-torrent, profanities flowing in a diatribe directed at a young photographer after an awards ceremony.

Although his fellow Parisians show a tenacious, irrational-seeming loyalty, verging on love, towards Marchand, he may not be regarded or received in the same way by the British.

Is Marchand really in a position to begin something so new, so daring, so fraught?

His friends, few in number, don't think so.

His enemies, many in number, don't think so either.

With interest, we shall watch events unfold and see if Jean-Michel still has what it takes to maintain his empire.

Whoa. I snap closed the laptop. Looks like the only person that needs this break more than I do is Jean-Michel himself.

I set my alarm for 5 a.m. but by the time it sounds, I have been lying here, staring at it, for an hour.

There is just so much to think about. So much to take in, so much to imagine that I couldn't possibly shut down my mind. Soon I'm showered, caffeinated and the sun has come up. I'm ready. New dawn, new day and I'm feeling good.

I get a text message from Alice.

Is it normal to be thinking about wine this early on a Tuesday? Asking for a friend. Ax

You're awake early?

Can't sleep.

Uh-oh. A sleep-deprived Alice does not bode well for the rest of the day. Most people would dream of staying away in a hotel all expenses paid, but to Alice, it is an anxiety-ridden hell.

How bad?

80%. Met new clients last night for dinner. The human resource guy is very cute. I'm supposed to be whipping his ass later today re: his client, but he's just too sexy. May have to wait here a few days for this to wrap up. writing on my name tag 'I'm not a bitch, I'm just jet-lagged'.

But you didn't fly anywhere, you're in Manchester!

Whatever. Good luck today. When you get this job we are going out! If Jean-Michel gives you trouble, just imagine him rubbing Nutella on his nipples. Blow them away today, sending all the love and luck, you beautiful culinary wizard-ess x

I stand in front of the mirror, combing back my hair into a slick, tight bun. I straighten as I button up my new tunic. It's tight-fitting, almost military, a French design of heavy-duty but breathable cotton to keep me cool in the heat of the kitchen. It is snug at my chest, tapered around the waist, with unconventionally high-capped sleeves that I just fell in love with. I have no watch, but I don't care because I know the time.

It's *now*.

CHAPTER TEN

'Good morning. You've all made it. Welcome to your new kitchen,' says a very dapper Pip in a blue checked suit.

Together, our small band of round-two candidates, competitors and jittery hopefuls enter the enormous bright galley kitchen of the new London Marchand.

'Please sign the confidentiality contract on your left and then take the station with your name on it. We will then give you a chance to prepare yourselves; wash your hands, don hats and aprons, place your knives on the block and then we will introduce ourselves.'

I look around and take in the shining steel reflections that surround me; brand new sparkling ovens, fridges, pots, pans, mixers and countertops. This high-design, ultra-modern kitchen is the perfect marriage of form and function. Clean lines, sleek surfaces, floor-to-ceiling unglazed white brick tiles with open shelving on every wall. It is gorgeous; every spotless, dazzling inch of it. Ten food stations are arranged perpendicular to the pass, which is where our dishes will be handed over for service. I turn on my heel to take in all the latest and greatest equipment, hopping slightly with excitement; there is everything you could ever dream of in here to smoke, freeze-dry, dehydrate or deep-fat-fry for the rest of your days. Wow, imagine working in here. Commanding this light, airy contemporary space. This is a far cry from the industrial kitchen at Parklands with its plastic plates and tinned soup. Just imagine walking across this sparkling chequered tile floor every day. This is the most impressive kitchen I've ever seen in my life; it looks like it belongs on a spaceship. I can see where a big chunk of the eight million quid has been spent.

'Please. Take a look round. Familiarise yourself with your surroundings.'

I draw my hand over the brushed-steel pass at the front, almost altar-like. Here we'll offer up our best work, our souls, to be carried off by the servers to the palates of the gods. The gods being, of course, anyone with a purse big enough to afford to grace these tables in the first place. I move towards the back, to the pantry; it is palatial. Walls of shelves laden with clearly marked tubs and baskets of fresh food, fruit, vegetables and herbs on one side, along with dried staples, liquors and oils on the other. The equipment room is fully furnished with every top-of-the-range appliance a chef could wish for; I spot a spanking new sous-vide in the corner. Just one of those costs the same as a small flat in some parts of the city. This kitchen really is every chef's dream come true, everything you'd ever wish to use, to play with, to experiment with.

Pip claps his hands together to summon us back to our stations. 'One of you will become the grand chef of this kitchen. One of you will have your name in lights. One of you will be chosen. One of you will win the ultimate culinary prize and live the dream of working with and learning from the most iconic chef on the planet, Monsieur Jean-Michel himself.'

At this, Jean-Michel walks through the swinging doors to our applause. He clasps his hands together, surveying all ten of us.

'I am not a monster. But by the look on your faces, I think you do not believe it.'

Jean-Michel places his finger on his bottom lip thoughtfully and blinks his eyes as if in conversation with himself.

'Many people have condemned me for being controversial. I am never controversial. I am never contradictory. I am pure.'

He raises his chin skyward. 'I do not pretend to be that which I am not. Most of my reputation is founded on ignorance and exaggeration. Hypersensitivity by those who have been offended by their lack of appreciation for what I do, for what *we* do.'

I watch the other candidates. They are nodding, so I start to nod too.

'Do I shout?' he whispers. '*Mais, oui*. I shout because I lead from the front,' he booms, lifting his fist high up into the air. 'I nail my colours to the mast and I fight for my profession, for *our* profession. For our most noble quest. If you are going to be a revolutionary, you must fight, fight, fight for what you believe in. And that is all I ever do.'

His arm lowers and he takes a deep breath, fingers on both hands fluttering in front of his chest.

'What made me a fighter?' A trace of a half-smile graces his lips. 'The same thing that makes everyone a fighter. Fear of our own insecurities. Insecurities make victims or victors of us all. My inadequacies – reading, writing, struggling in school. It gave me that fight to prove myself. Because they believed me to be nothing. Worthless. Destined for failure. I'd been belittled. I knew I could do more, be more, but they did not believe me. This was my fuel.'

He pauses a moment. And then raises his gaze to us, an angry, defiant tone to his voice.

'I did not waste time snivelling, pointing fingers and waiting for apologies. I fought. I showed what I knew inside to be true.'

The great hush that has descended upon us feels heavy, yet we are bound by it. Nobody is even breathing out of sync.

'We have all faced moments in our lives when the pressure mounts beyond what we feel we can handle, and we find ourselves thinking that we do not have the strength to carry on. Sometimes we have just gotten through a major obstacle or illness only to find another one waiting for us the moment we finally catch our breath. Sometimes we endure one loss after another, wondering when we will get a break from life's travails. It does not seem fair or right that life should demand more of us when we feel we have given all we can, but sometimes this is the way life works.'

I hear a sharp intake of breath behind me. I don't need to turn around. I know it's Ben. My senses lead me right back to him. That scent. His scent. I can't help but *smell* him for feck's sake.

He still wears the same cologne. My favourite. I can picture the dark red bottle in the medicine cabinet of our shared little bathroom. I still can't pronounce the name, even though I bought it for him every Christmas. It smells sweet and warm, a musky mix of coffee, chocolate, salt and leather. *Yum.*

Ben is the only person I know who wears this. Well, the only one I've ever noticed anyway.

Jean-Michel stops and stares at me. I hold my breath.

'When we look back on our lives, we see that we have survived many trials and surmounted many obstacles, often to our own amazement. In each of those instances, we had to break through our ideas about how much we can handle and go deeper into our hidden reserves. So here, you will be belittled. Here, I will shout, I will swear, I will scream until you decide to reach into those hidden reserves. To what you know deep inside to be true. Let the battle commence.'

Hidden reserves? Silly me, thinking I was here to cook up some great-tasting food. I attempt to breathe again.

Pip clicks his tongue and makes a steeple of his hands. 'The competition starts now. This restaurant will only be as great as the chef in charge of this kitchen. I am a businessman. I'm investing in a great restaurant and a great chef. I need to be absolutely sure that we have the right person in place or else the whole thing could fall apart. We will present you all with a task each day over the next three days to determine your competencies in different areas. We are looking for the best, and after each task we shall eliminate the worst. We have no desire to retain dead wood.'

We stand behind our stations. I look around. Where is Octavia? She's the hotelier, so maybe she's not going to be here every step of the way? My stomach flips. Dear God, me against Pip and Jean-Michel and all these other guys. Against Ben. Please tell me Octavia is involved today, I need all the support I can get.

Pip continues. 'Your first challenge. During pre-selection, you were able to choose your own dish. Now let's see what you can do when that choice is taken away. How creative are you? How well do you respond to pressure? What skills can you showcase that will blow our minds?'

A waiter arrives at each of our stations carrying a silver platter covered with a serving dome. They stand to attention.

What on earth is under there? Could be some really outlandish ingredient that I won't have a clue how to approach. Like some unusual fancy fruit or a rare spice or a controversial exotic meat. Rattlesnake? Beetle larvae? Grass? Something notoriously tricky to get right unless you know exactly what you are doing and are up to date on every single hot new trend on the food scene at the moment?

Oh God, I hope not. I'm finished if that's what this challenge is all about. Because I don't particularly enjoy cooking anything that I wouldn't eat myself. And if I can't put my heart and soul into it, I know that it won't be my best and I can't imagine anyone enjoying the loveless product I'll have to plate up. My cooking is about taste and about flavours, not so much about dressing the inedible. So if that's what Jean-Michel is after, I guess it'll be me first out that door today.

But then I think, this is Jean-Michel Marchand we're dealing with. That would be way too predictable. And the unpredictable is too predictable. This could be anything.

Okay. Yes. No. He's going to spring something on us that we're not expecting. Something that will really make us think, *dig deep in our hidden reserves.* But what if I don't know what the hell the thing is underneath that silver dome? What if it is something really obscure that I don't even *recognise*, never mind know how to prepare to a level befitting this kitchen?

I dig my fingernails into my palm. This is my worst nightmare. Even though I'm classically trained, I come from an ordinary background; I don't always have as sophisticated a palate as others who have travelled more and been exposed to a richer breadth of tastes from a young age. This is something I'm acutely aware of. My mother was a great cook, but she was a home cook. She learnt everything she knew from a Celia Sanderson Book called *Cooking From the Heart* which stayed splayed open, by her side, on the kitchen counter every dinner time until she became ill. Compared to other households, we were no-frills, bare basics. I really started to understand this when Alice moved into our village. Her parents were much older than my parents (older than some people's grandparents; her half-siblings from their previous marriages were closer the mark) and they were both really posh and well educated. You could tell that by the way they spoke, but mainly by the way they listened – none of the interrupting and eye-rolling and relentless teasing that went on in my house if you tried to say something in more than five syllables. Alice's parents were always writing and reading, always trying new things, learning languages and instruments, taking her out for adventurous meals, foraging wild leaves and inviting her to taste different wines and then discussing them even when she was just a teenager.

Alice didn't think it was something to be admired at all. She hated it, felt it was like she lived in a museum and preferred my house because it was 'less intense' – that is, more chaotic but no one cared what you did or what you thought or what you drank. I loved her house because it *did* feel like a museum to me:

a hushed, cultured place where you could learn about the past, enquire about the different, listen without the constant clanging of an overused washing machine or a sibling fight breaking out upstairs. And I built up my knowledge. I'm always trying to learn more but still, I guess I'm ashamed of my lack of worldliness and I always feel like I'm lagging behind. Alice doesn't appreciate that cultural capital that she just absorbed without even noticing. Like last year when we went ice-skating, some music came on and she just knew it was Vivaldi's something or other. And when I made my own flavoured gin for her birthday, she picked up on the hibiscus straight away, said her mum always put it in her tea. The one time we tried speed dating, which was so tragic we left early, I remember Alice said that the longer she stays in this city, the more her head feels scrambled and frantic and aimless, like a Jackson Pollock painting. I thought pollock was a fish. So these gaps, these voids in my knowledge – I've spent my life trying to fill them and rectify them and cover them up.

I look at the mystery platter, my mind racing as to what it could be. I start to panic as I think of all the things it could be that I haven't even heard of yet. My cheeks flare red. Oh God, this could actually be the end of me. Not only could I be out of the competition, but this could be a real exposure of my own fundamental ignorance. I know what I've been taught, what I've taught myself, but yeah, hey, got it in one Jean-Michel. I guess my unremarkably common, meat and two veg background is my great insecurity.

My heart starts to race. I could really show myself up here. Humiliate myself. If I stand here blank-faced when that lid goes up, it's not as if Jean-Michel is going to give me a kindly smile and help me figure it out.

And *where is Octavia*? At least I thought I'd have her support. After all, Pip didn't want me at all and Jean-Michel didn't love what I did before, so what chance do I really have?

To be honest, this is feeling more and more like the Hunger Games rather than a cheffing interview. And I don't know if I'm going to be standing at this station beyond today. Elimination feels very real.

I glance behind me for the first time. Possibly the last time. And there he is. Looking so strong and confident and tanned and handsome and so Ben. He gives me a smile. Yes, Jean-Michel, you are right on one thing, some stuff happens that breaks your heart so completely you just can't even believe that you got through it. I nod towards him and turn right back around before he sees my cheeks flush.

'Server, please reveal.'

I scrunch my eyes shut and swallow hard. *Please don't be something small and soft and pink and weird or large and green and gooey and weird or long and brown and hard and…*

I open my eyes and my breath catches in my throat. My hands fly to my face. *Thank you, thank you, thank you. Dignity saved for today.* I certainly know what to do here, no fear of unfamiliarity. It seems ridiculous now looking at what I've got before me that I let myself get so wound up about everything I don't know. This is where Alice diagnosed me (via a free online quiz) as having acute Impostor Syndrome. I don't really believe that I know what I'm doing and I'm always waiting for someone to say 'come now Katie, good try but the gig is up'.

Well, even so, that's not happened to me today. And I can't help it. I just laugh, right out loud.

'The humble potato,' announces Jean-Michel, a mischievous glint in his eye.

There's a little mound of different coloured, random varieties of potatoes on the silver serving plate in front of me. Nothing out of my depth. Nothing weird. I pick one up in my hand, rubbing the gritty, waxy texture. I raise it to my nose and breathe in the earthy, starchy scent. It reminds me of standing by the sink helping my mother wash and peel until our hands were red, raw and wrinkly and we had set the world to rights.

'We shall do more than scratch the surface,' says Jean-Michel. 'We shall start with what is deep down, under the earth, buried in the dirt. *Balance* is everything. Use whatever you like from the pantry, from the equipment room, whatever you wish, to lift up this humble ingredient and make it shine. You have one hour; your time starts now.'

CHAPTER ELEVEN

I dash to the pantry and go straight to the fresh section, deciding that this is my chance to show them that I know what's locally sourced and I know what's in season. I spot a nice leafy head of lamb's lettuce and think that could be a way forward. Light, fragrant, its long spoon-shaped dark leaves and distinctive, tangy flavour could be a great balancing partner for my friend the potato. I eye up the rest of the stock. Thinking all the time about balance, balance… How will I achieve balance in colour, flavour, texture, temperature – all on one plate in an hour? Balance. It's so hard to get it right, not only with food, but in every other area of life as well.

I wonder what Ben's thinking of? This is one of the things I miss most – *missed* most about us when he left. Our brainstorming, our chats about what would work with this, what could work with that. I'd love to slide up right now and ask him, *What do you think? Potato blinis with crème-fraiche and smoked salmon? Or perhaps sweet-potato gnocchi? Or a classic galette? Or maybe something radical and loud with shock value, like a dark chocolate fondant with potato foam?*

I bite the inside of my lip. I could really use Ben right now. He wouldn't even have to say anything, just the slightest shift in his left eyebrow, or rising of the corner of his mouth would tell me everything I need to know. Because yes, we're in competition, but we're not *directly* in competition as yet; we're both just trying to survive these elimination rounds, right? What harm can it do? I don't need him to give me ideas, I just need a sounding board;

I just need to someone to share my ideas with… Unlike most chefs, I am less of the control freak and more of the *taste-this-and-tell-me-what-you-think-team-player* variety. My dad says this is where my restaurant probably fell down. I should have been 'more commanding'. Should have made the hierarchy clear. Made sure I was perched at the top of said hierarchy rather than slogging away at the bottom. But I know that I'm better when I'm working with other people. I like to get out of my own head and communicate and talk and laugh and cry and taste and spit and swear and get excited with everyone else.

I take a deep breath and turn towards Ben. This is the first time I've properly taken him in since we've been here. He looks just the same. His hair is a little shorter, a little lighter just around the front, and he's a lot more tanned – probably all the Mediterranean sun on the deck.

'Excuse me! I need to get through.' A very agitated, bearded chef scowls directly into my eyes as if to say, *get out of the freaking way*, and reaches across me to the basket of fresh spinach.

I feel a shiver. There's something about him which gives me the chills. I step aside as he roughly snatches everything he can get his hands on and shoves it into his overflowing basket. There's no way he'll be using all those ingredients; it looks like he's poaching stuff so other people can't use it. The battle is on and it's every chef for himself.

I straighten up and look into my empty basket. C'mon Katie, time is running out. Forget asking Ben. He owes me nothing. We're virtual strangers now; we've had no contact in ages. That little smile he gave me earlier was clearly just his way of being civil. Of putting past differences behind us and moving on. He's probably smiled at everyone here in exactly the same way. Even the bad-tempered beardy guy seems to be hanging around Ben, maybe they are mates? Maybe he knows him from his new life? As in the life that happened after us?

I take a deep breath and glance one last time to my right. I can see that Ben's ready; he throws a final handful of parsley into his full basket and strides back to his station.

I'm on my own. Time is ticking by and I need to make a decision and get started. I need to come up with something. Something really bloody good.

I grip the handle of my basket harder and look around at everyone else. Half are standing around, squinting at the range of stock crippled with agonising indecision just like me. The other half, like Ben, have already grabbed their ingredients and are well underway.

I shake my head and try to refocus myself. I have a solid idea. I look again at the lamb's lettuce. It's a good idea. No one else seems to be thinking in this direction; most are over in the dairy and meat sections. I'm thinking rose-lipped parmesan and rosemary stacks with a lightly dressed lamb's lettuce salad. I can make the presentation impressive too – if I get cracking now. I have less than an hour. I want to showcase my knowledge, my skills *and* I want to make it to service on time.

Another indecisive contender is eyeing up my lamb's lettuce. I dart him a look and then grab the last fistful along with all the fresh herbs, seasonings, salad, veg, cream, cheeses and butters that I need. As I head out of the pantry, I realise there's already sizzling and hissing, clanging and banging coming from the other stations. I need to get a wiggle on.

I rock back up to my oven with my basket full, light my rings and start peeling at lightning speed. I've got to credit Parklands for that particular skill. I peel more than I need and stick a back-up saucepan of potatoes on the back ring. Just in case. If dropping my pre-selection steak taught me anything, it's to expect the unexpected and have a plan B.

When the potatoes are ready, I carefully slice each one into thin, round, delicate slivers. I add melted rosemary butter, grainy pink rock salt and a generous helping of grated parmesan and I fold them by hand. I'll need to layer up the potato slices carefully, building them in the tin mould like petals of a flower to give a rosebud effect; each one will have to be identical and perfectly crafted. I delicately brush a glaze of garlic-infused oil over the roses and then put them in the oven to bake. In about thirteen minutes, I'll expect the warm air to smell of roasting garlic and melting cheese. That's when the magic kicks in and all those wonderful flavours will start to sing. Crispy, crunchy, salty roasted edges working inwards to a gooey, cheesy, velvety middle. Oh my, Alice would be all over this.

I double-check my oven settings, mentally bless my baking blooms and start on my salad.

Somewhere to my left, I think I smell burning at someone else's station. In the distance, I hear a plate smash, the muttering of obscenities, and I feel the energy of intense pursuit. I smile to myself because my heart is pounding in my chest and I feel so excited, like this is exactly where I belong and God does it feel good. I'm back and it is *on*.

As I prepare my salad, I can't help but follow my nose. I definitely smell burning, I recheck my oven. It's not me. I sniff over to the stove at the back wall, nearest the pantry where I spotted my greedy, bearded buddy earlier on. No chef in sight, I open the door and smoke billows forward. Oh no, this is not good. I know from my own previous disaster that somebody's heart is going to implode when they see this.

I raise one hand in the air shouting, 'Attention! Oven at station three!' while I try to rescue the tray of ramekins which I assume contain potato soufflés… Burnt, sunken potato soufflés.

As I wave my dishcloth in the air to distribute the plumes of smoke, I hear Ben's voice right beside me.

'What the hell?'

I turn to see him. His eyebrows knitted together with incredulity and his cheeks flushed pink.

'Are these yours?' I ask.

'Yes! I only put them in five minutes ago… how can they be burnt?' He slides his fingers through his hair and swivels from side to side. 'That's it. That's me done. I'm finished.'

I glance down at the temperature dial; it's on 200 degrees! These need to be at 120 maximum. There is no way Ben would *ever* put soufflés on at that temperature unattended for even five minutes. We were trained the same way. It would simply never happen. I rack my brains and instinctively turn to the far corner of the kitchen, where I can see Beardy watching us out of the corner of his eye. He meets my gaze momentarily and then hastily turns away.

I saw him over here a few minutes ago. Clearly this isn't his station. He had no business being here unless he was in the business of sabotaging Ben… Ben being the one who has already impressed Jean-Michel's wife, and therefore the current favourite and the one to beat.

Beardy, you slippery, soufflé-destroying, greedy, cheating bastard.

I turn to Ben, who is leaning back against the wall, pinching his shut eyes, as if unable to even look at the charred remains of his black and smouldering dish. I can tell by his own low, shrunken shoulders that he's beaten. He's given up. There's only fifteen minutes left on the clock. There's no time to whip up some new soufflés, no time for potato blinis with crème-fraiche and smoked salmon, or sweet potato gnocchi, or a classic galette, or any other of the ideas I had earlier.

I put my hands on Ben's shoulders and give them a squeeze. He looks at me, defeat in his eyes.

'I thought I could do it. I really wanted to see how far I could go.' He shrugs. 'But I don't need to tell you that, do I? Of all people, I know you understand exactly what it means.'

He's right. I do know.

'You *can* do it, Ben,' I tell him and I find myself moving in closer, dipping my gaze to find his and make sure he's listening to me loud and clear. Because I've got an idea. '*Vichyssoise*,' I say, a smile breaking my lips. 'Ben, your vichyssoise is the best thing in the universe and that's a big statement for a chilled soup.'

He almost laughs at me. 'Thanks, Katie, but fifteen minutes?'

I stand straight and start firing orders. 'I've got extra potatoes boiled, you can have them. Just plunge them into ice and they'll be fine, two-minute job. I'll check my oven and then fetch you some leeks, you'll have time to sweat them, blend and finish with cream if you heat your pan this second.'

He stands to his feet, wiping his hands down his apron. 'You think so?'

'Yes, chef! Now get going!' And I whip the dishcloth across his chest.

'Thank you,' he mouths just before he sprints to the pantry.

I take my parmesan rose stacks out of the oven to rest and, I've got to say, they are *perfect*. I fetch the leeks, drain, rinse and cool the extra potatoes I've got for Ben, and leave it all by his station. Right, time to begin my own plating up. I decide that I'm not going to tell Ben about my Beardy suspicions right now, or maybe ever, because with everything that there is at stake and so many sharp knives around, it's not safe. Jean-Michel isn't the only one with a chef's hot temper. If Ben gets wind of this, he will go over and tear strips off Beardy. And even though he'd be well within his rights, it'll definitely get him kicked out of this process. And I realise, that's not something I'm willing to let happen just yet. Firstly, because it would be unfair, Ben's burnt soufflés were not his fault, and secondly, if I do dig deep down and let myself be truly honest for a moment, I don't want him to go. It's been far too nice seeing him again, even if it has been mostly out of the corner of my eye.

I can feel my cheeks flush at the thought of standing so close to him back there, looking straight into those eyes like we hadn't yet made all our mistakes – or maybe like we were on the other side of them. Is it possible? That it could feel like we were new? Different? Like we had it all to look forward to all over again but this time with a happy ending?

I have to stop to steady my hand as I lift my potato roses out of the hot tin. That one nearly slipped off the serving spoon.

'One minute left,' calls out Pip.

I stretch my fingers, pull back my shoulders and try to regain my composure. *Remember why you are here*, I whisper to myself. I think of Martha, her faith in me. Her conviction that I can do this. Rooting for me from her tiny corner of the retirement home, encouraging me to go for this in the first place. I think of Zoe and Mel sacrificing their shifts to help me out. I think of Alice who would share her last pound with me if it came to it. Dad and Rachel and even my brothers who worry if I'll ever find my way.

I can't let all these people down. I need to give this my all. I need to focus. *Katie, focus!*

Carefully, I lift a perfectly formed, perfectly baked, golden rosebud from the tin and onto my decorated plate. My hand steady again, I wipe the edges with my cloth, dress my lamb's lettuce and add the finishing touch, a dried gold-blush rose petal, to the centre of the dish to bring it all together.

'Three, two, one. Time is up!'

Wow. It's done. I did it.

I don't turn around to Ben this time. I keep my eyes forward. On my dish. On the judges. On this opportunity that I want and need so much. Because seeing Ben today, up close, is enough to throw me off my game and make me forget why I am here. But I can't afford to lose anything else. And the closer I'm getting to winning this position, the more I realise how much I don't want to go back to where I've been.

CHAPTER TWELVE

Jean-Michel whispers into Pip's ear as they inspect our plates and nod in solemn agreement before he addresses us all.

'We are looking to advance the best. But remember we are also looking to eliminate the worst. There are two dishes here today that really did blow our minds – by how bad they were.'

Pip walks over to the pass. He looks at the first plate presented by a tall, lanky chef with the biggest hands I've seen. He lowers to sniff the dish.

'Blinis.'

The tall chef nods.

'You know what this is like? To me, this is like going to the New York Philharmonic. You are excited, these guys are the best of the best, top of their game, selected from thousands, trained by the most celebrated in the world. Skilled, passionate, exemplary in every way. You are all dressed up, you've brought a hot date, or your wife. Everything is in place for something extraordinary, something memorable, something special… And then they play "Chopsticks".'

The tall chef's eyes widen. This sounds like it's going in the wrong direction.

'These blinis are "Chopsticks". A complete let-down. Patronisingly simple. Devoid of imagination.' Pip picks up his fork and begins to prod around the plate. 'And you know what? These may taste great; these may be out of this world. But here is the thing. I don't care enough to find out. I'm so uninspired by the mere word "blini" that I don't even care to try this. I wouldn't want

to read it on a menu; I wouldn't even want to ask my maître d'
to write it up because I suspect he may die of boredom before
the second letter.'

Jean-Michel nods his head. 'This challenge was about creativity.
This is not creative. This is *passé*.' He points to the door. 'Please
see yourself out, you are now eliminated from this process.'

Oh my God, he didn't even taste it! I was going to go with
blinis! Thank God I didn't. But what about my dish? What's he
going to make of it? I just cannot predict his reaction. My palms
start to sweat. Even though I have no idea what's going to happen
next, I'm going to have to act ready anyway. Stay calm. Stay rooted
to the spot. Stay professional. I can't let my insecurities leak out
and make a mess everywhere.

I try to console myself. What's the worst thing that can happen?

Well, except that both of them attack me, screaming, shouting,
throwing my food in the bin in front of all these people, including
Ben. And then they eliminate me and I have to break the bleak
news to everyone that I have, indeed, failed again with the one
thing that I'm supposed to be good at it. And then I wake up
in my sleeping bag on Alice's couch bright and early tomorrow
morning to head back to Parkland's kitchen with Bernie as my
superior for evermore. And this time I'll have no real hope or
practical way of escaping.

I clench my jaw tight. And decide that my attempt to cheer
myself up has actually just scared the living crap out of me.

I watch the tall chef slide his apron over his head and fold up
his knives. The kitchen is utterly still and silent. Nobody dares
move. I hear the swing door whoosh shut. And he's gone. And
we are one down, just like that. Nine of us remain. But for how
long is anybody's guess.

Jean-Michel steps up to the next plate, which belongs to
a young, dark-haired chef with a goatee. He regards the dish.
'*C'est quoi?*'

'Pommes purée, chef. I immersed the potatoes in the sous-vide at a high heat for twenty minutes before passing them through the sieve fifty times to ensure a perfectly even, silky-smooth texture.'

Jean-Michel's face stays unmoved as he samples a small forkful.

'Flavour is almost adequate. But texture? Colour? It looks like somebody already ate it, and brought it back up again.'

He considers the dish another moment, then puts down his fork.

'Just because the equipment exists doesn't mean we should use it for the sake of using it. I watched you as you cooked. You spent more time with the equipment than with the food. This upsets me. I am looking for creativity. And this should not have been created *at all*. It has no soul. To me, you have sucked the life out of this. *Impardonnable.* You have prepared your last dish in this process. Please, the door.'

A second chef stripped of his apron, he exits through the swinging door without looking back.

Jean-Michel dispatches the next four chefs in the same manner, one by one, a curled lip, a sigh, a grunt, a shrug of his shoulders, a shake of his head, and then a decisive nod to the door.

Eventually Pip looks towards me. 'So, let's get on to some better news. We were impressed with the talent that remains. Katie, you did yourself proud. I shall let Octavia know that her instinct about you proved correct. Today, you came out of your comfort zone. Your presentation is elegant, your flavour combination impeccable. This is what I would order at a high-end restaurant and if I was served this, I would be extremely satisfied. So well done, I look forward to more.'

I'm in. I passed. I'm coming back! I blow out my cheeks, letting a huge sigh of relief escape my lips. I stretch out my tightly furled fingers. And unclench my butt. And unlock my knees. My whole body loosens as the fear of elimination dissipates. That was tense. That was scary.

Pip then turns to Ben.

And I feel my fists ball and my butt re-clench and my knees re-lock. I'm as nervous for Ben as I was for myself. *Please let him survive this! Please don't send him out, away again, through those doors never to return.*

I hold my breath. If Ben doesn't get through I'm going to speak out about what I suspect Beardy did. There's no way should Ben be going home. I cross my fingers and hold my breath. Hoping. Praying.

'Vichyssoise. This was an inspired choice. A nod towards the British favourite of potato and leek soup, but light and elegant enough to serve as a summer's day appetiser. It's clean. It's clever. It's classical. It makes me think of all the other times I've enjoyed this great dish in other high-end dining rooms, and believe me, this is up there. It belongs here. And that tells me that *you* belong here.'

I unclench. God, that feels good.

Jean-Michel takes a step towards Ben. 'What I like is that you served it at room temperature. Not cold. Not chilled. Just right so the flavours shine. At the wrong temperature, you can't differentiate all the dimensions in there and it tastes as a plain potato soup. But, *this…*' He takes another spoonful, closing his eyes as he swallows. '*C'est vraiment très bon.*'

Ben bows his gratitude and I watch a modest smile relax his lips. He glances over at me and winks his gratitude.

Jean-Michel praises another quiet chef called Joe for his efforts and spares him the walk of shame. He's saved. He'll return tomorrow.

Pip pivots on his heel and raises his chin towards the back-corner station. He claps slow and hard. 'But let's not get carried away with commendations when there is a clear winner amongst you.'

There's only one chef remaining that he could be talking about.

And that's Beardy. Beardy the soufflé assassin is standing, arms folded across his chest, a proud, smug smile across his round, red face.

'Our grand chef of today, is Harry Trott. Harry, please talk us through your dish.'

Dirty Harry he should be called, the hairy, sneaking cheat.

Harry explains in a low, gravelly tone. 'It's a clam, pickled potato, and Sichuan oil salad. I sliced the potato finely with a mandolin, then placed the slices in a pickling broth of ginger and star anise, while the clams went into a saucepan to mingle with garlic, shallot, and a healthy glug of sake. With the fishy clams and the bright, luminous red Sichuan oil – which I made with plenty of chillies and peppercorns – I wanted to make a statement. I like loud, bold, in-your-face flavours. I like ingredients that intimidate: tongue, brains, jellyfish, cod sperm. I love nothing more than persuading diners to eat foodstuffs they wouldn't ordinarily appeal. I take what's intimidating and make it interesting,' he says, chin high, nostrils flared, as if he'd already been crowned grand chef and we're now his lowly minions. 'I like to challenge. I like nervousness, anticipation, but most of all I like drama, because that's what makes a meal great.'

Cod sperm? Did he say *cod sperm*?

Pip actually smiles. It is the first time I have seen his teeth. He walks forward and shakes Dirty Harry's hand. 'Now, I'm excited. The competition is hotting up,' he nods towards us, the remaining four.

'Go home. *Au revoir et à demain,*' says a big-chested Jean-Michel as he turns on his heel and out the door without a backward glance.

As I gather my belongings together at my station, I know I should be rejoicing at surviving today and having the chance to come back tomorrow, but I can't help but feel enraged that Harry has got away with what he did. By the smug grin on his face, he is very pleased with himself, and his cunning plan to trounce the competition got him to the top spot after all. And I'm the only one who knows what he did to Ben. I'm the only one who knows his dirty little sabotaging secret. To everyone else, Harry Trott appears a genius, a daring savant, an unbeatable new grand chef.

But I know different. So, as I slip my apron over my head and fold it carefully ready for the next day, I decide that tomorrow is not just about survival, not just about avoiding elimination. Tomorrow, I've got to set my sights on winning. If nothing else, I want to wipe that smug look off Harry Trott's cod-spermy face and serve him up his just desserts.

Ben calls out to me and I see that he's making his way in my direction. But I've had about as much as I can take today. Personally *and* professionally. So I nod my goodbyes and dash out into the fading evening light. With a surprising sense of relief and a swell of pride, I jump on my bike and start pedalling straight for Parklands.

CHAPTER THIRTEEN

As this is a late evening shift, the place is eerily quiet, empty and still when I arrive. I push through the heavy wooden doors into a deserted, dimly lit kitchen and I realise that I'm the only catering staff member here. No Mel and Zoe to chat to and have fun with, but likewise, no Bernie to harass me and bring me down. I change out of my lovely starched tunic into a well-worn gingham bib, slip on a blue plastic hairnet and take a moment to listen... to absolutely nothing. No shouted orders, no cynical guffaws, no snorted criticisms, no call for time. Nothing but the sound of my slowing heartbeat and the rhythmic buzz of white noise coming from the fridges. I pause a second to catch my breath. It is blissful.

I don't turn on the radio, grateful for the silence, happy to be alone for a while after the franticness of the day. For the first time ever, I'm actually looking forward to getting stuck into the mindless routine of this factory-line kitchen, the repetitive, brain-numbing nature of the work seeming almost meditative compared to the fraught intensity of Jean-Michel's kitchen. And now that I find myself completely physically and emotionally overwhelmed by the process, it is a great pleasure and relief that I get to come here and work in solitude, without audience, scrutiny, judgement or fear. I smile to myself as I hoist up the first of four huge bins of spuds for washing, knowing that once the prep is done, I'm free to go home.

I can do this kind of work with my eyes closed, so as my hands rinse and sieve and peel and dice, my mind wanders off to somewhere else altogether.

And I'd like to say it was on planning my next menu or quizzing myself on rusty techniques or even mentally psyching myself to bring out my best and not get intimidated by Harry Trott's cut-throat campaign to win.

But it's Ben that's on my mind.

I can't think of anything else but him.

I think about the way he mouthed 'thank you' to me earlier.

I've stared at his photo for so long, it is like I have a static memory of him in mind. So today, when we were actually facing each other again in real life and real time, it didn't *seem* real. It felt was like I was imagining the whole thing. Or more accurately, I had to check myself that the whole business of us breaking up and going our separate ways wasn't the illusion. Did that really happen? Because today, in that kitchen, in that moment that I was standing in front of him with my hands on his shoulders, it felt like we'd never been apart. That we belonged together and that was the way it was meant to be.

So, even though professionally, I'm moving on, getting back on track to recovery, I have to admit that seeing Ben has only shown me how little I've moved on emotionally. And how little I want to.

They say it's better to have loved and lost than to never have loved at all.

That is utter bollocks.

I'd have been better off never knowing what it was like to love Ben. Because then I wouldn't know how special and rare and impossibly unattainable it is with anyone else.

'There are plenty more fish in the sea,' I was told on about five thousand occasions. Which is great, if you like men with fish lips or fish scents or with wet fish personalities. Or sharks like Harry Trott.

Today I looked at Ben and I just wanted to press rewind, and bring us right back to just before we went off the cliff edge, in two separate directions. I think it's because I still see the waste, the travesty, the *wrongness* of us being apart. It would be so much easier to see him and think to myself '*You bastard*'. To steel myself with memories of all our shortcomings, to remind myself of all the ways he treated me badly or let me down or made me feel worthless.

But I can't conjure up anything of the sort.

Because Ben never did any of these things.

In fact, he made me feel like I was the most special, most beautiful, most cared for girl in the world.

And being around him again, all it has done is reawaken that ache. God, how I miss feeling that way. Special, loved, safe.

How I miss how we were. Loved up, hopeful, fearless for the future.

Who we were when we were together. Happy, confident, anchored.

Then came sad, confused and lost.

I was bereft when we split, but given that he was leaving the country there was no chance of me 'accidentally' bumping into him looking effortlessly drop-dead gorgeous, or spontaneously cycling to his house in my PJs in the early hours of the morning begging for another chance, or calling him up when I drank too much wine and pouring my heart into his voicemail. He was gone, he was unreachable. So I threw myself into the restaurant, and barely came up for air.

But now he is back. Footsteps away from me again every time we stand at our stations. And even if I don't turn my head, even if I don't make eye contact, even if I turn my back and pretend he is just another chef, just any other guy, I know he's there.

We were so good together. We really could have had it all. Everybody thought so.

That made the fallout quite unreal, and the thought of ever getting with someone else quite unnatural. So for me there hasn't been anyone else, not even close. But Ben has never had any shortage of admirers, Georgia was testimony to that. Maybe us breaking up turned out to be the best thing that ever happened for him.

I hoist up the second bin of potatoes, and start scrubbing them under scalding hot water, burying myself in the task, making a poor attempt at trying not to think about it all any more. We believed that we had to have it one way or another. Not trusting ourselves to find a way to realise both our dreams and ambitions, to find balance, to make time for each other. I want to run over to my twenty-six-year-old self and shake her by the shoulders. Instead I shrug my shoulders, because it's all too little, too late and it just hurts too much to wish that things were any different.

By the time the clock strikes eleven and I near the end of my shift, I have been so lost in the silence, in my own thoughts, busily ticking off the jobs on the list left by Zoe, that I've hardly noticed the hours pass, not drag as they usually do. My last task is to leave out the breakfast service ready for the early shift and do a quick whip-round the residents to see if anyone wants a last cup of tea before I knock off for the night and close the kitchen.

I walk the dimly lit, quiet carpeted halls, gently knocking on each resident's door, but there is no one awake now, nothing to hear except some deep snoring, the hypnotic mumblings of late-night radio and the odd sleep-talker whispering the other side of a dream. I pop my head around Martha's door, but she is sound asleep, a smile dancing on her lips. By her bedside is an open photo album, and I take a quick peek. A young, impossibly glamourous Martha sits at a very fancy dining table laughing while her striking moustachioed Oskar pops a champagne cork. The next photo shows Martha again in her finery, this time a very cute cream flapper dress, cuddled into Oskar as she kicks out her leg and smiles. I look closer and I realise I recognise the exterior of the building; she is on the steps of the Ritz. Wow, she really wasn't joking when she said that she wined and dined in the finest places in her day.

I look back at the dreamy way she is looking at her moustachioed soulmate. Her love for him is so easy to read, shining as it is from her eyes and her smile. I remember that Oskar died last year. And in this moment, I understand it. I understand about taking the trip and eating the cake and buying the shoes. Because joy is a gift and we should celebrate every second that we are granted. I feel so happy that Oskar Rosenblatt really lived his life philosophy, enjoying everything in the moment and not holding back on life's pleasures because, standing here by Martha's bed, I can tell the fun they had, from the photos and the stories, that the memories they made together are still sustaining her now. It's these that are keeping her heart lit with hope and, all this time later, still sending her to sleep with a nostalgic smile, even though she is now without him. How she must miss him. I hope she's had a good day.

I write her a quick note to say hi and that I'm through to the next round of selection and leave it on her bedside locker. I reach into my bag and pull out the Tupperware of sliced banana bread with cinnamon butter that I brought for my lunch but forgot to eat. 'Eat the Cake!' I scribble down on the bottom of the note, and leave the box on top. I know she'll be pleased as punch. Just as I am.

After I've closed up the kitchen, I start my cycle home in the pitch dark. Now, this is eerie. There is no one around and I feel like I'm in the trailer of a Stephen King movie. When I see someone at a carwash late at night, I assume they've just committed murder. And that they are probably in the mood to strike again. Pedalling as fast as I can, I hear nothing but my own shallow panting magnified in the dark alley that I need to take to get me home as quickly as possible.

I wasn't joking when I said I was scared of the dark. Especially deserted, urban darkness, crackling with the sounds of distant arguments, flickering street lights and rustling bin bags. I keep my eyes on the path ahead, and try to banish all thoughts of hooded men, serial killers and flesh-eating clowns out of my mind. I feel my phone vibrate in my bag but dare not stop to check it. I need to get home as quickly as possible.

When I finally turn the corner in to Alice's road, my heart is pounding in my chest.

I never want to do that again. I hated it even more than I imagined I would.

I completely underestimated how terrifying that was, yet every night this week I'm going to have to repeat that dark gauntlet run. I have no money for a taxi instead and, besides, I need my bike at home to get to the Rembrandt every morning. I swallow back the fear at the thought of doing this again tomorrow night. Of everything I'm putting myself through to win the chance to work for Jean-Michel, so far, this is the hardest.

I quickly lock up my bike by the railings and turn the key in the door, feeling along the wall for the light and that's when I sense it, sense another person, sense that I'm not alone as I stand rooted with terror in this tiny dark doorway. There is someone running through the house towards me. OMG OMGGGGAH-HHHH!

I am screaming so hard that I can't catch my breath. I've collapsed on to my knees and I'm holding two fingers up like a cross. I don't know what I'm expecting to happen; I'm not thinking, I'm just screaming.

The light switches on and when I open my eyes all I can see is a laughing Alice.

'What the hell!' is all I can manage to cry as I get my breath back – along with rasping snippets of, 'Why are you even here? I thought you were at work! I thought you were a burglar! Or a feckin' clown!'

I am on my knees begging for my life, and it's just Alice. Standing in her own doorway bra-less in her sweatshirt and shorts. Laughing. Laughing her little blonde head off.

My hands fly to my heart which feels like it is going to erupt out of my chest. 'Alice, it's not funny! Never do that to me again! Why didn't you say!'

'I texted you just ten minutes ago to say that I was back, but you didn't check it. This caseload is going to be way bigger than we thought so I figured I'd just come home and work here.'

It must have been Alice's text message I heard vibrating in my bag when I was cycling scared through the city. I rub my hands down my face. 'I'm sorry. Oh my god I need to get inside. You scared the living shit out of me.'

I collapse on to the sofa as Alice brings me a cup of tea and some of the last buttered slices of banana bread. I turn to thank her and notice her trying to cover her laughing mouth with her oversized sweatshirt sleeve.

'Get lost,' I smile at her, drinking in the hot milky sweetness that instantly dissolves some of the tension still in my neck and shoulders.

Alice throws her head back, letting all her giggles loose. She starts to mimic me screaming with two bulging eyes and a huge o-shaped mouth.

'You should have seen yourself! I swear I have never heard anyone scream so loud. It's like you saw a ghost.'

Now that I've regained my breath and know the door is safely locked behind me, I sink into the corner of the sofa. And I start laughing. 'Shut up. I hate you,' I tell her, kicking her arm.

'And you of all people are never jumpy!' Alice pours herself a cup of tea and snuggles in beside me on the sofa, tucking her feet underneath her. 'So come on, I want the lowdown on everything I've missed. I can tell it's already shaken you up. I'm not surprised that Jean-Michel has you jumping out of your skin like a nervous wreck. Nobody can work with that man.'

I shake my head. 'Worse.'

She raises a quizzical eyebrow.

'Ben.' I tell her.

Alice's mouth slowly drops and she shakes her head quizzically.

'Ben's also been selected. He's going for the same job.'

Alice puts down her cup of tea and turns to me fully, looking straight at me so there is no room for misinterpretation. 'Have I got this right: you and Ben are in the same kitchen, working side by side, in competition with each other.'

I nod.

'Whoa.' And she blows out her cheeks. 'So it really is like you've seen a ghost. Good luck with that.'

CHAPTER FOURTEEN

'*Bonjour, Mesdemoiselles et Messieurs.*' Jean-Michel greets me and the three remaining male chefs as we fall in behind our individual stations like military officers awaiting command.

Octavia nods her head towards us all. I am so glad to see her here today. Without her it would be just me and six men including the judges and maître d'; it's easy enough to be overwhelmed by the pressure without feeling in the minority as well. Her eyes stay on me a beat longer than the rest and a smidgen of a smile raises the corner of her lip. I feel a swell of pride carry through from my stomach to my throat, and I want to run over and wrap my arms around her and say, 'I'm still here! Thank you for believing in me!' But regal and dignified Octavia doesn't seem the sort to appreciate hugs and hollering. I blink my gratitude but I dare not put a foot out of line; as every day progresses, this gets more serious. As we've seen the competition whittled down to just four of us, we know that it will take every ounce of concentration, of imagination and of strength of will to make it through today. And if I make it through today, then I'm in touching distance of a brand new life as a Jean-Michel's grand chef: my career rescued, my status redeemed, my self-respect restored. I straighten my back and focus. Today is big. In this world, it doesn't get much bigger.

'Like every creative, every visionary, we are not always wonderful in a team,' says Jean-Michel. 'The vision makes sense to us, we know how to realise it ourselves, and it frustrates and delays us to involve other people in the process. Chefs are just the same and as a result can be the world's worst delegators. As perfectionists, we want to do it all ourselves. Not possible.

'We have these recipes in our minds that we are not patient enough to write down, and therefore we run the risk of becoming inconsistent. This cannot happen. Assembling the recipe, fine-tuning it, establishes a consistent high mark in terms of standard. This is paramount. This is what makes a great restaurant a *Michelin*-starred restaurant. Unfailing consistency. Every. Single. Time. Not just for the *Times* reviewer or the high-profile client, not just the signature dish or when the grand chef is watching. But every forkful, at every sitting. Perfection without fail.'

Octavia nods towards Jean-Michel and places both hands at the pass. 'So before you can cook perfection, you must taste it. If you don't know how it is supposed to taste, then you shouldn't be cooking it. But if you know how it tastes perfectly, then you will cook it one hundred times better. So today we will begin in an old-school way, focusing on taste. The ultimate culinary test, today you will be replicating a highly technical Jean-Michel dish.'

Jean-Michel steps out from behind the pass and begins to walk towards a vacant station. 'I am not going to tell you what to do. I am going to *show* you. You will have to rely on your eyes and your palate to recreate it – as I will not give you a recipe or a list of the ingredients I am using, nor will I answer any questions. I will cook it. Then it will be your turn.'

Jean-Michel slips an apron over his head and begins to cook. He's mesmerising to watch, moving with such speed and confidence, the likes of which I've never before seen. He uses so many ingredients, moves so fast, so smoothly. He places a fillet of white fish – *Is it halibut? Sea bass?* – into a pan. On another gas ring he is making a sauce, light, opaque and fragrant. *Lemon and dill? Garlic and fennel?* My mind is racing as I try to take in and analyse everything whilst listening to Jean-Michel's commentary at the same time.

'This is the exciting part,' he says as he nears the end. 'Plating up.' He stops and considers the round white plate. 'For me there is nothing so exciting as an empty plate. It is like a clean piece of paper, a blank canvas, naked, new, it is ready for your creation, ready to become. Just like your own life, it is up to you what you will do with it... You are the creator, the expression is yours, just like any artist.' Slowly, with eyes narrowed, he arranges his leaves. 'Using the plate as a canvas is key in mastering the art of presentation. Use sauces, leaves and other garnishes to frame the focal point. It's all about proportions and really following your instincts. Sometimes I need to take a few steps back to look at the plate like a work of art; sometimes you need a bit of distance.'

He continues to build and layer. 'Simplicity is always beautiful. But it must be executed perfectly. Can you imagine Van Gogh with an unfinished brushstroke? Jimi Hendrix playing even one wrong chord, Pavarotti's voice splitting on a high note? You would be disgusted. Even minute imperfection renders everything imperfect. Food is our medium. This is the standard expected.' He gently lifts the final various exotic vegetables from the pan to the plate, with the accuracy and sensitivity of a surgeon.

I watch him build the plate, complete his canvas. It is a masterpiece. In terms of colour, shape and balance. And I haven't even eaten the thing yet.

My eyes drift from the dish to the man himself. This is the first opportunity I've had to actually study Jean-Michel up close, almost touching distance. Usually it is us in the spotlight, under his scrutiny, and we have no time to look up, no time to get a sense of who this crazy genius actually is. He has a large head, ruffled unkempt black hair, pointing now in all directions, and a face of deep lines, like childhood scars. You don't see lines like these on a man who has just turned forty. Jean-Michel doesn't smoke, and is a mountain marathon runner. The lines betray something that exercise can't melt: Stress? Fear? Fury? Guilt?

He wipes the sides of the plate with a clean dishcloth and raises his hands in the air. '*C'est fini. Bon appetit.*'

We each marvel at the intricate fish dish in front of us.

'Food should be created with passion, thought and technique, but plated with a light hand, with direction from nature. Colours should reflect the seasons, with contrasting light and dark shades that evoke emotion. In the end, keep it simple and let the ingredients be the stars. Now, taste.'

Each of us takes a fork and digs in. The first mouthful is absolutely divine. Light, lemony, aromatic, slightly fruity with a real kick from the fresh herbs. How I would love to sit down with this and a nice, crisp glass of white wine! But I must remember that I am here as a student, as an apprentice. I dive in for another bite. Carefully, I try to decipher all the flavours I can identify. The fish is halibut, I'm certain. The sauce is a delicate combination of wine, stock and olive oil with a hint of marjoram and lemon for a light citrus tang. Okay, I think I've got it.

Octavia speaks. 'We need to see you working in a team. How you communicate with each other, how you reach a decision, how you delegate and deliver. So, Harry and Joe, you are Team A. Katie and Ben you are Team B. You have one hour to select your ingredients from the pantry and replicate Jean-Michel's dish. Your time starts now.'

I turn to Ben. He looks as shocked as I am.

'Katie and Ben, together again. Who'd have thought?' he says, rubbing his neck, eyes lowered to the floor.

We shuffle on the spot a second, unsure of where to start. How to restart.

In the background I hear Harry's voice screaming orders at mild-mannered Joe. Team A ain't waiting around bonding. And

I cannot let Harry beat us. I clap my hands together and take a deep breath. It is on.

'Right, let's do this. You raid the pantry for the vegetables and seasoning, I'll take care of the fish and get the stove on.'

'Yes, chef,' he says with a smile. And just like that, we are on our way.

Ben and I work like dancers. I move forward, he moves back. It is like there is a music that only we can hear. Everything that Ben brought from the pantry is exactly what I thought. Right down to the length and arrangement of our courgette ribbons. A sideways glance towards the pan, a slight eyebrow raise, a licking of the lips and we understand each other. Everything makes sense. And we just know what the other is thinking, we are perfectly aligned.

Unlike Team A.

Harry is pounding through the kitchen in a sprint-walk, disturbing everyone, taking over at least three stations, chopping carrots whilst muttering curses, tasting the sauce Joe has prepped ('We're not going with that! Get some water into you *now*! You must be dehydrated, your palate is fucked.'), wilting an endive ('No, *this* is how you do it – you start with a really hot pan, right? What the *hell* is wrong with you?').

I feel for poor Joe, just twenty-three, adolescently thin, long-limbed, with big ears and the quick-twitch temperament of a racing animal.

'You are cooking like a robot,' shouts Harry into his ear. 'How could you think that was OK? Use your head.' Then, seeing Joe start to become flustered, Harry claps him on the back, massaging his shoulder. 'It's okay. Stay calm. We are going to win this, Joe. Hands down. We are going to wipe the floor with Team B.'

Ben gives me a nudge but we don't take our eyes off the stove. This is too important. We need to stay focused. We need to make this right.

Harry's last words to Joe should have been reassuring, but then he whips his dishcloth angrily on to the floor, slamming his hand on the steel table. 'You are making me so nervous, man,' he says.

Joe stiffens visibly, which inflames Harry yet again.

'Did you hear me? You are making me very fucking nervous.' He stares at Joe and, not getting a reply, screams, 'Will you just fucking relax!'

Joe's ears turn deep red.

Once Harry has allowed himself to get angry, he seems to look around for other things to stay angry about, as though something has been switched on that he can't control. For Joe, the next task involves the fish. He's cooking it in a sauté pan.

Harry walks over and stands inches away. 'More oil in your pan! You're not cooking it. You're scorching it. Did you hear me? You're ruining the dish.'

'Yes, chef.' Joe quickly adds oil to his pan.

'Why are you scorching it?'

'I don't know, chef.'

'You don't know! Will you get a grip?'

'Yes, chef.'

'Will you focus?'

'Yes, chef.'

Harry continues to stare. 'You are so fucking insular. It's like you're wearing a straitjacket. Will you fucking loosen up?'

Joe seems, understandably, unable to loosen up while being screamed at.

We work hard to the final minute, plating up with the same surgeon-like accuracy we saw Jean-Michel use.

'Three, two, one. Stop!'

Both Ben and I raise our hands in the air and exhale for what feels like the first time in sixty minutes.

Octavia approaches the pass, where we stand beside our plate and Harry and Joe stand beside theirs. I try to catch Joe's eye, to reassure him, to give him some moral support. But he won't look anywhere but at his feet. I understand. His face has puffed up with held-back tears. He doesn't want sympathy or pity. He's humiliated enough by the end of a long and relentless haranguing by Harry.

Jean-Michel approaches the pass after Octavia, both of them with forks at the ready. Both our dishes are presentable. Both look elegant, balanced: a good replication of Jean-Michel's own dish.

He tastes ours first.

He finishes his mouthful. And points his index finger to the sky.

'Bravo.' He glances down to our plate. 'Stunning. You nailed it. Flavours, balance, presentation. It is like a symphony.'

I can't help but catch Ben smiling, which makes me smile too.

Then he turns his attention to Harry and Joe and tucks in.

'This also is a very promising effort. A few things wrong, not perfect. You over-seasoned your couscous and the garnish looks a little sparse, but overall, not bad…' He looks to Octavia.

'Yes, we threw you in at the deep end,' she says. 'Yes, we asked you to replicate a three-star Michelin dish whilst working in a team. Jean-Michel is satisfied with your food. However, what we are also really looking for is potential. *Leadership* potential.' She turns to Joe first. 'You have the potential, but you need to find your voice. You are not taking control. You are being controlled.'

Jean-Michel winces. 'Look at you,' he whispers. 'When there's a problem, you shrink, you sulk. It's not good enough. You need to find yourself still. Please go. Leave. You are not ready for my kitchen.'

I am shocked. I can barely believe that it's Joe that is being sent away, not Harry. Harry was a complete brute! All of us know that this industry is not an easy ride. We are all more than aware of the sacrifices it involves: the hours, the scrutiny, the weeping, spending the night on a dining-room banquette because there wasn't time to go home and be back for the morning prep. And then it dawns on me. Maybe *Harry* is what Jean-Michel wants.

Maybe it's this behaviour that he wants perpetuated. I guess we've put up with it because it was Jean-Michel: god, genius, legend. But seeing it in someone lesser shows it for all its monstrosity. It is nothing to do with being in a position of authority. It is clear that Harry is a bully, and now I see that Jean-Michel is too. He is no better than Bernie or that man who shouted at my mother in the car park all those years before. All this about pushing us beyond our limits is crap. It's just about pushing us as hard as he can, ruthlessly pushing some of us over the edge.

He watches as Joe slips his apron over his head and tries to stop his bottom lip from trembling. He looks up one more time and, for a split second, I think he is going to say something, that he is going to find his voice and stick up for himself, scream down Jean-Michel and Harry and let them know that he *is* ready, that holding his tongue was his brand of courage. That putting up and plating up was his way of being strong and making sure the job was done, not because of Harry but in spite of him.

But Joe closes his mouth again and walks out the door, his head bent low.

A heavy, tense atmosphere descends upon us. Part of me wants to rush out and see if Joe is okay. Another part of me wants to find my own voice and ask Jean-Michel why on earth he thinks it is necessary to treat anyone that way. I look to him. He too has paused and become reflective, seeming to savour the effects of his punishment. Then his face breaks into a smile.

'Did you see that? Did you see that young chef's face?' His voice is high-pitched, almost shrill. 'The way it was all knotted up? Wasn't it fantastic? He was in terrible pain. Isn't it fascinating how food can make for such pure emotion? He was desperate. He wants to be here so badly it hurts.'

I clear my throat. I need to speak out. This is vicious, cruel. I open my mouth but nothing comes out. Again I cough, but something only akin to a squeak escapes.

Jean-Michel raises his arms above his head and meets each of us in the eye.

The moment is gone. I missed it, choked with a mixture of horror and fear.

'My final three. Ben, Katie and Harry. Prepare your taster menus: three courses. Tomorrow night, here at the Marchand, we will test you for the final time.'

I am in the final three. I look to Octavia.

She smiles at me as she says, 'You shall all run your own kitchen, serving your own menus to ten of the most influential diners in London. The most successful will be appointed the new Grand Chef.'

Tomorrow night I will run my own high-end kitchen. I will prepare and serve my own menu. Tomorrow night, I will make or break my career forever.

'*Bonne chance,*' they both say in unison, and with that we are dismissed.

As I unlock my bike outside, Ben catches up with me.

'Hey. Why do you always run off so fast? I've been trying to catch you every day so far.'

'Really? For what?'

He widens his eyes and looks up at the sky awkwardly. 'To say hi. Properly. To, you know, catch up. See how you've been, what you've been up to.'

I throw my leg over the crossbar. 'There's nothing much to report.' I don't want to tell him that everything I've been up to has fallen flat on its arse.

'How about a quick drink?' he says. 'My shout. There's a cool Italian place I spotted right there across the road. It's busy all the time so they must be doing something right. It'd be nice to check it out and… celebrate. Besides, I feel like I owe you one.'

'Owe me? For what?'

'For the vichyssoise. If you hadn't suggested it I'd be gone by now and it would just be you and Harry against each other. So please, one drink, just to say thanks.'

I stop and think. I know I should just decline, but what could a little drink hurt? After tomorrow we're going to be going in different directions again. I may never ever see Ben again. And besides, I've got to be at the home for my shift in a couple of hours so there is no chance of me drinking too much and getting maudlin, or divulging way too much because I stay too long. It's literally one drink. Between two chefs who work well together. Two people with something to celebrate. That is all.

'Okay,' I tell him. 'But just the one because I've got to be somewhere else for 7 p.m.'

Ben's mouth breaks into a wide smile and his eyes flicker wide. 'Great! That's great. Here, let me take that.' He leans over and takes my helmet for me. Then he looks at me and says, 'That's the best thing I've heard all day.'

CHAPTER FIFTEEN

We slide into a low-lit booth by the front window. There's an Aladdin's-cave-like quality to this traditional trattoria, cosy and intimate with jars of decorative oils, nests of dried pastas and long, red hot peppers preserved in glass bottles. The walls are covered in an eclectic mix of landscape paintings and mirrors with a distinctive Sicilian feel, wild and rustic with muted earthen colours in the stonework. It's gorgeous. I wish the owner every success; this place is a gem. It smells of onion and garlic and freshly baked bread and melting cheese. I love the informality of it: waiters and waitresses rushing by in aprons with pads and pens sticking out of their pockets, customers straight from work, swivelling on stools, murmuring and talking and laughing and slurping their forkfuls of spaghetti.

'Peroni?' Ben asks, snapping me out of my own thoughts.

I nod. 'You've got a good memory.'

He tries to catch my eye, but I'm afraid of what I'm going to find there. This is weird. It's me and Ben, alone again, having a drink and eyeing up the food on everyone else's plates. This is who we were, how we used to spend our time. But I don't know who we are now, so I smile curtly and continue my inspection of the tables covered in paper cloths and the steaming trays of little plates weaving their way past us. It all looks and smells so good. Why have I never been here before?

Ben orders our drinks and once the waiter leaves we both simultaneously reach for the tall card menu in the middle of the table like two kids playing snap.

I ball my fists and hold them in the air in defeat. 'Go for it, don't mind me. Force of habit.'

A smile rises in the corner of his mouth. Then Ben gets up from his seat at the opposite side of the table and slides into the seat beside me, opening the menu up in full view for both of us to read together.

'Just like old times, eh?' he asks, again giving me a side glance that I refuse to meet.

I can't trust myself. If I meet his eyes there is every chance that I will give everything away: how much I've missed him, how un-over him I am, how badly I've been doing since we split.

I take a deep breath and keep trailing my finger down the menu.

'You very hungry?' he asks me.

Oh he knows my bloody weak spots. At this, I can't help but give him a look as if to ask if the Pope's Catholic.

'Maybe we should just order a few things. Research, just a few bites to wake up those taste buds,' I tell him.

He nods excitedly. 'It would be rude not to! This place is famous for their antipasto. And the way this cold beer is going down after the day we've had, I could destroy this entire menu without coming up for air.'

I love this about Ben. He's always ready to eat! I start throwing out some suggestions. 'We'll get the platter, right? Artichoke hearts, black mission figs, cherry peppers. Some meat, cheese.' I know that should be enough, but our fingers are still skidding across the menu card. I pause. 'Oh, we've got to. Shrimp romesco, I want to see how they do that.'

Ben flashes a thumbs up and moves over to the top of the next page, tapping the first item. 'Breaded courgette blossoms with goat's cheese. *Deep-fried.*'

'No-brainer,' I say, rubbing my hands together; this is going to be amazing. 'Right just one more thing each, I'll count to three and we'll both say our choices out loud and then we'll stop, we'll just shut the menu. Okay?'

Ben nods, and I count down on my fingers. Three, two, one…

'Lemon and black pepper calamari,' we both say at the same time. I try not to look freaked out. Like the Venn diagram of me and Ben isn't like two circles placed one on top of each other.

'Sounds perfect, you're on,' he smiles. 'But make sure we order two, can't have you pulling your little stunts, because I'm telling you now, I am not sharing the calamari…'

'What little stunts?' I gasp in mock offence.

'Oh, you know exactly what I'm talking about, Katie. Claiming you just want to try a mouthful and then eating the whole lot. You may look like the high-end gourmet, but remember I know all your secrets.'

I pick at the label on my beer bottle as a jolt hits me.

Ben's wrong. He only *thinks* he knows all my secrets. He *used* to know all my secrets. But so much has happened since the time we shared a life, a bed, since we thought we shared a future. We are two different people now. No doubt with a whole host of new secrets.

The food comes and it is glorious. With every bite we are groaning and yelping and licking our fingers and shaking our stuffed squirrel cheeks with delight. This place is amazing: my new favourite. I've already had so many ideas just being here. And Ben was right. I'm really glad I got my own calamari; there isn't a crumb left.

Ben stabs a bite of the melted goat's cheese from the platter with his fork and raises it to my lips. 'This! Just taste this. I mean, the balance of sweet and salty is pitch perfect…' He puckers his lips to kiss the air.

Without a second thought, I lean in and bite it off his fork.

He turns to me and for a moment our eyes are locked, and it's like we have never been apart. I nod my head and let myself hold his gaze.

'What do you think?' he asks.

'I love it,' I tell him.

And then I pick up my spoon and dip it into the romesco sauce. I raise it to his lips and he opens his mouth. In that second everything feels right, and I imagine myself leaning in and passing my lips against his. I think about my hand following the gorgeous curve of his face and sliding my fingers across his skin, his cheek and into his soft dark hair.

Oh Ben... He squeezes his eyes closed as he swallows, and I watch the rise and fall of his Adams's apple as the mouthful slides its way down his throat.

'Sensational,' he says finally, his eyes bright and wide and the same deep brown colour as melted chocolate.

'Sensational,' I echo. *If only you knew.*

He looks up to the ceiling shaking his head as if he's posed himself a question that he can't answer. 'It's been such a long time since I've done something like this. Francesca doesn't really... How can I say this? She's a picky eater. An extremely picky eater. She wouldn't really like the scene in here, you know, bit too loud, too casual.'

I raise my eyebrow. 'Francesca?'

He nods, biting down on his lip. '*Francesca*, she's my girlfriend. She works on the ship too, in the casino. She's great, very supportive, ambitious. We've been together quite a while. About six months now I'd say.'

'Right.' I try to smile and not dissolve all at once, distracting myself by taking the neck of my bottle to my lips.

'So when this opportunity came up, it made sense, you know?'

I drink my beer and nod and squint my eyes like I can empathise with every single word and mumble 'absolutely' at least three times.

'How about you? You seeing anyone?' Ben asks me.

I shake my head. 'No. Not at the moment. Not since— Not for a long, long time. You know me. Work, work, work.'

A silence swirls between us. I hate the feel of it, heavy and electric. I take deep breath, conscious that I've ripped the beermat in front of me. I need to break the tension; we're just two old friends having a drink, no need for things to be so solemn and serious.

'I'm really glad, Ben. Truly. I'm really glad that it all worked out for you. The ship, and all that travel, a serious girlfriend, that's a great life and you deserve it.' I raise my bottle to toast. 'To the future, right?'

He clinks his bottle against mine. 'To the future.'

Our chat drifts back to the food and then about our families, about Octavia and Pip and Jean-Michel, what he's really like, what he's really after.

'Another drink?' Ben asks as he finishes his own.

I shake my head and go to look to my wrist out of habit. My *bare* wrist. A sad look clouds Ben's face as he registers that I'm not wearing my watch any more. I twist my wrist and start making my excuses to leave, eyeing up the nearest waitress for the bill.

'I can't, I need to be on my way,' I tell him. 'My shift starts soon.'

He nods. 'So where exactly do you work now?'

Hmm. Parklands Care Home isn't something to brag about. It's hardly Casino Royale where Francesca works. I bet she's super glamorous. I bet she works out and never eats bread. Or fat. Or sugar. I bet he's in love with her. I bet she's in love with him.

Nope. I'm not coming clean with Ben. There isn't any way I want him to know the full extent of my fall from grace.

'Oh, just a local place, local to Alice and me... Nowhere you'd know.'

'Is it a restaurant?'

'It's more of a hotel really, lots of residents. Booked out in fact.'

He nods. 'And you like it?'

I want to tell him I hate it, but we've had such a lovely time. I don't want to put a downer on things.

'There are some great people. Some not so great, but that's life right?'

He nods knowingly. 'Speaking of not so nice, do you remember Ozzy from college?'

The dreaded name… *Ozzy*. I've not heard that name since the day we graduated.

I feel my skin prickle and my hand reaches up to the back of my neck.

'You can't have forgotten Ozzy?' says Ben, probably confused by my muted response.

I shake my head. 'No, sadly. I haven't forgotten him. Despite my best efforts.'

Ben stretches his hands out wide. 'He came to work on the ship! Complete moron. He was fired within the first few weeks. Never met anyone as up their own arse as him in my whole life. Actually, I take that back. The way Harry was acting today – screaming abuse, shouting, yelling, creating drama – brought it flooding back to me.'

'I bet,' I say. Ben isn't the only one who has drawn parallels between Ozzy and Harry. It's been flooding back to me too and, to be perfectly honest, not in a way that I'm finding easy to deal with. He completely rattled me way back then, kept trying to tell me that I wasn't up to it, that I wasn't good enough, that I didn't belong.

I drain the end of my beer and push it into the middle of the table.

'Do you ever think about what could have been?' Ben asks.

I look at him, confused. He reddens.

'I mean if you'd come to work on the ship too? Mediterranean skies at this time of year are really spectacular.'

'Sounds like you still love it?'

He nods. 'What's not to love? Open seas, a new adventure every day.'

'Then why are you here? Why did you apply in the first place?'

'I didn't. I was put forward by Jean-Michel's wife. She insisted I come for interview. And then Francesca told the Captain and he told me not to upset such a high-profile guest, to comply with what she wanted and go from there. And so, I came. And now I'm here. Sitting with you, through to the final round.'

'And so you're glad you came?'

'Very glad. I'm realising that I kinda miss the crazy, you know?'

I nod. I know.

'Once I set foot back in London, I couldn't believe how much I missed it. I miss lots of things. Or maybe deep down, I *did* know how much I missed it but just blanked it out. Pretty deep right? So, win or lose on the big night, I'm going to have to figure out the next step. The thing is, it's easy to forget the real world when you are on the ship, living in a gorgeous, glamourous luxurious bubble. Life is simple: you work, you sleep, sun comes up, sun goes down and we wake up in another beautiful port. And don't get me wrong, it's amazing for a while, but still, it's transient, it's not real. And I feel ready for real.'

'So what happens if you win tomorrow?'

Ben blows out his cheeks and runs his fingers through his hair. 'I almost can't even think about it. It would be incredible. Absolutely incredible. To be back here, as a grand chef in one of the most anticipated openings in the world. Cooking for the good and the great, learning under Jean-Michel, close to family, loved ones.' He blinks as if to shake himself out of a daydream. 'I want it so much.' He presses his hands against his chest, that side smile of his appearing. 'It hurts how much I want this.'

It hurts to see him like this. But I know exactly what he means because I want it just as badly – but by the sounds of it, I *need* it more too. At least Ben has a luxurious, exciting, loved-up bubble to return to. And he's got Francesca. I have Bernie and Alice's sofa bed. I can't afford to suffer another failure, another disappointment, another dissolution of a dream.

'How about you?' he asks me.

'I feel the same. I need this. I don't know if you know but the restaurant? I had to close it down.'

He reaches an arm around my shoulder and hugs me into him. 'I'm sorry, Katie. I'd heard it on the grapevine. I know how hard you worked for that.'

I try to swallow back any tears in my throat and catch my breath. The heat of Ben's body, the scent of him, shuttle me back through to a time that everything was right…

'So I guess I've got to prove myself all over again. My dad thinks I'm mad.'

'No change there.'

This brings a smile to my face. 'Alice thinks I'm mad too.'

'Well, maybe they're on to something.'

I give him a gentle nudge in the belly, and he cuddles me even tighter.

We hear a jingling and look up to see a Romany lady with a bucket full of red roses. She stands by our table and offers them up to us.

I can imagine what we look like. A cosy couple enjoying food and drinks together without a care in the world.

'Rose for lady? For sweetheart?'

I shuffle up in my seat, shaking my head whilst waving my hand politely. 'No! No, thank you.'

She pushes out a bottom lip and I realise that I've patronised her.

'Sorry, it's because we're just friends. Old friends.'

She smiles and nods her understanding and carries on to the next table.

'It's getting late; I've really got to go now,' I tell Ben, glancing out the front window to the fading light. 'I need to get to work while it's still light.'

He nods. 'You and the dark, eh?'

I shrug. 'Some things never change.' I raise my hand for the bill so they know I really do have to go this time. The waitress nods and touches her temple indicating that she forgot, and starts to tap into the cash register straight away.

I zip up my jacket as Ben's phone vibrates on the table. 'Francesca calling' appears on the screen. He looks at me sheepishly.

'Take it!' I tell him.

He tilts his head, uncertain.

'Please, take it, she'll be dying to know if you got through.'

Ben and I are not the same as we were, and we will never be. Old times are just that. Old. Gone, past, belonging to a different era. Impossible to resurrect or recreate. Not after everything that's happened. If Ben is in love with someone else now, what's it to me? What business is it of mine? I had my chance.

Ben's phone is still ringing out, he's still not answered it, and I can see the awkward conflict darken his features. Francesca's call just ringing out on the table between us.

Where is the waitress with the bill! I need to go. Outside the streetlights are flickering on and I'm on the wrong side of town for work.

Unable to stand it another second, I plunge my hand into my bag and pull out a twenty. My bloody *last* twenty, my last note, but I can't start scrambling around with coppers and coins. I want to disappear right now, before he takes this call.

'Right, I'm off. Seriously, just answer it, before you miss it. Tomorrow is a big day and we need to get on. And just a word of warning, keep your eye on Harry. I have reason to believe that he can be just as devious and underhanded as Ozzy was. And it's no secret that he wants to win – whatever it takes.'

I toss down the note in the middle of the table and grab my helmet, waving my last goodbye and dashing out of the restaurant to start pedalling my way to the home against the fading evening light as fast as I possibly can.

CHAPTER SIXTEEN

All the cycling must be paying off in terms of speed and fitness as I arrive at Parklands twenty minutes early. That's certainly a first, so I call up to see Martha straight away.

She claps her hands and shifts up in her bed soon as I enter her room.

'Peppermint tea?' I offer.

'Yes, please,' she says as she plumps her hair for me, batting her eyelashes theatrically.

'You are looking very well!' I tell her. 'New hair?'

She slides a soft, waxy hand over her freshly coiffed, dyed bright red 'do. 'Zoe did it for me this morning. Isn't it gorgeous! I feel like Rita Hayworth. And that was always Oskar's secret crush.' She giggles, looking fondly at the photo by her bedside.

'Any particular occasion? Another handsome doctor caught your eye?' I tease.

'Much, much better!' she laughs, widening her eyes with excitement. 'My son and grand-daughter are coming to see me! It's been ever so long, it certainly feels that way. But he promised he'd be here for my birthday this weekend. He's never missed one. So that's what really lifted my spirits. I can't wait.' She raises up her hands and wiggles her fingers. 'I just can't wait to get their beautiful faces in my hands and smother them with kisses. Once I get to do that, I don't care what happens! He can take me for a hot dog for all I care.'

I laugh, thinking of Martha's high-end palate and imagining her grappling with a saucy hot dog in her finery. I open up my bag, slide out my notepad and begin scribbling down three courses that I've been brainstorming the whole cycle ride over here.

'Can I run something by you, Martha?'

She takes a sip of her tea and meets my eyes. 'Of course, my darling, anything.'

'What do you think of my menu? Tomorrow is the big day. I need something that'll really blow them away. Show them what I can do and make an impression. What do you think?' I fill her in on what's expected and who I am up against. Harry's got a bold, daring, confronting style. With him I'm expecting the unexpected, nothing we've seen before, dry ice, sharp angles, new flavours… and that could be anything. Some rare, exotic reptile poached to perfection? Tempura grasshopper? I just haven't a clue what he's going to do. When cod sperm is his starting point, I know I'm up against a wild card.

'Sounds like a wild dog,' says Martha, sipping her tea. 'A mini Jean-Michel in the making. Not necessarily a good combination, two huge creative egos along with fiery tempers. It won't be long till they will clash, mark my words. Jean-Michel may not even know it himself yet but he needs someone who can keep calm, stay focused as well as be a great chef. I think you've got the edge on Harry; don't be intimidated by his puffed chest and loud noises.'

She slides her glasses up her nose and starts to read aloud.

'So, three courses, taster size. The guests will sample from all three of you and then vote after each course, is that right?'

I nod. 'Exactly. It sounds so simple, so straightforward on paper. But I'm not just cooking for guests; I'm cooking for chefs, for critics, for industry moguls who know how to scrutinise every mouthful. I have to exceed their expectations and then I've got to make sure that exceeds the efforts of Harry and Ben. This is tough; this is probably the toughest thing I have ever done.'

Martha slowly follows the words with her finger as she reads them, pausing and then moving backwards and then forwards again. I don't want to rush her but I'm desperate to know what she thinks. I sip my tea and wait. Martha's an amazing resource: a seasoned, well-travelled diner. In my father's words, I'd do well to sit up and pay attention to what she's got to say.

She takes off her glasses, placing them back on her bed side locker. She takes a deep breath through her nose before flattening her hands down on the bed and pursing her lips.

'So, you've given everything you have to get this far. You've made it past Jean-Michel and you are facing the final pass, and from your own admission, against some tough competition.' She shakes her head. 'They are not there to eat food. They are there to experience *your* food, your story. So, I think that's what we've got to give them.'

'What do you mean?'

'At the moment, these dishes all seem technically enchanting, but I don't know how much I'm learning about Katie Kelly here. You've got cocotte of vegetables with smoked orange peel, foie gras soup with sarawak pepper, and white root vegetable tart with beetroot syrup and purslane. And for dessert a Montélimar Nougat glacé, persimmon with clementine and orange in a rosemary syrup. Why this menu? You could choose anything, tell me, why this?'

I'm stumped. I was not expecting this reaction from Martha at all. I thought she'd be impressed! I find myself biting my thumb. She's waiting for an answer. And I can tell by the look in her eye that she's prepared to wait all night.

'I chose it because I thought it sounded impressive, because I didn't want them to think that I'm basic. I was taught how to prepare these dishes at college and I know I can deliver on them. They tick a lot of boxes in terms of skill and flavour and presentation.'

Martha hears me out and then grabs a pen from her bedside locker. 'All very respectable reasons. And now, I want you to imagine you are writing a menu that tells me the story of you. Would this be it?'

This time, I shake my head.

'Really think about it, Katie. What does it mean to you? Why these dishes for the most important cook-off of your life?'

I look down at my handwritten menu, lying flat on Martha's bedspread. She's right. Why have I chosen these dishes? I hate foie gras. I've never even been to Montélimar. And I'm not a big fan of nougat come to think of it. I think it tastes like stale marshmallow. A quiver begins in my right hand. Martha's right. I realise that I chose them to show off, as a vanity. And I can do better than this. I can give much more. These dishes don't mean anything to me. I may as well serve up Harry's dishes if I'm just going to be in the business of replicating other people's work.

What the hell am I going do? The final is tomorrow and now I haven't the faintest clue what I'm going to cook, never mind how I'm going to cook it, plate it, present it. My left hand is shaking as well. I feel sick.

Martha hands me her silver fountain pen, turning over the piece of paper to a fresh side. 'Now, don't you panic. Take a moment to listen to yourself and you'll find your answer. This is your chance to make your mark, Katie. Make it as exceptional as you are.'

Where do I start? With Rachel and I sharing a bag of pink toffee sweets that looked like melted Legos, Fruit Salads and Wham bars, tasting sharp and sour and sweet and sickly all at once. Or do I choose eggs Benedict, the first breakfast I made for Ben the morning after we 'officially' moved in together. Happy times: happy, joyous times. It's quite overwhelming to review your life in food, in dishes and dinners, in tastes and smells and textures. The buttery crunch of popcorn during a sleepover, the merciful comfort of a bacon sandwich when hungover, the velvety warmth of a bowl of soup after running home from school in the wind and rain. The way tea was always sweet and silky when my mother made it. The sheer pow! of excitement the first time I tasted fresh coriander or wild honey or a lychee. Or indeed, when Alice and I got smashed on lychee vodka. I smile at the thought, Alice singing in a karaoke booth after-hours, without any words, perhaps without any music. Certainly without any shame.

She waits patiently as I scribble down my ideas only to cross them out and rewrite something completely different, making additions only to take them away again. And then, all at once, I know exactly what I'm going to do. I'm going to plate up my story, shamelessly, fearlessly, proudly. And my hand starts to move across the paper, an even flow of perfect cursive, as if this menu has always existed somewhere forgotten, some place hidden. A menu that has been shelved in an old drawer in my head, a menu that's been standing at the back of the dance hall, biding its time, holding out for a particular song, waiting to be invited to dance.

I scribble through everything I wrote before, and I write my menu, three courses, rooted in memory, in love and perfectly representative of me, my upbringing, my taste, my experience. My life, my heart on a plate.

I clear my throat. 'I think I've got it now. Are you ready, Martha?'

She nods, patting her hair and smiling at me. 'Absolutely, chef.'

I begin, sharing it with her, sharing who I am and where I'm from and what's important to me.

Wild rabbit and leek turnover with piccalilli. (We always had piccalilli sandwiches on a beach day out, and it reminds me of sand in my toes, the sound of waves and laughter.)

Best end of new season lamb with a pine nut and wild garlic crust and tarragon gnocchi. (The first meal I prepared for my dad that made him really think 'wow, this tastes professional'.)

Sherry trifle. (Reminds me of every Christmas, birthday or family celebration we had growing up. It had its own, exclusive cut-crystal bowl that nothing else could be served in. I loved licking the cream, layering the custard, finding the cherries, watching that that gorgeous oozy pink sponginess soak up all the sweetness. When I think of sherry trifle, I think of family gatherings, of times when I felt like everything had fallen into place and I was smiling. For real.)

'Now, that's more like it,' Martha says. I realise that I'm holding my new menu with a rock-steady hand. 'But I have an idea, Katie.' She leans forward and snaps her fingers. Her eyes sparkle as I watch her nod to herself and find my eyes. 'Golden rule: you should always put your guests' enjoyment first. You are not cooking just to amuse Jean-Michel, or impress reviewers. Take care of the guest, focus on service, keep your goal clear and true and everything else will fall into place. You know what is the funny, contrary thing about your diners? All of them are rich, high achievers, each with celebrated talents in their own fields. They can pay for anything they want, nothing is denied to them. So give them something they are not expecting, something that they didn't even know they wanted – surprise them, excite them, *move* them… They've been to a thousand meals just like this one so it's got to make a connection with them, emotionally. Make it special. Something that deserves a page in their memory book. They will appreciate a gift even more than most. What do you give the person who has everything? Something they didn't know they didn't have.

'Oskar and I were once staying overnight at a beautiful winery in Spain. It was breath-taking and the family who ran it were simply the most gracious people in the world. Barbidillo it was called.' She thinks a moment and then a certainty brightens her face. 'Yes, Barbidillo. I remember. Anyway, I could tell you everything about our meal there right down to the very last detail, you know why? Because we weren't just served, we were welcomed, celebrated… But you know, what really made that meal was a little surprise. A little something that we were not expecting…

that's what makes the experience. That's what brings the excitement. What they eat will not be as memorable as how you make them *feel*. The owner gave us a very special bottle of his finest Sherry. Versos 1891. A superbly rare mixture that contains an old family recipe. Very intense flavour. Incredible quality. Served in a beautiful inkwell bottle. It made us feel like the most special guests they'd have ever had. Here I am forty years later telling you of it! So, let's take your sherry trifle to a new level. That's always how I did my business, how I attracted and retained my clients. I would always surprise them with offering something a little bit more, a little bit special. And I think that's what could make all the difference here, Katie.'

She's really got me thinking now. She's right. Utterly spot on. I watch as Martha points a red-painted fingernail to the corner of her room.

'Go over there to my locker please. The one with the combination lock.' She scribbles four digits on the notepad.

I open the combination lock and wait for my next instruction.

'Now, if you look inside, in a small sandalwood box, you will find a set of keys with an address written on the tag.'

I nod as I open the box and hold up the keys she's described.

'Bring them here to me, my darling.'

Again, I do as she asks.

'I want you to do me a favour. Do you promise?'

'Of course, Martha, that's no problem. It would be my pleasure to do you a favour after all the advice you've given to me,' I tell her genuinely.

'Good. Go to my house, Katie, and downstairs in the cellar, is a bottle of that sherry. In an inkwell bottle. It was a gift to me and now I want to gift it to you.'

I'm shaking my head. 'Martha, I couldn't possibly...'

She rests a hand on mine. 'I want you to have it. And, you promised, remember? So please, for me, take it out of a dark and empty house and bring it to the table. Serve it. Celebrate it. Surprise them. Blow their socks off, Katie. Sometimes it only takes one small thing to make all the difference.'

And I concede. Because this one small thing, her faith in me, is making all the difference to what I'm beginning to believe that I can achieve.

CHAPTER SEVENTEEN

After thanking Martha, I bid her goodnight just in time to start my shift downstairs. As I leave her room, I can't help but try and process everything that's happening in my head. I am bowled over by Martha's kindness, her faith in me, and her wisdom. This menu feels right; this menu feels like a friend, a memory, a self-portrait. If I'm going to put my best foot forward with anything, it's going to be this. I want to cook it right now!

But I need to steady myself and not let myself get carried away, because the reality is I'm a catering assistant at Parklands clocking on for the late-evening shift. I look around as I pat my way down to the industrial kitchen, pitch dark besides the humming bars of fluorescent blue light. It feels hauntingly quiet as always; there's a thick oppressive stillness in the air that seems more claustrophobic when I am here all by myself. I let out a deep breath, stamp my feet, flick on every light switch, speaking my menu out loud so that I can hear how it sounds, play with the syntax, practice my pronunciation. I need some chatter or music tonight; I feel the need for company, for something to fill the atmosphere and help the time pass quickly until I can go home, collapse on to Alice's sofa and wake up a Grand Chef finalist.

I reach into my bag to take out my phone, to turn on a playlist or tune into a comedy podcast… Or maybe, I could ring Rachel. I look up to the clock; with the time difference, she'd just be getting up around now and wouldn't have to be at work for an hour or so. I smile to myself; what a perfect idea. I can't wait to hear her voice, tell her about all the good things that are in the pipeline. I might even tell her that I'm planning on serving piccalilli to the most sophisticated palates in London; she will just love that, I know she will. I rustle around to the bottom of my bag, but I can't feel my phone anywhere. I recheck my pockets, then the counters, drawers, shelves, my locker, and then back to my bag to empty the entire contents on the floor.

But there's nothing. My phone is not there. It's not anywhere in here, it's nowhere to be found.

I rack my brains. I definitely didn't take it out in Martha's room and the last time I checked was at the Italian place – so I either left it there and it's probably been stolen by now or I've dropped it whilst riding here and it's smashed to pieces somewhere on the roadside.

I hold my hands in my head. Please. Not this. Not now. All of my contacts, hundreds of screenshots of desserts and cocktails and deli counters and everything that influences me and makes my heart skip a beat. But mainly all my photos; they can't be replaced. Scans of Rachel's baby, pictures of my brothers on expeditions, my nights out with Alice, a couple of photos of me and Ben that I couldn't bear to delete, and almost every single picture I had of my little restaurant. Without any photos, it really will be like it never existed. What have I done? What if someone hacks all my accounts and runs up a huge debt? I just can't absorb that right now; I haven't got enough left. I'm running on empty as it is, trying to keep myself afloat. And now I'm phoneless.

I slide down the wall tiles on to the lino floor, my head on my knees. Tomorrow is my last chance to stop the ripple effect of previous failures from ruining yet another part of my future. I love seeing Martha but this job here at the home is all wrong. I can't stay on at Alice's any longer, so, as much as I love her and we love being together, I'm going to say goodbye to our London dream of being two city success stories. We work all the time, and by the end of the week I have no money and Alice has no energy to do anything as basic as even going out or having fun. The truth is we are living nowhere near a dream. We are shattered, we are beaten. We are the rat race. We are what the rats chase down. If I don't get the job tomorrow, I'm going to give it all up, stop pretending, change tack altogether. Give up on cheffing. Give up on London. Give up generally.

I will pack the few things I've got left worth salvaging and book my one-way budget airline ticket home. When people ask where I've been, I'll just tell them 'nowhere special'. Because the truth is I've now been in Parklands longer than I've been anywhere else – so technically, this is my place, this is my story, and this is not special. When they ask me, 'What did you do?' I'll tell them the truth, *nothing special*, nothing even average. And I'll change the subject. I'll talk about weather or TV or holiday destinations or anything else. If tomorrow goes tits up, I'm going home as Dad has suggested. But if he does sell the house, I'm not sure what kind of home that'll be. I'll have to find somewhere new. I'll have to start from scratch. Again.

I sweep up the contents of my bag and unfold my new menu. This is my ticket. This is my last shot. I pat my trouser pocket to make sure I've got Martha's keys. I take them out and thread a piece of string through the small circular key chain and tie them around my neck. There's no way I can lose these. Absolutely no way. I double-knot it just in case.

I've got to keep hopeful. Because, with this menu, everything could work out just fine if I pull it off tomorrow. I'm excited, not scared to share these dishes; they mean the world to me. Martha seems to think I have a fighting chance. And the more I learn about her expertise as a diner, the more I realise that it's high praise indeed when she approves. And Martha Rosenblatt hasn't been wrong yet. So even if I doubt myself, somehow I don't doubt her.

I'm a finalist.

I'm still in the game.

I'm good at what I do and I deserve to be there just as much as anyone else.

I'm going to give it my everything.

The clock strikes midnight and I wipe down my area for the final time tonight. That's my last shift done for the week so I'm happy to wave this place goodbye. I unhook the apron from around my neck, take off my hairnet and shake out my hair whilst gathering my things from the locker. I take a deep breath as I push through the double doors and psych myself up to ride home through the darkness. I zip up my coat and bring my collar to my chin. It's freezing; the wind is whipping around my ears. It looks like it's going to teem down with rain so I better pedal extra quick tonight if I'm going to escape the downpour.

As I head out of the driveway, there's a figure by the gate that looks incredibly familiar, but I can't be sure. It's so late, the blackness unrelenting except for the pale yellow beam of the security lights, and my heart is starting to pound in my chest.

'Hey! It's me! Katie, over here, it's Ben!' shouts the figure. It certainly sounds like Ben.

But really? Ben? What on earth? What in God's name is he doing here? At Parklands in the middle of the night?

I shake my head in confusion and gesture a finger to my lips. 'You'll wake the residents!' I whisper loudly.

'Sorry!' he yells back, with absolutely no effort at all to lower his voice. I guess he doesn't fully realise that all the residents are octogenarians.

He waves a hand in the air. 'I brought you something.'

As I walk my bike towards him, a smile breaks his lips, because my phone is in his hand in one perfect unsmashed, unhacked piece.

'How did you know to find me here?'

'I called Alice from your contacts and she gave me the address.'

Heat rushes into my cheeks that Ben now knows where I work, that for all my sacrifice and burning ambition, I'm here on the late shift at a care home. But he doesn't say anything, saving me the embarrassment. I take the phone from his hand and place it into my bag. 'You are a lifesaver.' I hold it to my chest. It's back. Things are starting to look up. Maybe all's not lost just yet. 'Thank you so much, I couldn't bear the thought I'd lost this.'

'I knew you'd be panicking so I thought I'd come and find you,' he says with a mock salute. 'Lost and found!'

You could say that. And some.

CHAPTER EIGHTEEN

We shuffle in the gravel, it's cold, the wind is blowing around our ears and it's beginning to drizzle.

'I can walk you home if you like,' says Ben. 'Now that I'm here anyway.'

And then I get a brainwave. 'Actually, I've got to go somewhere close by, I promised to pick something up for a friend if you fancy coming along?'

Ben clasps his hands together and nods. 'I'm intrigued. Any more clues or do I have to guess what you are talking about?'

'Well, telling you will mean revealing my secret weapon for tomorrow. And obviously, you are the opposition.'

This means trusting him with the extra secret of my menu. But it is Ben after all. Not just any other competitor. And I really don't want to try and find Martha's house in the dark all by myself. He's never let me down before. But then again, the stakes have never been this high before, never have I competed with him so directly or over something so life-changing.

'Right. Well, to make it fair, how about I tell you my menu?' he says.

'You sure? You don't have to.'

'Actually, I want your advice on it. I know we are technically in competition, but the menu is only one part of that. Admittedly a big part, but we've got to cook, plate and serve the thing too…' He holds out his hand. 'So. Let's help each other do as well as we can and then leave the rest up to the judges, eh?'

If I win tomorrow, I will lose Ben. He will move on to another top job somewhere else or go back to the ship, and our time together will end as quickly as it began.

If I lose tomorrow, I will also lose Ben because I will have to buy my one-way ticket home.

So with everything to lose as well as everything to play for, I shake his hand, curling my fingers around his warm, soft skin. 'You've got yourself a deal.'

It's only about a twenty-minute walk to Martha's house. We chat the whole way so it feels like no time at all until we turn the corner into Martha's street, just in time to escape the downpour. This is a lovely part of town, spacious and tree-lined with large double-fronted red-brick houses with beautiful gardens. We reach Martha's door and I slide the key into the lock, turning it carefully.

It feels like we're trespassers, despite the fact that I've been instructed to come here and was given the keys. Nonetheless, we whisper and pad our way through the darkened porch, careful not to disturb anything or anyone. Once inside, we close the heavy door behind us and switch on the hall light.

Oh my, Martha's house is like a bazaar! She is indeed a magpie. We gaze, fascinated by the bookcases crammed with such a vivid wealth of colourful and curious things. Hand-drawn calligraphy in foreign languages alongside flags and hats and rugs and pottery and little pipes and bright mosaic tea-light holders. And that's just the hallway!

As we step through to the living room, it's clear that Martha has picked up and brought home a little bit of every place she's ever been to. And by the looks of things, she's trekked across the globe more than once. It is dazzling; utterly impossible to stop your eyes from darting from one curio to another. Glass cabinets of tribal jewellery and intricate beadwork are strewn for display alongside gorgeous lacquered boxes and stocky phallic wood carvings. Ben nudges me at the sight. I cannot help but giggle. *Martha, knowing you now, it is no wonder these treasures caught your eye. In my eyes, you're the treasure.*

On the mantelpiece in front of an enormous fireplace, I am drawn to the dozens of framed photographs. Some sepia of Martha as a young debutante, perched on a staircase, legs crossed laughing to the camera with her unmistakable smile. As I walk along the gallery of her life, I see her proudly linking arms with Oskar at the Taj Mahal, then with a lovely chubby baby in her arms, then that chubby baby as a well-groomed smiling school child, a football captain, a graduate. Then that same smiling boy as a young father holding a baby girl of his own proudly in his arms.

I point to the photo of Martha and her son together, laughing as they raise two champagne flutes, and begin explaining to Ben how my relationship with this special old lady began, and how it's developed, and how she's managed to turn my life upside down just when I needed it most.

'Her son looks so much like her!' I explain to him.

Ben leans in for a closer look. 'That's Leo Rosenblatt.' he says matter-of-factly. '*Sir* Leo Rosenblatt.'

'Sir Leo?'

Ben raises an eyebrow. 'You don't know him?'

I shake my head.

'He's a famous businessman. A self-made tycoon. He's got investments in everything you can think of. He's been on the ship a few times, Captain's table, obviously. Nice guy, always sends his compliments to the kitchen, which is rare with people as rich and powerful as he is. I heard he went through a messy divorce with a supermodel a while back, it was in the news… you know the one, she did the perfume ads for that scent you used to wear, the one with the silver bottle…'

'Oh my goodness, you mean Julianna Marquez!' I exclaim. 'Wow. She cheated on him with an actor I'd not heard of, I read all about it in a magazine.' I look up at the mantelpiece and, sure enough, there are no photos of the golden-haired, leggy Julianna. Martha must have edited her eclectic gallery to reflect the changed circumstances.

'Well, that might explain why her son lives in America now. Martha misses him and her granddaughter like crazy.' Poor Martha… One moment she lives independently surrounded by all her memories and belongings, has her family on the doorstep, the next they move away, she loses her soulmate and she has to move into a home.

Ben turns on all the lights and opens the doors to have a look around, breathe some warmth into all the sealed, still rooms. It feels like a museum at night, somewhere we certainly shouldn't be and I'm terrified of setting off an alarm, breaking something or disturbing the house in any way.

'Right, let's get what we came for,' I announce. 'To the cellar.' I open the door and look down the narrow dark passage.

A cold, damp feeling descends upon me.

Ben stops and looks at me. He flicks the light switch but it's not working.

The cellar is completely black; I can't even make out the second step, it is so dark. And cold. And fathomless. I shake my head. Nope. I can't go down there. The sherry was a lovely touch, but I know I won't be able to convince my feet to take one step into that cold underground room.

I begin to imagine all the horrors the darkness may cloak. Spiders, rats, escaped snakes. My mind flits to scenes from horror films that my unsupervised brothers used to make me sit through after Mum died. People being buried alive, scratching at their coffins, dark dungeons and torture chambers where the undead hid until…

'You okay, Katie? You're white as a ghost.'

'I'm sorry, Ben. I can't go down there.'

'How about I go first and you follow me down.'

I shake my head again.

'I'm happy to go down for you but only you know exactly what you're looking for.'

I clench my eyes shut and take a deep breath. Thank god Ben is with me because if he wasn't I'd never be able to go down in that cellar all by myself. I would have legged it by now, that's for sure.

But he is here and I've made it so far. Even if I do get startled, he'll be with me. To either calm me down or be captured and tortured with me.

'Okay, but I apologies in advance if I scream my head off. Or cling to you too tightly.'

And I wrap my arms around his chest as tight as I can, pressing my face deep in between his shoulder blades as we descend down the staircase into the cellar together.

Ben feels along the wall, and finds a second light switch. This one works, but only just, but a very weak, flickering light is all we need to find the incredible bounty that is before us.

On our left-hand side, there are floor-to-ceiling racks full with at least a hundred bottles. We try to work out Martha's system, but then give up and decide we'll have to take a close look at each one until we find it. She's got everything here; whisky, bourbon, rum, port, cognac and, finally, the inkwell bottle, which I spot and point out to Ben. *Versos 1891.*

He carefully slides it from its place and holds it towards the light to read the label. 'This is a seriously impressive gift. They are going to love this, Katie. It's special, very special. This old lady Martha, she must like you a lot,' he says, holding the bottle up to the single crackling bulb.

I smile to myself. 'Yes, I guess she really does.' And for a second, I don't feel like I'm in the bowels of the earth, but on top of the world. 'Come on then, let's get upstairs and pour ourselves a little taste.'

Once upstairs, we can hear a full-blown storm rage outside, whipping against the windowpanes and making the whole house rattle.

Ben is the one to suggest that we wait till the worst of it blows over. 'No use us getting soaked to the skin when we've got shelter here?'

As I am more than happy to stay inside a little longer out of the cold and wet – and dark – I turn on the gas fire and snuggle up on the couch, trying to warm myself up after our cellar expedition while Ben opens the bottle of sherry, selects two cut-crystal sherry glasses from Martha's drinks cabinet and pours us a generous share each. I know Martha would certainly want us to take shelter and stay in the warmth for an hour rather than venture out and get drowned in the gale.

He lifts his glass to eye level, swirling the dark red nectar to study the colour and the way the light takes it. 'Do you actually know anything about sherry?' I ask, teasing.

'I do actually. It's not just for your nan at Christmas, you know, it's massively underestimated. I agree with your friend Martha. This is great stuff. Great for pairing with food. Superb with Spanish cheeses, Manchego in particular. There's a range, from super sweet to bone dry. Generally, the darker, the sweeter. So I'm guessing this is going to be very sweet indeed.'

We take a sip. Wow! A sip is about all I can manage, such is the sugary punch. But I like it. I really like it. It's warm, dark and oaky, with a distinct nuttiness and caramel coming through. Perfect to sip during a storm to warm you right to the core.

I take another sip. And soon another. Each time it's going down easier than before. If sherry is an acquired taste, then I've acquired it. Soon, we are pouring ourselves a generous second glass to 'warm our bones' as the wind continues to whistle through the house.

'So, talk me through your menu,' I say as we both sit on the couch, huddling to feel the heat from the gas fire. Ben slips his hand into his jeans pocket and hands me a folded piece of paper, his scrawled handwriting instantly recognisable in black pen.

Roasted cod with champagne and honey
Crispy oysters with pickled vegetable salad and citrus mayonnaise
Chocolate orange mousse, spiced fruit brioche and yoghurt sorbet

'What do you think?' he asks me.

'Fishy!'

'Well, that's my forte now after spending so much time at sea.'

I nod my admiration. 'It's fantastic, Ben. I think it sounds like an absolute showstopper.'

We sip away at our sherries as we chat and he raises his glass to mine.

'After tomorrow, whatever happens, I'm glad that we're here. I'm glad that we got this chance to meet up again and to hang out, even for just a short time.'

I swallow hard. It is such a short time. And soon it will all be over.

'It's good to see you again, Katie.' Ben finds my hand and squeezes it. 'To the finals!'

'To the finals,' I echo.

But I notice that Ben doesn't release my hand. He's still holding it in his.

He furrows his brow slightly and brushes his thumb over the melted skin across the back of my hand, my souvenir from a scalding. Again, he gently brushes over my scar. But he doesn't ask. And he doesn't let go. And neither do I. Our hands drop back down between us. Still holding on to one another.

Maybe it's the adrenalin or the sherry or the exhaustion or the temptation that he is right here in front of me, I don't know, but I can't ignore it, I can't help but look down at my hand in his and wonder what exactly is going on here? Just hours ago he told me all about his glamorous girlfriend? Of course I want him – I've never stopped – but what about Francesca? We can't just pretend that she doesn't exist. And I can't just pretend to forget all about her. I drift my gaze slowly back to Ben and immediately, as if we were both having exactly the same thought, at exactly the same time, he snaps his hand back from mine and grabs at the nape of his neck.

'I'm sorry. I'd better go. Big day tomorrow, so we should both brave it and try to get home. We'll need at least a few hours' sleep to make sure we arrive looking bright-eyed and ready to roll.' He says all this while looking at the ground.

'Of course. You're right,' I agree, more loudly than I mean to. 'Definitely the biggest day ever.' I shuffle up in my seat, trying to hide my crimson cheeks from burning.

And so we wash out our sherry glasses, turn everything off we turned on and shut up Martha's home again, leaving it as dark and empty as when we found it.

We walk in silence now, our hoods pulled tight around our faces to protect us from the wind and rain and giving us a perfect excuse not to talk, not to discuss what nearly did or did not happen. Mercifully soon, we reach the main junction, which is well-lit with street lights and twenty-four-hour petrol stations and supermarkets.

'You okay from here?' he asks me.

I nod and point in the direction I'm going in. The opposite way to him.

'Good luck for tomorrow!!' I call out as he staggers against the force of the wind.

He smiles and waves me goodbye. 'You too, Katie.' And then he turns away and disappears into the distance.

I hop on my bike and ride with the wind to Alice's. Bloody hell though. That was intense. That was close. That was downright dangerous. But now I need to focus because Ben is right. Tomorrow is the most important day of our lives so far. And he's gone to catch some shut-eye because he knows what's at stake. And so do I.

A few minutes later I get home and put my bike away, letting myself quietly into Alice's flat.

So here it is, I say to myself as I find the mirror in the downstairs bathroom, shaking out my knotty hair and splashing cold water on my face. 'Everything,' I say to my reflection. 'Give it everything.'

I've got to put everything that happened with Ben tonight to the back of my mind because tomorrow is as big as it gets.

And I want to go all the way.

CHAPTER NINETEEN

'Welcome!' says Pip. 'Firstly, I want to congratulate all of you on getting this far. There can be only one appointment, so two of you will be leaving here today extremely disappointed.' We all straighten behind our stations, match ready and raring to go.

Jean-Michel continues where Pip left off. 'But rest assured, that even if you fail to make the grade today, now you have made it this far in such a high-pressure, demanding environment, you will no doubt be snapped up by a lesser establishment.' He flashes a cheeky smile. 'I'm joking. You have risked a lot being here and here is the only place you want to be. Otherwise, you would have walked a long time ago. Win or lose, today is our last day together and a glittering career awaits one of you as we discover our new Grand Chef.'

Octavia casts her eyes over us all. 'More than 1,000 applicants, 50 shortlisted, and now only the three strongest remain. We've watched you grow. We know what you are capable of, and it really is quite phenomenal for chefs so young. I could not pick a winner right now. The next three hours are going to be some of the most important hours of your cooking career. Not only will the grand chef work in this new restaurant, learning under the great Jean-Michel, but they will also become a resident of this hotel on a permanent basis, accommodated in a luxury suite here, so in every sense this will become your new home. And we will become your new family. The stage is set; three courses separate just one of you from this life-changing opportunity.'

My stomach flips. And I do feel sick, very sick. My only comfort is that I couldn't possibly throw up because I've not eaten a thing in ages. Too busy and too nervous to eat, even though all that's on my mind is food. It is shocking, daunting and exciting to think that three dishes of food will determine *everything* for me from here on in.

Pip steps forward and gestures for the three of us to follow him. Ben and I have only exchanged half-smiles. I'm going to avoid him altogether today; I've got to stay focused. Ben is my opposition. He is somebody else's boyfriend. He is one of the people standing in the way of me and the rest of my life. This I know. All I've got to do is remember it. I'm buoyed with well wishes texted in from Dad and Alice and Mel and Zoe. I missed my chance to call Rachel last night; by the time I was reunited with my phone, she'd gone out to work. But once this is all over, calling her is one of the first things I'm going to do. I can't let that keep slipping.

Harry clears his throat. He looks like he hasn't blinked in the last twenty-four hours, his eyeballs red, veiny and protruding. I'm going to have to watch him today. Who knows what kind of stunt he'll pull in order to emerge victor?

Until now, the dining part of the new Marchand restaurant has been portioned off while they complete the interior. Octavia leads us through to the front part of the secretive section, pushes the 'no entry' sign aside and lifts back the draped sheets.

'Completed in the early hours of this morning, our interior designers worked around the clock to ensure that it was ready on time and up to the highest possible standard to compliment your food on this special night,' she says.

Two waiters appear dressed like stylish beefeaters in tailored reds, blacks and gold and draw back the heavy dark velvet curtains.

'I present to you, for your eyes only, our grand dining room à la restaurant Marchand.'

You can't help but look up first. Hanging in the middle of the vaulted ceiling is a colossal tiered crystal chandelier, glittering in the soft light. The walls are embellished with scalloped edging, finished in brilliant white and gold. The light draws your eye upwards and I hold my breath at its dazzle. I spin around on my heel. This feels like a vintage ballroom in an old-style mansion house. The circular dining tables are set with crisp white tablecloths, sparkling wine glasses, perfectly polished and set silverware with dainty flower centrepieces all in keeping with the luxuriant colour scheme of red, white and gold that defines the space. It is fantastic. Well, it is certainly *fantastical*. It looks like it was drawn straight out of *Beauty and the Beast*. I decide not to mention this to Octavia.

We follow Pip as he talks us through the layout and the decor, the seating and the service. Then he turns to us and gestures towards a small army of kitchen and waiting staff, all immaculate in the same reds, blacks and gold as the lead waiters. 'For front-of-house service, I have brought in my best staff from my other restaurants. They are experienced and have been trained to the highest degree, and are here to support you in your endeavours tonight. Each chef will be assigned a brigade of staff, three waiters and a sommelier out front. In the kitchen will be you, one sous and two line chefs, who you will communicate and lead as necessary. Remember, you are not just cooking. You are Grand Chef tonight. If anything goes wrong, no matter who is at fault, the buck stops with you. Tonight, we discover who you really are. And what you can really do. Or not as the case may be.' He holds up his hands, each finger outstretched. 'Each of you will have ten diners to serve in each area.'

Ten diners sounds reasonable. But then I really think about it. We're talking three courses, three *perfect* courses, which means *thirty perfect* dishes. All that with a new team of staff and a judging panel.

Whoa. I hold my hands together and squeeze them before any trembling can overtake me. *This is doable. I can do this.*

'These are no ordinary diners,' Pip continues. 'Tonight you are serving a party of the finest, most successful chefs, hoteliers and independent reviewers in the city. Along with our own friends and family.'

So basically Jean-Michel multiplied by ten.

Oh my, now this isn't seeming so doable. This is the hardest challenge I have ever faced as a chef. And this time, I have the most at stake, because if I don't make it I'm hanging up my chef whites for good.

'At the end of the day, the chef that delivers the goods, on time, to the highest standard, and receives the most votes from our guests will become part of our family and reign king' – Pip chuckles and darts me a look – 'or *queen* over this grand kingdom.'

Octavia steps forward. 'There isn't much between you three right now, so give it your best. Your menus are being paired with wines as we speak, and all your ingredients are in the kitchen. Any questions before we commence our preparations?'

I shake my head, keeping my promise to myself not to look over at Ben today. We both have to keep our minds clear and neither of us can afford to be distracted from the reason that we are here in the first place. To win. To be selected by Jean-Michel. To prove our worth and change our lives. Instead, I snatch a quick sideways glance at Harry. Even he has beads of sweat collecting on his lip, and is baring his teeth. I draw my gaze over his body, his shoulders back, elbows cinched in, and his hands in tight fists. It looks like he is entering a boxing ring rather than a kitchen.

He throws me a look that I can only describe as rabid. I swallow hard, push out my chest and weave my fingers together, holding them in front of me so he, and everyone else, can see that I haven't got even the slightest tremor. Because I'm not letting anything slip today.

CHAPTER TWENTY

I gather with my team in the white marble lobby. We sit in a circle in high-backed leather chairs around a low glass-topped coffee table. We shake hands and smile our introductions; a few light questions about where we are from, where we live, why we want to be here to break the ice and everyone seems a little more relaxed. I think of my first impressions of Bernie based on the gruff, dismissive way she introduced herself to me on my first day at Parklands and decide that I'll do the exact opposite, which seems to be a reasonable strategy. Once everyone has settled in to their seats and knows who is who and where we'll be positioned, I take out my paper folder and talk them through the menu, the service and timings. I want to let everyone know how to be the best they can be and how we are going to roll as a team.

'Communication is key, you guys; if you are confused, speak up! If you are lost, speak up! If you are in trouble, speak up! And we will work together to sort it out, quickly and efficiently.'

I hand them each a printed copy of my kitchen rules that I hung up in my own little restaurant. I see them raise eyebrows and nudge each other in agreement. I keep watch as they read through, nodding and smiling to themselves. I'm not rushing this bit. If we stick to these rules, we'll save ourselves a lot of tears and tantrums. There are a few knowing smirks. Yep, I can tell these guys know where I'm coming from and we're all on the same page. This is a good bunch. I can feel it. But it's always best to be clear, so we all get an idea of the tone, of the way things are going to work, the way that we are going to work *together*.

I stand to finish, mindful of the time and the amount of prep that we need to get underway. 'My biggest nightmare would be that someone freaks out because they make a mistake or we turn on each other because of the pressure. 'We know it is going to be crazy, right? We know it's going be hard work. But we're here for each other and I want you to promise to speak up if you need something, however big or small, the tiniest detail is still important.

'Remember, tonight, it is not about me, it's not about you.' I think of Martha and the way her memories sustain her in her little Parklands bedroom. 'It's all about our guests. Let's give the guys out there something they are not expecting, a real night to remember. We want them to go to bed smiling in their sleep because we created something special. We're in this together. Let's make it happen. Let's make some memories tonight.'

My team look to each other and then to me, warm smiles breaking their lips.

Sara, the lead waitress, nods her head, raises her hand and they all follow. 'A-game tonight, guys. Let's go.'

And so it begins. This is it.

And somehow, I just know that it will be special. But special enough? That's what we're here to find out.

By eight o'clock, the dining room is starting to fill up and a sneak peek around the door makes my stomach flip. Limousines have pulled up outside, a red carpet leads the guests in through the main doorway. Ladies wrapped in fur stoles with long black gowns and glittering jewels air-kiss each other as they mingle and sip flutes of champagne. The candlelight flickers across the tables and in the dancing glow I catch a glimpse of my own childhood heroine Celia Sanderson arrive.

Pip wasn't kidding when he said the movers and shakers of the industry were coming to test us tonight. Everyone who is worth their rock salt is here.

I decide that it's probably best that I stop gawping at the guests and get back to work.

I can't see Ben, which is a small mercy; his station is hidden from my view, on the other side, with a different entrance to the dining room. But I can see Harry. Our ovens are side by side and we are sharing the same pass. He is like a hurricane, side-stepping and pirouetting frantically with fantastic speed. He is a hard ball of energy, charismatic but also frightening.

For the past few hours, he has done nothing but dominate his space and his staff with the erratic frenzy of a malevolent dictator. Firstly, the sommelier made the mistake of approaching him while at the oven – he had a question about oranges and got momentarily in the way – and was so humiliated that, by the end of a long and relentless haranguing, his lips were pursed in disgust. Minutes later, Harry's sous-chef committed a variation of the same offence, simply asking a question regarding the ever-changing menu and he was verbally tortured until, finally, he too was ordered out.

'Go, get the fuck out of my sight. You are morons, how can I get to the next level surrounded by morons?' Harry had wailed. But I watched him as he seemed to calm again, as if the outbursts were a valve mechanism for his own mounting pressure.

But that calm doesn't last long, the smallest trigger proving enough to blow his top all over again.

'What the hell?'

I watch now as he jabs a finger into the back of the line chef making the starter of pork snout with green radish and tomato micro-salad, dressing the rye croutons in advance.

'Do you work for Subway? Pretend you're the customer. Why would you want a soggy crouton?' Harry slams his hand down on the counter. 'And I told you to halve the tomatoes, not quarter them. Bin now!' He picks up the tray of miniature plates and slides them all into the rubbish. 'How many times? How am I supposed to do it all by myself? Step up! Step the hell up. It's my way or the highway, you losers.'

Harry starts slicing furiously into the tomatoes, his mounting anger and frustration evident in the tight scowl on his face and the red tops of his ears.

To my surprise, he catches my eye and points his knife directly at me. 'You two want to fanny about and stay cooking at the same average level, churning out pimped-up Marks and Spencers' plates, then go work with her,' he announces to his line chefs.

I take a deep breath and try to ignore him. I tell myself he's just trying to goad me, distract me. I purse my lips into a tight smile as my mother would advise and I keep my head down, trying to stay focused on my station and refuse to be drawn into his temper.

'There's a reason women stay in the pastry section.'

I stop my own slicing as my hand is shaking and I don't want to make a mistake. I need to pause, to steady and compose myself. He's wasting my time. He's been in my ear all day, but now he's actually succeeding in holding me up. I can't let this go. I can't let him go on. I know he's spoiling for a fight and I should rise above and be the bigger person, but I've had enough of him. I see that Sara has entered from the dining room and stopped in her tracks, a concerned look spreading across her face.

Harry claps his hands together and cracks his neck.

'Very interesting reading about your restaurant, Katie. Do your team know that you've already tried and failed? Closed down. NO leadership. NO business acumen. Didn't have a handle on your staff or your books. The problem with you is that you're too afraid of not being liked. On top of the fact that you have NO imagination. I saw your menu: boring. That's why you haven't made any mistakes yet, because everything you do is old hat. No disasters but no fireworks. Your idea of originality is a ten-second Pinterest video that you copied.'

Oh you bastard. I'm not here to lose to Harry. Or because of him.

I wipe my clammy hands down my apron. Despite my greatest effort to stay cool, I'm fuming, even my hands are burning up with rage. I can feel all eyes on me. If I stay quiet but look so obviously worked up, then it will look like Harry's won, or worse still, it will look like he's succeeded in intimidating me. I've got to stand up for myself, and for the line chefs and for all the other staff he loves to terrorise. My brigade will lose faith in me if I cave in to this, and without them behind me, I'm finished. I'm the only other chef in here at this time in a position to take him on, and this has to stop right now.

'See, nothing more than a withering look... that's exactly what I'm talking about, right there,' he says with a smug smile as he turns back to his station. He thinks he has had the final word.

I can't let him have it. I've held my tongue before. But this is different. This is a time to stand up and speak out.

'Harry.' I take a deep breath to steady the tremor in my voice and I take a step towards him.

'I'm busy so I'm going to keep this short. And I get that this concept may blow your mind but I am here because I'm as good if not better than you.'

He snorts. 'Better than me? Don't make me laugh, neither you or sailor boy are better than me.'

'Is that so? Then why did you turn up Ben's oven during the selection? Why would you sabotage his dish?'

Harry squints at me and his mouth closes again, he swallows back.

'You'd do that despite your confidence in your own ability?' I take another step towards him. 'See this is what confuses me about you, Harry. All this time you've been screaming and shouting and agitating everyone and everything, treating all of us like we are snivelling, loathsome insects who deserve to be degraded and humiliated, but I've been watching you.' I walk right into his station so we are now face to face. 'You're hyper because you can't decide on what you want or who you are. All this shouting is just masking that.'

I pick up his menu and point to the grill. 'Look here, you've already changed your mind at least a hundred times. After all the drama and indecision, you are revising yet *again* – adding dishes, redoing others, embellishing them with caviar, truffles, foie gras. You introduced a venison main on roasted beets halfway through the day. Then an hour later, you add cabbage, then a purée of roasted parsnips along the plate rim. Then you change the scallop dish. "What about quail eggs on top, fried in goose fat?" Then: "And white truffle on top?"'

Harry runs his fingers through his hair grabbing it at the scalp, his lips gaping like a caught fish gasping for air.

My eyes are fixed on his. 'Harry, you are giving us all a fucking headache.'

I turn to the line chefs. 'For the record, he told you to quarter those tomatoes the first time, boys, I heard him, so you're not in the wrong. If you do want to join my brigade, you are more than welcome.'

Harry's eyes drift behind my shoulder, his face is now purply red. Except for the blotches of grey. His hand drifts down towards his chin but he pinches at his neck.

I turn behind me to follow his gaze. It's Jean-Michel and Octavia, standing together and looking grave. I realise they've heard every word.

Uh oh. I don't know how this is going to go now. Another blow up? Another meltdown? Another stand off? Or are we all going to be kicked out and sent packing?

The two line chefs step from Harry's station to mine. Then one by one, all his other staff follow until he is standing alone.

Jean-Michel shakes his head. '*Quelle catastrophe.* You cannot continue without a brigade. It appears they have abandoned you.'

Harry swivels in utter disbelief. There is no one left to work with, no one left to shout at. He bites at his fist a second. No one steps in, we all just wait for his next move.

Octavia tuts at him like a naughty schoolboy. 'Oh Harry, you came to win but have only succeeded in defeating yourself. Let this be a lesson to you. Truly. Learn from this.'

With a sharp breath through his nose, Harry rips off his apron, throws it on the ground and storms through the swing doors.

And he's gone.

All eyes are now on me. Octavia's hand is clutching at her necklace and Jean-Michel is massaging his forehead, his eyes clenched shut. Are they going to expel me now? Has standing up to him made me look a tyrant, unable to manage my emotions, to stand the pressure? Have I come across all wrong? In their eyes, have I acted a little more similarly to Harry than I thought? What if Octavia and Jean-Michel think that *I'm* the loose cannon, the wild dog?

What if they think I've cracked under the pressure? That *I'm* the one without a handle on my temper? I decide not to face them but just to keep my head down and get on with the job. I've not got the time or the mental energy for anything other than the task at hand: running this kitchen. So I straighten my hat, glance up to the clock and call for everyone's attention.

'The show must go on. Harry's brigade, please divide yourselves up between Ben and me. The more the merrier, you are very welcome and we appreciate the extra pairs of hands. It's one hour till service, whatever happens behind the scenes, back here in the kitchen, the bottom line is that we still have guests to serve. So let's get to it.'

I put my head down and start chopping, avoiding meeting Octavia or Jean-Michel's gaze.

Seconds later, Pip bursts through the doors, phone in hand for Jean-Michel. I hear Octavia clear her throat, and despite my best efforts, I sneak a glance upwards to try and read her expression, her body language, try to get an idea where I now stand in light of what's happened.

And she winks at me. And that's all I need to know.

CHAPTER TWENTY-ONE

Pip approaches me at my station, my menu in his hand. 'Rabbit? Piccalilli? Really?'

'I know it's something you would never dream of serving in a restaurant like this, but that's why I think it's worth trying. Trust me, Pip, these flavours are going to blow you away. Just you wait and see.'

'I'm liking this new confidence, Katie. Very best of luck. Your diners are ready, so service as soon as you can.'

I nod and start plating up. Sara takes my starters from the pass, out the swing doors and into the dining room. And we're on a roll. Every morsel cooked perfectly, every plate presented beautifully, everyone fed on time. Every. Single. Time.

So far so good.

After half an hour, Pip re-enters the kitchen, shaking his head.

'The votes are in on the first dish, and Katie, you won that round, you are in the lead. You got the majority of votes over Ben's cod and they loved it. Plates are clean, happy faces. Well done.'

I'm thrilled but I can't stop. I can't let that go to my head or hold me up. I'm in the middle of plating my main, so I keep my eyes ahead of me the whole time, even though Pip stays by, half-impressed, half-bemused.

'I've never seen anything quite like it; camping tucker that was not. It is genius, wonderful, completely unique, you've played with the classics and, to my mind, that is a triumph, I really like it. No, I *love* it. You're mad, you know that?'

'Thank you,' I answer. 'Maybe I am.'

One course down, two to go. I plate up my lamb and hit the bell for Sara to start collecting the mains from the pass. Pip disappears out the door with her, but Jean-Michel comes in again to take his place. I think this is all part of the process, the selection, the test. Right when you are at your busiest, when the last thing you want is someone watching you or asking you questions, that's when they show up.

'So, explain your choice, Katie, what is the inspiration behind this dish?'

I continue building and layering the elements on the remaining plates as I talk, aware that Jean-Michel isn't just here to listen but also to watch.

'Well, I was very quiet at school, couldn't always find the words. They'd just get stuck in my throat, my cheeks would burn and my hands have always given me away. I'd get the shakes. I'd get very nervous speaking up or reading aloud, I've never felt comfortable in the spotlight or under the intense pressure of exams. And then there was a group who picked on me a bit, for being so quiet, an easy target. But you get stronger, more determined, you want to prove them wrong, do better, try harder. But with food it was different. For others it may be singing or dancing, sports, but for me it's cooking. And the first time I served this lamb dish to my father, who was worried that I wasn't meeting my potential, it spoke to him, helped him understand that I was serious, that I could be professional, that maybe this was something that would take my life in a new and fulfilling direction. And once I knew that he could be proud of me, that he understood that this wasn't a hobby or a phase, I jumped in with both feet. This dish made that happen.'

I finish my last lamb plate and hand it to Jean-Michel himself. 'I hope you enjoy it.' And for once Jean-Michel doesn't say anything; he just nods and takes it away with him.

*

Pip returns into the kitchen. 'The verdict is in. A quote from Celia Sanderson who sends her compliments to the chef. "You've taken a traditional dish and turned it on its head. These are meals to give you comfort, they illicit feeling as well as deliver tremendous flavour. That's why they're favourites; they just work. I loved every mouthful." Well done, Katie.'

Praise from Celia Sanderson! *Oh Mum!* How you would love to hear this! Good old Celia was always your favourite; I can picture her recipe book perched by the stove as you made our Sunday dinner as clearly as if I saw it yesterday. Tears are close. God, could I sit and cry now. Floods of proud, happy tears. But I bite my lips and blink a few times and escort that idea right to the back of my heart for a little while longer. There'll be time for tears later. Right now, I've got to be strong and keep my eyes on the prize.

'So who won that course?' I ask.

Ben is on the other side of the kitchen, a partition between my station and his, so our brigades run parallel. The fact that we are kept apart and I can't see him and he can't see me is the only merciful part of this process so far. I'm really relieved that we don't have to compete right under each other's noses. Or hear the results, the votes as they come in after each course. I imagine it's Octavia or Jean-Michel who is delivering the same news to Ben right now. Bet he's just as nervous as me. I know we can't both win, but I don't want either of us to lose.

Pip smiles into his clenched fist. 'A tie! It was straight down the middle. Exactly the same number of votes for your lamb and Ben's oysters. So, here's where it gets interesting. You've got one course in the bag already so everything is riding on this course, Katie. No pressure.'

A tie! Oh my god. Right well, I haven't got a millisecond to think on that. I've got one last course and I've got make it count.

Octavia arrives this time to interview me as I prepare my dessert, despite the fact that any of these questions could have been asked earlier when I submitted my menu in the first instance. But I know they want to stay close, see how we respond under pressure. And I guess after Harry's episode earlier, it's important. Besides the food itself, it might be the most important thing of all.

'Sherry trifle? What an extraordinary choice, Katie. Please, talk me through it.'

There's a big reason behind this one. I'm relieved I can explain it to Octavia. Knowing that she lost her husband, she may understand a little more easily what I mean.

I clear my throat. 'Sherry trifle was at the centre of the table, at the centre of my family, at the centre of every happy occasion I can remember. But times and families change, and sometimes, grief sticks out its leg and takes you off your feet. Today is a day I would love to share with my mother. She would really be proud of me. But today I'm not crying. Today I'm grateful. I was blessed with the best. She taught me how to follow my beliefs – kindly. How to be known as a person who is true and trustworthy. To work hard and try to have fun. She taught me that I was wonderful and to never let anyone treat me as anything less than that. But more importantly she taught me to treat others as wonderful too. My mum didn't come from privilege but from hard work. She gave to charity: her money and her time. She put others before herself. She loved my father, me and my siblings. If I could give a gift to others it would be to have the foundation of love that I had. She was special, but, thank goodness, she was not unique.' I smile as I think of Martha. 'There are many wonderful people who have shown me great kindness, and this dessert is a celebration of that.'

And I hand Octavia a bowl of trifle for herself. The last dish of the last course. And I notice a glistening in her eyes that I've never seen before. She blinks back and thanks me, and then she's gone. And now there's nothing to do but wait.

*

Sara walks through the double swing doors and tells me it's time. It's time to come out of the kitchen and step in to the light, the spotlight and scrutiny of the dining room.

I take off my hat, shake some volume into my hair and follow her through.

Ben walks out the opposite door from his station at the same time, and he looks like he's been just as absorbed in the process as I have; the steam in the kitchen leaving a sheen across his forehead and cheekbones. He has a look on his face I recognise. Hot, intense, his heart racing, his chest rising and falling with fast breaths.

I remind myself that I'm not here to look at him. That there's important business afoot. I straighten up and look to the diners sitting around the circular tables. There are faces here, smiling up at me, chancing an encouraging nod, that I imagined I'd only ever see on screen or in print. My hand jolts upwards and I venture a quick wave as I spot Celia Sanderson sitting by the window. She beams back at me and gives me a double thumbs up.

Celia Sanderson! She brought so many meals into our house. I am honoured and privileged and overwhelmed to be here now, serving her. I bite back tears. I've got to stay composed, professional. The big announcement is about to come. And one way or another, I'm going to need all the strength I can find for that.

Jean-Michel steps forward and stands between Ben and I. He takes a moment to think, to choose his words. First he turns to Ben.

'Ben Cole. I'll remember your name. Simply stunning. You could serve your menu at a Michelin-star restaurant and no one would blink an eye. You are a star in the making. Some things in life you have to learn and some you are born with, and you, Ben, are born with a gift. Stunning... Well done.'

Everyone in the dining room applauds and for a moment I think that maybe I missed it. That Ben has been crowned Grand

Chef and somehow I've got mixed up, because I didn't hear him say the exact words. But this is Jean-Michel. It's not like he's going to stick to the script. I clap along with everybody else in the room, still unsure if I'm standing here as first loser.

And then Pip turns to me.

'Katie's menu, we loved it. It really is very, very clever. I'd order this just to see if you could pull it off, and wow, you've done that. It's wonderful, it's joyous, it's refreshing, it's exceptional. You are a chef completely and utterly in love with your craft; you understand the connection between life and food, and it shows. You recognise that what grows together, goes together, and that works in terms of flavour and colour palettes. Your combinations are divine. The thought process, the execution, the presentation. It is all there.'

He nods over to Octavia, she stands from her seat and walks towards me.

'For me, your dessert was the absolute highlight of the evening. Sensational, a time-honoured pudding at its most glorious, many-layered best: the jam-slashed and sherry-sodden sponge, the sharp fruity layer of syrup-oozing berries, the lashings of custard with smooth, cool whipped cream. On top, my favourite colour combination: the Victorian pink of crystallised rose petals with the tender green of chopped pistachios. Perfection.'

'Thank you,' I say but I'm still so confused! When are they going tell us who the winner is?

All of these flattering comments are great, I'm blown away. But is it enough to win? How is it going to feel to hear all this and then be told 'It's not you!'? What's going to happen now if, after everything, they tell me: *Sorry, Katie, but it wasn't enough*? If, after everything, I've got to walk away from all this without being selected I will be devastated. It's unthinkable, unbearable. But it is possible.

Jean-Michel claps his hands. A hush descends. This is it. This has to be it.

'Take excellent ingredients, key techniques passed down through the generations, add a table full of family and friends, and a good meal should ensue. As people become busier and busier, the appeal of a cuisine that celebrates the culture of the table – not just the eating, but the ingredients, the preparation, the company – is ever stronger. "Balance is the key to life," they say, "You need family, food and time." And therefore, there is one clear winner. There is one chef here tonight that brought all of that.'

Jean-Michel looks to Ben first and then to me. And then he takes a step in my direction, stretches out his hand and says:

'Katie, *félicitations. You* are my new Grand Chef.'

CHAPTER TWENTY-TWO

'Grand Chef! My heartfelt congratulations,' Ben says as he offers me more champagne. 'I'm really happy for you, Katie. You did it and you deserve it, you really do. And now, all this, living and working in a five-star hotel, that's a pretty good reward for all your hard work.'

'Thanks. It hasn't quite sunken in yet… And congratulations to you too,' I say as he tops up my glass. 'I heard Pip made you an offer.'

He shrugs, smiling. 'Can't complain, running a restaurant for Pip Taylor in New York isn't a bad second place.'

We clink our glasses and sip the cold, crisp bubbly, surrounded by the most glamourous and well-connected professionals in the industry. This is haute cuisine heaven. In fact, it's not just chef heaven, it's *my* heaven.

I look at Ben. He's just as awestruck as I am.

I am now the Grand Chef. I now live in a palatial hotel suite.

No wonder my head is swimming.

Everything is perfect. Everything is beyond my wildest hopes. Everything is about to change! I can't wait to tell my dad and I can't wait to get Alice here for drinks and thank everyone who has supported me and I really can't wait to let Bernie know I quit. But mainly, I can't wait to share this news with Martha, because without her I'd never have believed this was possible. I've kept back some trifle for her birthday celebrations. Just to say thanks, for backing me, for believing in me, when I couldn't even muster that belief in myself.

'Oh my god! New York!!' I hear a shrill, yelping noise getting louder. 'New York! New York!!' I turn to see a tall beautiful woman in a black silk dress with a mane of golden hair flowing down her tanned, toned arms shrieking the words 'New York' over and over. 'I've been looking for you everywhere!' She takes Ben's face in both her hands. 'I am so, so proud of you!' And then she closes her eyes as she kisses him on the mouth, softly, slowly, fully.

Ben's eyes are wide open. They are looking at me, staring at me, startled. He looks as taken aback as I am.

She pulls away and slides her hands down towards his shoulders. 'I know! Surprise, right! I docked into Portsmouth this morning. I wanted to be here win or lose.' She gathers him tight into her. 'Oh I'm so proud of you! I have missed you so much. So, come on, introduce me. Who's who?' She spins around on her gold strap stilettoes, looking beyond me into the designer-clad clusters.

I watch Ben as he pinches his lips and then slides his fingers down to his chin, his eyes still wide, his forehead furrowed as if he was refocusing, presumably looking for Jean-Michel. He juts his chin forward, raising up on his tiptoes to study the crowd as she hooks into his arm, snuggling into his chest. But this girl is impatient, her eyes are darting around the room and she swipes herself a flute of champagne and a canapé from a passing waiter.

I take this as my cue to slink away, remove myself from my close proximity to Ben, but her eye catches mine and she registers my new black grand chef hat and apron.

'Oh my god! You must be the winner!'

I smile sheepishly, nod and try to keep shuffling backwards.

This girl's eyes… Wow. They are bright green. I've never seen eyes like them. It's like they've been photoshopped.

She throws the whole canapé into her mouth to free up her hand which she then thrusts in front of me. 'Francesca,' she manages through a mouthful of salmon mousse. 'Ben's girlfriend. I can't believe we're going to New York! No offence, but I actually think that the runner-up prize is far, far better, don't you think?'

I take my hand in hers and shake it, smiling my best smile, but not knowing quite what to say in response, wanting to stay friendly and composed and distant. 'Congratulations,' is all I manage before I excuse myself and slip back into the kitchen.

I take a deep breath and savour being on my own for the first time in the last crazy, frantic, high-pressure fourteen hours. I try to stop and be grateful. I try to enjoy the moment. This moment that I've wanted so badly. The winner's announcement already feels like so long ago. That may be due to the excitement and the exhaustion and the alcohol of course.

When Jean-Michel announced that I did it, that they chose me, that I was the one, I felt like I was watching myself on television. He went on to tell me that all three of them loved the maturity that I showed in the kitchen. They loved the way the staff were treated with respect and patience. That the food was accomplished and elegant. Jean-Michel said that I was perfect protégé material and that it was clear that I was keen to learn and I took instruction easily.

They presented me with my new chef whites along with black hat and apron – which I put on proudly straight away. Octavia handed me my hotel pass key, and made me promise that I would make myself at home. I got a business card, already printed with my name on it. New jacket, new hat, new title, new start, new luxury hotel suite. It feels like a fantasy, like I am just having another daydream in high definition.

But what I'm really buzzing about is that they loved the menu. Especially because that was the most autobiographical, true-to-self menu I could have dreamt of. And I created it all from scratch. So here I am, selected based on my own style, my own skills. Not as an impostor, not as a 'best pretender', not as a convincing imitation of a classic French chef far removed from who I really am – but on my own, with all of me invested in every little bite. And that makes me feel hugely proud and relieved and unburdened. I guess that's what it means to feel free.

So I've got to enjoy right now because I know everything from now on will be different. Soon I'll start the hardest job I have ever done. Soon I open myself up to a whole new level of scrutiny and exposure. And soon Ben will leave my life all over again.

But right now I feel like the luckiest girl in the world.

Somewhere by the bar, I hear Francesca squeal with joy.

Okay. So, maybe I'm the second luckiest.

CHAPTER TWENTY-THREE

Even though the party is in full swing, I don't feel like staying. I don't want to watch Ben and his girlfriend laughing and drinking and dancing. No wonder Francesca can't stop smiling; I don't blame her. So why hang around and torture myself? I came to win. And that's what I did.

So I slip out the back, not wanting to draw any attention to myself. It's late and I'm exhausted, wired as a result of all the emotion and the alcohol, but still I want to pop into Parklands as it's Martha's birthday tomorrow. I know it's pitch black out there now, but I figure that if I could find it in myself to cycle through the darkness for Jean-Michel, then I sure as hell can do it for Martha. And ultimately, I survived. The darkness I imagined took on a life of its own, the horrors lurking in the shadows don't really exist. I've not caught sight of one serial killer. I appear to have escaped the zombie-clown-flesh-eaters. I haven't been attacked or captured or strangled. I am on the other side of all that now, I've pushed through the fear and have managed to live to tell the tale. City streets at night? Not a problem.

Even if Martha's asleep, I want to leave her something to wake up to. It's the least I can do. I'm not sure I can ever repay her faith, her advice, or the expensive sherry which made the menu so special, but I can give her a little something to show her how much it meant to me.

In my rucksack, I've got her trifle alongside a little cheese plate and a small flask of port for her, which I know she'll enjoy.

I cycle across the street-lit city, the fog so thick that I almost lose my way several times and have more than one close call with angry drivers who don't see me fully despite my neon vest until they need to slam on the brakes. By the time I arrive and take off my helmet, steam rises from my head, a mix of adrenalin and physical exertion. I feel my cheeks, which are cold and red, and try to comb through my hair – now a damp, sweaty mess – with my fingers. I'm a long way from the fur stoles and tuxedos and the flowing champagne of the Rembrandt now.

I reach the second floor where Martha's room is, and oddly her door is wide open. I poke my head around and see that Martha's bed is empty. Perhaps her son has taken her out for her a pre-birthday meal? Can't think of any other explanation and there's no one around at this time of night to ask, so I leave the port and cheese plate by her bedside with a note to say I'll call in again tomorrow with some trifle.

The place is so still and quiet, I decide that I may as well pop down to the kitchen to say hello to the girls and tell them my news.

That I won't be coming back here to work.

That I'm the new Grand Chef.

Looking around here, I can hardly believe that it's true.

A flutter stirs in my stomach. I actually can't wait to tell them. And my dad. And Alice and Martha of course. I can't wait to share the news, the good news, of what so many of them helped me achieve.

I take a deep breath and have to stem the tears.

It's actually happened.

I won. I'm the winner.

I spot Zoe through the glass panel of the kitchen door and as soon as I get inside I stretch out my arms and give her a big hug. 'Hey! how great to see you!' I say. 'I won! I'm here to tell Bernie to stick her job!' but the serious look in Zoe's eye interrupts me, and there's a grave tone to her voice.

'Oh Katie, that's great news, and I'm sorry to be the one to put a dampener on things but Martha has been taken into hospital.'

'What? What happened?'

Zoe shakes her head. 'She collapsed earlier. She's just really gone downhill. Her son was supposed to come for her birthday, but he had to cancel the trip and then she just got rapidly weaker. They called an ambulance and took her to St. Mary's. And Bernie's been suspended. The cleaner put in a grievance, so the union has taken action for bullying and aggressive behaviour, so I guess you won't get a chance to stick it to her either.'

I grab my bag and run through the door out onto the street, up the road to where the taxis congregate and I jump in to the first one, with instructions to take me to St Mary's as quickly as possible. I don't care about Bernie now. I don't care about anything else. I just want to get to the hospital and find out where Martha is, how she is. *Please God, let her be okay. Please God let me not be too late.*

Once I'm there, I run again along the corridors, around the corners, up the stairs until finally I find someone who can direct me to where she is.

At the ward door there is a sturdy nurse, broad and upright in starched navy pinafore, holding a clipboard.

'I'm here to see Martha Rosenblatt,' I tell her breathlessly. 'Where is she?'

The nurse glances down at her pocket watch and knits her bushy eyebrows together. 'Visiting hours ended hours ago, you're too late I'm afraid. Family only, we've already had Ms Rosenblatt's son on the phone. He is on his way.'

'I am family,' I lie, the words escaping my mouth before I even process the thought.

The nurse looks at me through narrowed eyes. 'Are you her granddaughter?'

'Yes!' I tell her.

She regards me a moment longer. 'Ten minutes. And not a second over,' she says. 'My patients need their rest; I can't have this place filling up at every hour of the night.' She points with her pen. 'Third bed on the left and no noise or disruption. Make sure your phone is off, I don't want you waking the others.' She turns away, muttering something that sounds like 'always the way, too little too late.'

I slip between the curtains which have been drawn to make a cubicle. Inside is Martha. She has an oxygen mask strapped over her face, her coloured red hair is pasted back flat from her forehead and her skin is greyish white. This is the first time I've seen her without lipstick. She looks so frail, much more so in this large, clinical hospital bed that seems to envelop her.

One eye opens slowly. 'Katie?' she mouths from behind the mask.

I can just about make out a smile. I immediately climb onto the bed and put my arms around her. 'Look at you!' I say. 'I turn my back for five minutes and you end up here in the hospital! That's the last time I leave you again.'

She blinks in a kindly way and puts her damp hand up to my cheek. 'How did it go?' she asks, lifting the mask away from her face.

'All fine, perfectly fine,' I tell her, 'but that's not important, how are *you*?'

Martha starts to cough and I motion towards the oxygen mask, remembering the nurse's orders.

'Actually, don't answer that. It's better that you save your breath,' I tell her. 'And I suspect your nurse will have a few choice words with me if I tire you out.'

Martha inhales as deeply as she can and lifts her mask again. 'I'm absolutely fine,' she rasps 'All this is a lot of fuss about nothing.'

'It doesn't sound like nothing. Zoe said you collapsed.'

Martha makes a dismissive flick with her hand. 'I had a moment of dizziness, that was all. But it's nothing, a touch of pneumonia they say. I'll be back on my feet by tomorrow. I can't miss my own birthday.'

I squeeze her frail soft hand and remember how much she was looking forward to going out with her family and how, instead, she is here alone and poorly in a hospital bed. I feel a heavy sadness swell in my chest.

'Actually, it's after midnight, so happy birthday to you!' I whisper in a sing-song voice and her hand reaches towards me to stroke my hair.

'Right. Time up.' The nurse is suddenly behind me, holding the curtain open. 'I am afraid I must ask you to leave now, it is the end of my shift and I can't have any visitors when I hand over.'

But Martha grips me tighter. 'Does she have to go? Can't she stay just a little bit longer? We'll be ever so quiet.'

But the nurse shakes her head. 'I am afraid not: house rules. And besides, you need to get your energy up.'

I bend down to kiss Martha's cheek and she seizes me, pulling me towards her and whispering 'thank you' into my ear.

'Ms Rosenblatt!' the nurse scolds. 'Put that mask back on! You are a naughty one.'

'It has been said before,' Martha nods with a twinkle in her eye. 'You should have joined the army. Has anyone told you that?'

'It's my job to get you better.' The nurse whips the curtains back and I know it's time to go. 'You can come back tomorrow at six o'clock. Visiting hours.'

'Can't I come any earlier? In the morning?'

'No. She needs to rest, that's why she's here.'

I nod my understanding. 'I'll be back tomorrow, Martha. For your birthday, we'll have a treat, something special,' I tell her and

I walk out of the little cubicle and across the ward to the door, where I stop and wave to her from the end.

She lifts her wrist to wave back, her oxygen mask now firmly back in place, and I can see a definite smile in her eyes just before they close.

When I arrive the next day, Martha isn't wearing the mask any more and she is propped up on some pillows with the newspaper in her lap. She looks a little brighter and snatches off her glasses when she sees me and pats the bed beside her.

'Quick,' she says. 'Draw the curtain before The General returns.'

I pull the curtains around the bed and sit in beside her. She immediately envelopes me in an embrace, summoning all the strength she can muster.

'I have something for you!' I say. Out of my bag, I take a small, foil takeaway tray with my now famous sherry trifle inside, covered in gold glitter with an M inscribed in icing on the top. 'They loved it. And it was all thanks to you!'

She eyes me carefully. 'Does this mean…?'

I nod. 'It does.'

She places a hand on each of my cheeks and squeals. 'I knew you could do it! What a girl, Katie! This is absolutely wonderful!' She claps her hands together and calls out over the drawn curtains to the elderly lady on the other side. 'Katie here is the Grand Chef! You know!'

'Well done!' chirps back her neighbouring patient. The smiling lady nods and gives me a thumbs up. Martha is beaming and I see a flush of redness in the apples of her cheeks.

'Here I am in a hospital bed, on my birthday. Just like when I was born, eighty-nine years to the day. And you know what? I only want for the same things, food and love. Give a human being food and love and everything else is joyful distraction. Once I get out of here, I will insist my son brings me to your fabulous new restaurant. If he can ever untangle himself from his business affairs, that is. Now let's have a cup of tea and some of this beautiful dessert and you can tell me all about it.'

We chat for the next hour. I tell her all about what happened with Harry and then the judges, and the reaction I got to my menu. And then I tell her how I congratulated Ben and left him to party with his beautiful girlfriend.

'The one that got away,' Martha smiles gently.

I nod.

'Life can be so unfair at times. Wonderful of course, but, also unbearably unfair.'

And we sit together in silence. I'm grateful that she doesn't tell me that 'there will be another guy' who'll sweep me off my feet when I least expect it or that I'll forget him, that time will heal. We both just sit with it, accepting that it is what it is. A loss that can't be helped or changed or rectified but deserves to be acknowledged. And then she pats me on the hand. 'Try not to cry that it's over, but smile that it happened. Easier said than done, believe me.'

We both sip our tea and Martha dabs a stray dollop of cream from her trifle from her lips.

'Oh that was glorious. I can't thank you enough for coming, Katie. It really makes all the difference. I had a dreadful night last night. I don't know how anyone expects to get well in hospital. Kept awake at all hours by spluttering and snoring and the second you do fall asleep the nurses come to shake you awake again: time for prodding, time for tablets, time for injections. It's unbearable. I've decided that I shan't put up with it. I'm ready to check out.'

I laugh at her indignation. 'Martha, you're getting better all the time. So they are doing a very good job.'

She opens her mouth to protest when she is caught by a coughing fit. Her little chest heaves as she tries to draw breath. I put my hands on her shoulders and help to tilt her forward to ease her chest, something I used to do regularly when my own mother was ill. The fit over with, she lies back on her pillows, biting her lip. Her forehead creased in deep thought. 'We have been lucky, you and me.' She takes my hand and folds it between both of hers.

'What do you mean?' I ask. Her hands, around mine, are now hot and clammy.

'To be here. Survivors. When you love something dearly and it leaves you, it's very hard to let love back in. To open yourself up to that kind of hurt. But look at us, we are here. Knowing full well that we will feel that again one day, still, we are not afraid.' She looks at me. 'There is nothing to be afraid of except fear itself. Promise me you'll remember that.' She smiles in a lopsided way, as if a full smile requires too much energy, too much strength.

I nod my promise.

'Good.' She smiles, turning her neck back and forth as if trying to get comfortable. 'I was never one for fear.'

CHAPTER TWENTY-FOUR

It's 6 a.m. I'm standing on the balcony of my penthouse room. In an oversized, super-soft bathrobe, watching the world wake up beneath me. I moved my bits and pieces out of Alice's over the weekend and finally, into a bed of my own. A suite of my own. This morning's sunrise was a staggering display of radiant colour. Bright streaks of red, pink, and orange slowly overcame the dark blue and purple of the twilight sky and then all blended perfectly into each other. Mighty reds and flaming oranges splashed the clouds with endless rays of pink. I'd hardly ever seen anything so gorgeous. I've never been so high up, never had such a broad and clear view of the London skyline. I can't believe this has happened to me. I can't believe that I'm going to wake up like this every day. And then button up into my Marchand London whites and join Jean-Michel downstairs for a day of magic. Whatever I've loved, lost and left behind, however much it hurt has brought me to this point. So now, I'm forward-facing. This is a new dawn and I'm ready to make the most of it.

Everything feels altogether new and exciting and achingly beautiful from up here. It's still so early, the city is just rousing, softly, slowly, and there's a special, subdued quiet that only us early risers share. A handful of road sweepers, joggers and coffee-sipping office workers zip across the otherwise deserted streets. Every one of them oblivious to me, watching them from up here, like a queen in a castle. The sun itself is just peeking out of the horizon, and its brilliant rays already shining brightly are beginning to warm the air. A thrilling feeling of awe sweeps over me. The trees beam as if they are wearing golden crowns and I let the soft amber glow of the sunshine pour through my fingers and onto my upturned face. This is it. I can't wait to begin.

Jean-Michel is in a neon vest and shorts when I enter the dining room. I take my seat beside him at the table by the window and say good morning. He is still sweating from his run, a towel hangs around his shoulders and he has two phones, a laptop, a newspaper, a triple espresso, a tube of tablets, a box of vitamins and a single boiled egg laid out in front of him.

He knocks back the espresso, throws back two tablets and a handful of vitamins, swallowing with intense concentration, both eyes scrunched tight. He makes a very low, almost primal sound through his closed lips. Banging on the table to an unknown beat, he breathes deeply, then he opens his eyes, smiles and wishes me good morning back.

Right. Today is going to be interesting.

'So, your first day, Katie. Excited?'

'Very!' I tell him. 'This is a dream come true. I'm so happy to be here, Jean-Michel.' I take out my cardboard folder. 'I've got lots of ideas, so I thought I'd bring them along and see what you think?' I start to spread out all the different handwritten menus I've designed. 'I was also thinking maybe some theme nights? A bit like a pop-up, where we can feature new techniques or showcase new ingredients, that kind of thing? Something to make us stand out from your standard fine-dining experience.'

Jean-Michel nearly chokes on his egg. '*Standard* fine dining? You know this is a paradox.'

'Sorry, I didn't mean "standard", I meant usual or expected… Sorry, nerves, I just got muddled… We can scrap it, I was just brainstorming really, you know, trying to think outside the box and all that,' I tell him nervously.

Jean-Michel finishes chewing his egg. Slow, deliberate bites. All I can do is sit here and wait till this egg mastication ends and he gives me a green light to resume talking to him. Once he finishes, he dabs the corners of his mouth with a napkin and then tells me to tidy up my papers. Which I guess means, put all of my new ideas away. So I do. Jean-Michel runs a tongue over his teeth and takes a long breath through his nose.

'Katie, your enthusiasm is sweet. I like it. It is a good thing to dream and imagine and fantasise. However, here, now, you may be grand chef, but whose name is it above the door?'

'Yours,' I answer.

'Whose name is on the top of every menu card?'

'Yours.'

'Whose name attracted you to come and work here in the first place?'

'Yours.'

'*Exactement.* So, as long as my name is attached to every tick of the clock in this restaurant, you follow my lead, *comprends*?'

I nod and close over my folder. I understand perfectly well. I may be Jean-Michel's grand chef, but it's still his kitchen and I'm the apprentice here.

He slides over one of the phones to me. 'Here this is yours. Ensure it is charged at all times. This is your work phone. If I need you, this is the number I will expect to reach you. Bring it everywhere, keep it by your bedside, and answer it no matter what. Preferably by the second ring.'

I take it and see that all the contacts I need have already been entered: Jean-Michel, Pip, Octavia, suppliers, plumbers, staffing agencies, delivery drivers, you name it, it's on here. This phone is my link to everything in this new world.

'Okay. Now, this is the new taster menu I've created. Your thoughts?'

I take the heavy cream paper from his hand and read through the ten courses he's selected. All are classic Jean-Michel signature dishes, except for the last one. I look up at him, blinking my disbelief.

'You've got my trifle on there?'

He smiles. 'You okay with that?'

'I'm honoured, thank you. That means a great deal to me,' I tell him, meaning every word.

'Good. Onto our next point of business. Staffing. We've had some walkouts, you know the score. Oversensitive, overinflated egos that go running home to mama first time we forget to say they are wonderful. So, I need you to find me a new sous-chef. By Wednesday service.'

'But I'll need longer than that!' I tell him. 'By the time we put a job description out and then shortlist and interviews... I'm afraid that's not going to be possible.'

Jean-Michel raises a finger to his lips to silence me. 'You are the grand chef. You will find a way. Now, today – I need inventory of the entire kitchen; everything we have in stock, fresh and frozen, we need it itemised and uploaded to the central database before we let a single customer through the door.' He stands from his chair and nods towards the phone. 'Call me when you are finished.'

So I guess that means I'm doing it without him.

'And I don't want any shitty sous-chef, you know what I expect.' And then he takes his newspaper under his arm, and he's gone.

It takes me nine hours to inventory the freezer alone. And I still have the non-perishables to do. And I have no idea where to find a decent sous-chef in practically no time. And what decent sous-chef is going to drop everything on a Monday night to start work for Jean-Michel on Wednesday?

It's impossible. He is impossible. He has his infamous reputation for good reason. I remember all those crying candidates back on day one of the selection, crying from ridicule but also frustration. He was impossible then and he's impossible now.

And then this gives me an idea. I know exactly who would drop everything for this chance. I know someone who's desperate for this call. Not only because it's Jean-Michel but because it's a sous position. That'll take her out of pastry and the chance to show what else she can do, not just to him but herself as well. I just hope she doesn't try her dehydrated turd dish on my watch. I laugh to myself and give Georgia Jacobs a call. Why not? It could work, chances are slim, but I've got to try because now that I'm grand chef, nobody else is going to solve this for me.

The next day, I arrive at St Mary's just as the clock strikes visiting hour. I'm met at the doorway by the sturdy nurse in navy. In a low voice she tells me that Ms Rosenblatt passed away during the night. I can hardly take this in. On my last visit, over the weekend, Martha had seemed to be getting better, laughing and smiling like the Martha of old.

'Martha's died?' I hear my own voice say the words again, questioning, disbelieving. 'Last night? Are you sure that's what you mean? Are you sure that's right?'

'She just slipped away,' she tells me more than once. This nurse, The General as Martha had called her, was with her when she drew her last breath. Martha's son hadn't made it on time. I look around the ward, the plastic sheeting, the TV set on mute, a well-worn visitor chair, the beep of a heart monitor, the metallic slide of a curtain rail being pulled, and hear the hushed inflections of family members trying to make upbeat small talk with their bed-bound loved ones. This is all too familiar. All too heart-breaking. I remember being in a hospital just like this before: this dreadful news, these sights, and these sounds. The smell of antiseptic and boiled food. My vision is beginning to blur, to swim and melt with tears.

I find myself repeating the nurse's words back to her, expecting her to correct me, to explain that I misunderstood. But she doesn't, she tries to guide me out by the elbow but I stand still. Unable to lift the lead of my legs. The nurse nods again, this time keeping eye contact and adding how it was very peaceful, like she drifted into a dream.

'Thank you,' I say at last, with a tight, sad smile because I don't really know what else to say. Because it's best to remain composed, to hold yourself together… at least in public, until I am away from here. So I keep walking and don't turn around. I don't check the bed where Martha had lain, where we both had tea and trifle. Where quietly, selflessly, bravely, Martha had made her last birthday wish.

Quietly, selflessly, bravely. Just like my own mother did. She waited for me to go and then she left.

CHAPTER TWENTY-FIVE

The days and then weeks that follow are hard to describe. They all blur into a frantic sequence of dark mornings in the markets, then prepping until lunch and then cooking and conducting the kitchen choreography until it's time to knock off the lights and take the lift five floors up to bed. All with Martha's passing looming large in the background. She's on my mind every day.

I don't know what day of the week it is, never mind what the weather is like. I haven't seen sunlight since I started. A twenty-metre walk to the elevator has replaced my cycling commute. I just press a button and seconds later, ding! I'm home. Don't get me wrong, it's luxurious. But it's more of a luxuriant gilded cage. It means that I'm accessible and therefore available to Jean-Michel and the Marchand 24/7. I've got nowhere to hide. I am always on call.

Tonight is a rare exception. I'm going to have drinks with Alice. I haven't seen her in weeks and weeks so she's come to the hotel and once I finish clearing up this kitchen, we're going to sip our drinks watching the glittering skyline from the rooftop bar. A scene straight out of our original visions of London life.

After I've ticked off the final pastry inventory and counted bags of flour, we drink wine and help ourselves to whatever we fancy from the dessert fridge; the meringue-topped cheesecake with a side of white chocolate ice cream and hot salted caramel sauce getting our vote.

Alice is awestruck. 'This is the most amazing job in the world, free food, free hotel room, fame, fortune. I know it was hard-going at times, but when you see this, you must think: wow, it's been worth it, right?'

I laugh, 'We've only just started! Jean-Michel won't rest until we get a Michelin star. That's what this is all about. We are on high alert until then.'

'Well, star or no star, hats off to you, Katie. You just never gave up. No one would have blamed you for calling it a day after the restaurant but you didn't. And look where it got you! It's world's away from being stuck in Parklands, then weaving through the backstreets to drink cheap wine with me every evening.'

A pang of nostalgia hits me. I don't want to let Alice know that, already, being grand chef is not all I thought it would be. And there's been more than one occasion so far when I've locked the toilet door, held my head in my hands, battling against tears, as I consider the possibility that this was all a big mistake, that I am running myself in to the ground.

Was my pre-grand chef life really so bad? At Parklands I had friends. When Bernie wasn't around, we always had a laugh. But there is no laughter in this kitchen, no one would dare to glance at each other in humour, even when Jean-Michel is not around. The pressure is always on, the stakes are always high, the risk of destroying the ingredients, screwing up the presentation, the taste or the service is too great. And besides, Jean-Michel is here *all the time*. I swear he sleeps in the pantry. I put in a solid sixteen hours a day – 6 a.m. to 10 p.m. is my norm and often I don't get away that lightly. And still I've never yet arrived or left before him. Except for tonight, but only because Jean-Michel is upstairs in the office meeting with Pip and Octavia, going over the books, his plans for the future, his menu ideas, his expanding wine lists. All the stuff I imagined I would be doing as grand chef, but alas, no, Jean-Michel has no intention of handing over any responsibility. Not the slightest iota of control.

My assigned work phone rings. I scramble to answer it because it can only be one person and place my finger to my lip to let Alice know to keep quiet. It's late; it can only be Jean-Michel.

'You need to find a new patisserie chef.'

'But what about Pierre?'

'Pierre is gone.'

'You've fired our only remaining pastry chef?'

'*Oui*. He talked too much and made a mess everywhere he went, I told him, "You are too slow, your station is dirty, and you have a haircut that makes your head look like a testicle." He had to go. Replace him in time for tomorrow's service.'

And he hangs up. It's nearly 11 o'clock, but he expects me to find a pastry chef in time for tomorrow. This is typical Jean-Michel: erratic decision-making and fiery temper, gruelling hours even by cheffing standards, and, just like now, he hires and frequently fires staff and then orders me to pick up the pieces.

I'm grand chef only in name. Really, I'm Jean-Michel's lackey, his mere underling when there are jobs that need doing, and then in his softer moments I'm expected to be his life coach and counsellor. Jean-Michel is a complex man. I've realised that he's a man without boundaries, especially between his personal and professional lives. If he fights with his wife, expect hell in the kitchen that day. If there's hell in the kitchen, expect an explosion. That's when I try to talk to him, calm him down, reassure him that everything is going well, that we're doing great. That we have his back, we understand, we won't let him down.

Of course, when we are in full flight of service everything feels worthwhile and I feel so lucky to have such a mentor. I'm learning a lot. I'm enjoying that side of things, but I can't say that it's turned out to be exactly the dream job I thought it would be.

I can't admit this to Alice though. Or my dad or anyone else, so I paint on a smile on and crack on. This is what I signed up for, so I'm just going to have to suck it up until I find my stride.

As Jean-Michel says himself, it is early days. Establishing everything, recruiting and training the new staff, waiting for our orders to come through, setting up new accounts and contacts all takes a hell of a lot of work and time to put in place. Making sure it is exactly right before we open fully and officially is crucial. We've been open only a month, starting with just weekends, then dinner service and now we are lunch and dinner six days a week. I approached him last week and told him that I needed the evening off. Rachel had emailed me to say she was passing through London on a work trip in a few days, and I knew this was my chance to make amends. I needed to make sure I met with her.

'Not possible,' he told me.

'Jean-Michel, I wouldn't ask unless it was really important. She's pregnant so she won't be able to fly for much longer and I haven't seen her in a long time. I'm giving you reasonable notice and I'll sort the rota so someone will cover my shift. It's just one evening, Jean-Michel, please. I haven't had a single day off in twenty-two days.' And I need some time. Not just to do other things, to meet people, but to give my body a rest. I'm physically banjaxed. The heat of the kitchen means I'm constantly dehydrated, which means I've got a banging headache all the time and I'm still adjusting to standing so much. My calves are killing me. And with such huge pots, and so many of them needed for a restaurant of this scale, my forearms are killing me as well.

The first time I asked for time off was to attend Martha's funeral. He did not even look up. He just shook his head and snarled. 'You begged me to accept you and now you beg me to leave. You go, you don't come back.' I sent flowers and a card to Martha's son Leo, explaining myself, my absence, praying he would understand.

I backed down. Afraid of what was going to happen next. Afraid and utterly convinced that he would show me the door. The spectre of getting fired constantly looming over me. I was afraid I would get fired for not being good enough, for not being strong enough, for disappointing him by not meeting his exacting standards. But now I know that no one can meet his impossible standards. But this was different. And I'm different. Rachel is stopping over in London *especially* to see me. It will be the last time I get to see her before the baby comes; who knows when I'll get to Australia, especially with Jean-Michel as my boss. I was determined to catch her. It's already been too long and I've already let things slip too badly.

Jean-Michel looked up, staggered that I was still standing in front of him. But I was not going to budge.

'What time are you meeting her?'

'Nine p.m, at Heathrow, just for an hour, then she takes her connecting flight.'

He pressed the heels of his hands into his eyes. 'Book a taxi. Leave here at 8.30 be back for 10.30. Two hours, no longer.'

And I thanked him, knowing that these measly two hours was the best offer I was going to get. So we're getting there, steadily if not smoothly.

'Right. That's it,' I say as I put the phone down and try not to think about how I'm going to find a pastry chef at this time of night. 'This kitchen is now *closed*.'

Alice jumps down off her stool and pivots on the spot. 'Excellent! Cocktail time!'

I drop her off at the hotel lounge on the top floor whilst I quickly run to my room to shower and change. When I catch up with her she is sitting at the bar, giggling flirtatiously with the barman as she sweeps her hair over her shoulder. She looks wonderful, happy and confident and for a second, I think, yes! We are here! This is exactly what we always dreamt of, this is what we came to London for in the first place, excitement, glamour, fun. She waves over to me and points to the Martini she's ordered for us.

'Something's different with you. Tell me everything,' I say. 'I want to know all.'

'Well, you know how I've hated work since forever.'

I nod.

'And you know how much I admire you for going after your dream no matter what.'

I take a big slurpy sip of my cocktail whilst nodding. The last thing I want to do is start complaining about how life in The Marchand is not all it's cracked up to be so I just smile and play along. Did she get a promotion? Is she transferring to a different office? A different country? Whatever it is, it has brought Alice right back to the girl I knew, a sparkle in her eye and laughter in her smile. 'So?'

'I told my boss to stick his job. I'm done. I walked,' she says with a shimmy.

I double-take. 'Alice, you did what?'

'I marched straight in to the office, and gave it to him, Jerry Maguire style. I told him I hated the job, hated the culture, hated the meaninglessness of everything they stood for. Once I started, I couldn't stop. It was quite the spectacle, even if I do say so myself.' She is saying this so gleefully it's as if someone has imposed a voiceover.

'And you said this directly to his face?'

'Repeatedly. And in front of the other board members. And in an email. That I cc'd to everyone else in the company.'

I flatten my hands on the table, my mouth wide open. 'No, tell me, you didn't…'

'Katie, I did! I did it! I thought you'd be proud of me!'

I take a gigantic deep breath and lean into the bar counter for support. 'I am. Of course I am proud of you that you made a change, but… To do it so dramatically, they may not give you a reference.'

She finishes her Martini in one slurp. 'I don't care.'

'But how are you going to live? How will you get by?'

Another gleeful smile as she wiggles her shoulders. 'I sold my flat!'

Oh my god. 'Alice, what's going on with you?'

She takes a deep breath and clasps her hands together. 'I felt like I wasn't really living. If I'm honest with myself, I was just hanging on here because I thought it was the right thing to do. Lawyer in London sounds great, right? So it took me a long time to realise that just because it's something I can do, doesn't mean it's something I *should* do. And then when you moved out, I realised how lonely and sad and tragic my life had become. So just like you, I figured, I'm going to make it better, I'm going to make a change.'

Alice opens up her bag and takes out a card.

'Remember Ryan, the HR guy?'

I nod.

'We're both doing this course together, well-being in the workplace type of thing. Soon I'm going to have passed my first module: Coaching and Stress Management.'

I nearly spit out my drink. 'You! Stress Management! Seriously, Isn't that the pot calling the kettle—'

Alice laughs so hard she snorts, her hands flying up to her nose as she checks if anyone else at the bar has heard. 'I know! Who'd have guessed right! But I can't tell you how much better I feel. How much better I *am*. And I just can't wait to do this.'

I raise my hand to the barman and order two more drinks as I realise how much I've neglected Alice since I took on this crazy journey to working for Jean-Michel. How could all this have been going on with her and I didn't know? So, even though I am utterly exhausted and need to be up again to buy fresh scallops at Billingsgate in six hours, I don't care.

I genuinely don't care. Jean-Michel won't be happy of course. But I'm starting to care less about that too.

Because I need to toast my brilliant, beautiful, beaming best friend.

Because we've got to take these rare moments with the people who are special to us, as who knows when I'll get the chance to see her like this again.

I raise my glass and make a silent toast to Martha. Feeling her winking her approval at me from on high.

CHAPTER TWENTY-SIX

'Right, Georgia, you can take over Pastry. Lewis, you can move into hot sides and garnishes.'

Lewis nods and gathers his knives. Georgia stands to look at me with narrowed eyes, her hands on her hips. This is all I need. Two drinks with Alice turned in to six and it felt like my head barely touched the pillow before it was time to get up again. But I did; I threw myself under a cold shower and buoyed myself by remembering that today I'm seeing my baby sister, up close and face to face.

'What's the problem?' I ask Georgia, our recently appointed sous-chef.

'Pastry? The whole reason I agreed to drop everything and come and work here is so that I could come out of pastry! Why on earth would I do exactly the same thing that I did at The Buckingham?'

'Firstly, the reason you agreed to drop everything was that you were clearly unhappy at The Buckingham, otherwise you wouldn't have dropped the job as soon as a better offer came along. And this *is* a better offer, Georgia. You wanted to work in Jean-Michel's kitchen and now here you are. However, we need a pastry chef *tonight*, as in right now, your strength is in pastry so that's the way I've decided to reshuffle the team.'

Georgia bites down on her lip.

'What's the big deal?' I ask her.

'It's just that everyone thinks the crappest chefs do pastry. You know what they call it at The Buckingham? They call it the

Pink Kitchen. They think it's all we can do, rolling and piping. I wanted to show them that I can do more than that.'

I take a deep breath, I get it. 'Do you like pastry?'

She widens her eyes slightly. 'Of course, I love it but that's not the point.'

'That *is* the point. This is where your strength is. I can't say which came first; did your love of it lead to your talent or the talent lead to love? But it doesn't matter now because you have both. No doubt about it, Georgia, you are one of the best in the business. And nothing anyone thinks or says should push you out of that if you are doing a great job and you are happy. Don't feel you need to prove anything – to anyone. Pastry is where you shine, be proud of that.'

Georgia's face softens and she picks up her apron and dusts off her hands. 'Pastry chef for Jean-Michel, it's not too bad really, is it?'

I hand her the menu and a smile breaks her face.

'Dark chocolate cylinder with smoked hazelnut praline and salted milk ice cream and our signature trifle with Barbadillo sherry. Wow!'

I can see her fingers starting to twitch as she looks around her new station for ingredients, for equipment, planning how she's going to approach making a trio of all these marvellous sweet creations for our hotly anticipated brand new, taster menu.

'Exactly,' I say, knowing this is a much higher skill level than she was working at The Buckingham. 'You can do this, Georgia, pour all your love into it and knock Jean-Michel's socks off.'

She beams at me. 'Yes, chef.'

Jean-Michel is in a dark mood when he bursts into the kitchen. It could be because I'm nipping off to meet Rachel, but then again, it could be something entirely unrelated. Family? Business? Dill shortage? It could be anything. I feel sorry for him. Sympathy for Jean-Michel? It's like having sympathy for the devil. I know, not something you hear every day.

But being with him all this time, observing his moods, his bad days, the unwavering, relentless dedication he sinks into every tiny detail, over such long hours, with such intensity, I have to say he's grown on me. He isn't a monster but he is a slave to perfection. It's like a severe case of OCD. He can't be any other way; he can't even imagine or tolerate any other way.

His entire career can be made and unmade in the space of a setting. I think it's probably worse now than before, as prior to this London venture, the last restaurant he opened was over a decade ago. A new business is like a new baby, it takes its toll. It needs every piece of you, every moment of the day. I now see a chef's life involves much more than the culinary arts; it involves being a personnel manager, a marketing and public relations specialist and special events coordinator. Opening a new restaurant isn't like what you see in the movies. There's a ton of unsexy things going on behind the scenes and everything has its own timeline – recruitment, advertising, contracting, building, hiring, training, writing menus, testing recipes. You're dealing with it all from broken plumbing pipes to food orders. And most of the time, something is going wrong or someone's too slow or starts crying or throws in the dishtowel. You have to deal with issues constantly while still being hyper-creative. Jean-Michel's already outlasted his generation of chefs. Most of whom are either burnt out and in rehab programs or hosting reality cooking shows on television. Jean-Michel is a one-off all right, still at the helm, still standing the heat.

But sometimes, I can really see the exhaustion in his body, the dark bags under his eyes, the triple espressos he knocks back like shots, that third whisky during service that is coming earlier and earlier. Sometimes, I think even he regrets it all, regrets this whole venture. I figure he let nostalgia take over and underestimated the stamina, the physical and mental energy required to start a new restaurant from scratch. Especially one with such high expectations and when he's so defensive about his infamous reputation. I'm trying to keep things calm for him, trying to deal with things myself so I don't have to bother or agitate him. How well I'm doing on that front is anyone's guess.

Jean-Michel emerges from the walk-in fridge, his face pallid grey and creased with stress. He raises his hands, blows out his cheeks and twirls on the spot. I give him an encouraging smile.

Service starts. Jean-Michel is right when he says we are doing well. Word is spreading fast. We are booked out for the next three months and a *Time Out* review read, 'go here when you want to say to your mouth, you SHALL go to the ball! But book now because it won't be long before these guys take over the world'. Jean-Michel had just shrugged when I showed him.

'Cute but irrelevant. I care only for Michelin stars.' He stopped what he was doing and turned to me, meeting my eyes with full seriousness. 'I am married but Michelin is my mistress. It is a love-hate affair with the stars. Gaining that recognition, that validation can send you crazy, make you obsessive. Is it the lady at the corner table who ordered the blackened cod? Or is it the gentleman at table five with the steak tartar? Which of my diners has the power to change my life? Who is the Michelin inspector? When will they accept my offerings and raise it to their lips and deign it worthy for the world?'

'Is it really that secretive and undercover?' I asked. 'Surely after so much time, you have an idea of who they are or when they are coming.'

Jean-Michel inhaled sharply, placing his hands flat on the counter. '*Mais non*, if only! If I could tell when they were coming I would look half the age I am now because I would have had double the sleep. All I know is that we should be expecting them at all times. They will come to us, sooner rather than later, because of the profile of the newest restaurant in town. They will be keen to see if I am still the chef I was. I have much to prove. Achieving this level is one thing, sustaining it quite another.'

He paused a moment. 'However, I have learnt some clues over the years, purely based on my own experience. They are unofficial of course. From what I have picked up, they always book a table for two so as not to arouse suspicion, but then, when they arrive, there is only one. They dine alone. And always this lone diner is well-dressed, polite, middle-aged. Mostly it is a man. They order from the taster menu, and always the house wine and a still water. They are paying attention to the quality of service as much as the quality of the food. They try to stay under the radar as much as possible, to slip in and out unnoticed to give them a real idea of the typicality of the place, so that they can really focus on the food and the ambience and capture the entire experience.'

'I'll keep my eyes peeled,' I said, half-jokingly. But I saw that Jean-Michel was not joking.

'You should. They can turn an unknown chef into a superstar or a superstar in to an unknown ball of shame.'

It is nearly eight o'clock. So the last bookings are arriving and I'll get everything in place so I can catch my cab in half an hour to take me straight to Heathrow to see Rachel. The reality is dawning on me now, I'm actually going to wrap my arms around her, hold her face in my hands and look at her beautiful, freckled face for the first time in god knows how long, shamefully long. Well over eighteen months, this is the longest we've ever been apart. I'm just going to lift her up and hug the almighty out of her, carefully of course! Got to mind the bump! It's so exciting and I just cannot wait. She could be landing right now, so we're already a little bit closer, in the same time zone. I'll just start off this last service and I'll be out the door. I'm not nervous about slipping off at this stage of the evening; we've got a great team and it feels like it's starting to come together. Not one glitch tonight in the kitchen or out on the floor and that's a first. Everything has gone pitch perfect. Georgia's desserts have been really well received; she's even had the confidence to add her own little twist on Jean-Michel's recipe and he has given her an uncharacteristic thumbs up on everything so far, so there is a real spring in her step. I'd say The Buckingham team will want to eat whatever words made her eager to leave.

Everything is going so amazingly well that I start to think that Jean-Michel is right, that the setup is always the hardest part, but that once everything is in place we'll find our stride and really will take over the world. When things settle I'm going to book some time off. I'm going to go home and see my dad and help him with the house clearance. Just because I live far away and I'm busy is not a good enough excuse for losing touch. I may approach Jean-Michel later tonight, see how it goes, chance my arm and ask for just a few days.

I place my dishes up on the pass for inspection by Jean-Michel. He quickly studies each of them and gives the nod that they are service-ready, presented to his exacting standards. I call service Table Eight and press the bell for Sara to collect the plates and serve them out front. When she comes back into the kitchen, pushing through the doors and leaning into the pass, her eyes are intense and her voice is hushed.

'Top table booked for two but now only one diner. Well-dressed gentleman dining alone, just ordered the taster menu, half a carafe of house wine and a still water. What do you think?'

Jean-Michel arches his back, cracking his knuckles. He raises an eyebrow and blows out his cheeks. 'Mid-late forties?' he asks.

Sara nods.

'The booking was originally made for two?'

She nods again.

'Michelin?' he asks, a slight crack in his voice. He looks skyward, blesses himself and then slaps his hand against his chest. 'Michelin! We are on!'

Jean-Michel turns into a hurricane.

A sweating, shouting, swearing hurricane.

He snatches the order ticket from Sara. 'Is this it? Is this the order?'

'Yes.'

'Okay, Katie, I want you to make the short ribs for the beef starter and I want you to make the sauce for the sea bass main. Nobody else, only you.'

I open my mouth to tell him, No! I can't! My taxi is due to arrive in ten minutes. I've got to meet Rachel! I've promised her. She's arranged a stopover in London, pregnant, *especially* for me. And what am I going to say? What can I tell her? That I have to work?

But Jean-Michel cuts me dead. 'Let me finish! And when I finish the only thing that comes out of your mouth is "Yes, chef!"'

There is a mad, almost murderous look in his eyes.

He glares at me. Unable to understand why I've missed a beat. Why I've not answered him.

An incredulous laugh reaches his eye. 'Haha! You think you are leaving? You think you're still going to meet your sister or auntie or fucking long-lost relative? I don't care if you have a date with the Dalai Lama. You are the grand chef, YOU stay here.'

My feet are rooted to the spot. What the hell? There is no right thing to do. I hate to let Rachel down. My dad is going to be furious. Pregnant Rachel stressed and upset in an airport all by herself because I bailed.

Jean-Michel spins around and steps right into my face. He licks his lips and then speaks to me in a voice I've never heard him use before. A slow, calm, measured voice.

'You accepted your title, your uniform, your hotel room. You signed your contract. And that contract states that you shall meet the standards of grand chef as deemed appropriate by me. If you leave, if you cost me this star, I'll fire you, but trust me, Katie, that will only be the beginning.'

He wipes a hand down his face. When he reopens his eyes, they are wet. The madness, the rage has dissipated, replaced by something much softer.

'Katie, please. I thought you wanted this. You begged me for a chance. I gave it you. Now, I am the one begging you. Please. Stay. I need you. I need you right here, right now.'

And I know that I can't do this to him. As much as I'm going to upset Rachel, I just *can't* walk out on Jean-Michel. This is his moment. I know what this means for him. To him. I promised him at the first selection that I would give him everything I had and now is not the time to break that.

I pause, and then nod. 'Yes, chef.'

'I will make the sauce for the sea bass,' he says, changing his mind. 'Katie, you do the starter, I will begin the main.'

'Yes, chef.'

'And I will plate up the fish and the beef.'

'Yes, chef.'

He turns to Lewis. 'Where are my knives? Get them for me. Bring them now!'

Lewis dashes to the back station calling, 'Yes, chef!'

Jean-Michel turns to the whole team, finger jabbing at the air, his teeth clenched tight. 'And I want to see every element of every garnish. *Nothing* goes out without my approval, you hear me? I have *everything* riding on this. EVERYTHING.'

'Yes, chef,' we all say in chorus.

He turns back to Sara. 'And remember, he is not just watching his own table! He'll have eyes on *everything*, down to the last thread. So everyone, everything has to be pitch perfect!'

We are all nodding frantically.

Jean-Michel slams down his hand on the chopping board. 'Do you fucking hear me?

'Yes, chef!'

The next ten minutes is the most intense of my life, Jean-Michel standing over me, standing over us all, breathing heavily, his eyes watching our every move and commenting every millisecond, like a machine gun in our ears.

'Katie, turn it now. Two more minutes. Yeah. That's good? Taste it. Too insipid? Season lightly… Be careful! Yeah, that's right. That should be thick. That's good, that's good. More salt. Off the heat. Good crust… How's the sauce? Taste it… Like silk, *oui*? Is it silken?'

'Yes, chef. Yes, chef.'

I do as he asks, to the standard he expects, at a speed that even blows my mind.

'Yes, chef,' I repeat for the millionth time. But I dare not mess around. This is serious. This is *everything*. There is no way that I can leave this spot even for two seconds to text Rachel to let her know what's going on. I can feel Jean-Michel's breath on my neck.

Come on, got to thicken up the sauce.

Come on, this is the dish.

'Katie, you are looking at that all the time, yeah?' he shouts as I finish off searing the vegetables in the pan, spooning butter over them with the speed of a machine. 'Don't look up, don't blink. You have eyes on it the whole time till you hit the pass,' he tells me as he wipes his own brow with his cloth. The heat is coming from everywhere, the flames and the pressure.

'Yes, chef.'

'Yeah? Look at me.'

I do as I'm told, despite my earlier instruction. Because this is life with Jean-Michel. One second it is up, then it is down. First it's look left, then it's look right. I meet his eyes.

'You can do this? You can handle it?'

'Yes, chef. It's all in hand, chef. You don't have to worry. I've got your back.'

Because it's true. I know I can handle this. I know I can handle him. I can handle all of it.

And I won't let him down.

Just before service, Jean-Michel inspects everything one final time.

I turn to him. 'What do you think?' I ask.

'I think it's perfect, chef. I trained you well.'

I press the button for service and let my plate seal our fate.

Sara returns to the kitchen, calling, 'His plate is clean!' Her eyes flash and she chances a single thumbs up. I turn to the kitchen and give them two sure thumbs up.

'Starter is finished. All going well, team. The light is at the end of the tunnel now. Time for the main.'

Jean-Michel has taken complete charge of the main so we stand and watch the man, the maniac, at work. He shoos Lewis out of his way.

'Away, give me space,' he says as he starts to build the plate, layering and drizzling and positioning with the finesse of an artist. But the visual is only the beginning of food at this level. In a moment, every shape, every texture, every colour on that plate will have to play its part in terms of taste. And then it will disappear. Not immortalised like an oil painting or a watercolour. It lives only in this moment. And only for two people: the chef and the diner. Only they know it existed. How it existed. Only they will ever know what it means.

'Is it okay?' he asks me, his eyes wide like a little boy's.

'It's perfect, chef,' I tell him. 'Exactly how you like it.'

'Are you absolutely sure, my friend?'

'Absolutely. It's wonderful.'

He bites his lip, unsure. Scared. He takes the cloth and wipes the plate rim again, just to be sure.

I place my hand on his wrist. 'Jean-Michel, it's time. Let it go.'

He dips his head to his chest and blinks his understanding, pressing the bell for service. '*C'est tout.*'

Sara takes the plate and exits the kitchen.

And it is now out of our hands. In every sense.

CHAPTER TWENTY-SEVEN

Sara comes back into the kitchen, a smile breaking her face. 'Empty plate. He sends his compliments to the chef!'

I see a look wash over Jean-Michel that I've never seen before. He looks genuinely happy. Genuinely proud. He claps me on the back.

'Good job! Great job. One last course, I know it has been tough. I have been tough and you may think I'm not paying attention, Katie, but believe me, I always pay attention. You are a very special chef and you have impressed me. If anything, I've learned from you, from your self-control. You stayed. I know you were supposed to go, but you stayed. Thank you.'

That would mean the world to me had it not cost me my meeting with Rachel.

Although Jean-Michel is more relaxed with the dessert, he still scrutinises it before he lets Sara take it from the pass. I have to say Georgia's skill is incredible, and she's pulled out all the stops. When she said she wanted to be part of this team, she wasn't kidding. She's given her all and the way this is going, it looks like she's the last part of the puzzle.

It leaves the pass and Sara swans out through the double doors, a trio of deliciousness in hand.

Jean-Michel leans back against the wall and presses his hands into his face, breathing out all his tension. 'So there it is, we have done all we can do. Katie, you need some time. Why not take maybe three days? Visit your family.'

I thank him. It's like he's read my mind. I'm going to need some time off to try and make it up to my sister, how exactly still remains to be seen. But I'll think of something, something really special. Things are looking up; just this one last course between me and the life I've been trying to create since forever.

No sooner have I started to daydream about being back in my home, hugging my dad, hanging out with Alice and actually sleeping for more than five hours at a time, than Sara bursts through the doors, her face stricken. She slides a full plate of the trifle dessert back across the pass to us.

'Took a forkful, looked at it like he'd never seen it before, like he was actually going to cry and then he just dropped his fork to the plate, called me over, asked for the bill and his coat.'

Ohmygod.

Oh my GOD.

'What do you mean? What is going on?' Jean-Michel starts to shout. 'You, what have you done?' He lifts the plate and I'm afraid that he's going to throw it. Georgia is trembling. I stand in front of him, two steady open palms held up in an attempt to reason.

'Jean-Michel, Georgia is the best pastry chef I've ever seen. I have every confidence in her.'

He presses his fingers to his forehead. I hand him a fork. And we both take a mouthful. And then a second. And then a third.

Jean-Michel nods. '*C'est parfait.*' He plunges a finger right down to the bottom of the sherry trifle, sniffing it before putting it in his mouth. '*Je ne comprends pas.*' And then he shakes his head, lifting his eyes to mine, confused. 'You are telling me that he didn't even *taste* it?' he asks Sara.

She shakes her head. 'I watched the whole thing. Not one bite.'

I can see the fury flood into Jean-Michel's chest, up his neck and into his face. He throws down the fork and wrings his hands in his apron.

'Saboteur! He is trying to ruin me! He thinks he can destroy me like this! *Non*! I cannot allow it! I *will not* allow it!' He grabs the dessert plate and races out into the dining room, me chasing after him but barely able to keep up.

Jean-Michel storms over to the gentleman at the top table, one arm already in his coat, and slams the plate down in front of him.

'You will make a judgement of me without even tasting? You think you know so much that you don't even need to try the food now? You know nothing! Why do I care for you and your judgement? Why do I care for you and your stars when here—' He beats his chest where his heart is. 'I know that I have more knowledge, more expertise, more *passion* than any of you. Why should I listen to the opinion of someone who is less than me?'

The gentleman is clearly taken aback but he retains his composure. He takes a slow sip of water and then straightens his tie. His composure provokes Jean-Michel even further.

'How dare you send it back to the kitchen uneaten? Slapping me in the face! You owe me an explanation. So tell me! Tell me what is the problem with this dessert?'

Every other diner has now stopped eating, stopped breathing and has turned to witness this grand eruption. I move forward to try and get in between the gent and Jean-Michel, so that I can apologise to him. And just as I do so, he turns to take his bill from Sara's hand.

'My apologies if I've upset you,' he says in a calm, measured voice.

I offer a nervy but gracious smile, thankful for his understanding, and I find myself drawn to his face. I don't know him, I'm sure of that, but there is something so familiar about him. The almond shape of his dark eyes, his strong jawline… It's like I've seen him before and vaguely recognise him but can't quite place how or where. But I don't have too much time to dwell on this as the situation still feels very fraught, like it could get a lot worse before it gets better.

Jean-Michel takes an angry step in front of him, blocking his exit. By now, he is beyond listening to me or anyone. He is in a blind rage, screaming and shouting and ranting. It isn't just this incident. It's everything, the pressure he's put himself under, the pressure he's put his marriage under, the pressure he's put us all under. No one can live like this and stay sane. But right now, in full view of all these strangers, I need to stop him, get him to calm down. I used to avoid confrontation, run from it, but then there was Bernie and Harry and times that called for someone to stand up speak out and bring things to a stop before they escalated further. But how on earth can I tell Jean-Michel to calm down?

I look around, but there isn't anyone else who can step in. Not his wife or Pip or Octavia. I am the grand chef. Most of the other diners are now looking concerned and uncomfortable, shuffling in their seats and waving for their coats. Some are taking out their phones, getting ready to film. This is getting worse by the second: viral footage of Jean-Michel in meltdown mode with a Michelin inspector within weeks of opening will be the nail in the coffin of this restaurant. And of both our careers. And what will Jean-Michel do then? What will I do then? I shudder at the thought. This needs to end now.

I lower my voice, try to put on my most soothing, hushed tone and place my hand gently on the small of his back. I'm actually touching Jean-Michel. This is like sticking your hand into a shark tank. But for a second, it does cause him to pause, to take a breath, to run his hand up to his eyes. And I look toward the inspector and make eye contact, to de-escalate, to somehow explain with my eyes that this isn't about him, this is Jean-Michel battling his own paranoid demons. But something else happens instead.

I know him! I know this man! I remember who he is and how I know him. This man, this guest, standing in front of me is someone I've seen before.

In a frame, on Martha's mantelpiece.

'Leo Rosenblatt?' I ask.

He looks at me startled. 'Yes?'

I can see the confusion in his eyes, trying to scan where on earth he'd ever have met me before.

'I knew your—' I stop. Rephrase. 'Your mother Martha was a wonderful friend to me.'

Jean-Michel jolts upwards, looking stunned, his face rippling with conflicting emotion. He looks to me and I nod my assurance.

'Sir Leo Rosenblatt. He's not an inspector.'

Jean-Michel pales. A look of horror sweeps over his features.

'But… You had wine, sparkling water. The way you are dressed; you are dining alone.'

It dawns on Leo what's happened, that there's been a grave misunderstanding. And he takes Jean-Michel by the elbow. 'Chef, I am dining alone because my mother booked this table for us both to come together, weeks ago. But she passed away. And I have many regrets. Many, many regrets. So when it came to dessert, always her favourite, it reminded me of moments we enjoyed together and how much I miss her – and how I took those moments for granted and now there is nothing I can do to get them back.'

Leo swallows and holds the back of his hand to his lips a moment.

'I loved your food, but I couldn't even manage one mouthful of the dessert because it was too painful for me to do so. I'm ashamed of how I left my mother alone, when she needed me.' Leo closes his eyes, pinches the bridge of his nose as if to stem a memory. 'My apologies for the upset I have caused.'

And that's the moment that Jean-Michel takes off his apron, and hands it to me.

'It is me who is ashamed. Please, accept my deepest apologies.' He bows and then walks out the front door of his own restaurant into the street, without looking back once. Leaving us all behind in stunned silence.

When I eventually get to my room, at 2 a.m., after apologising again to Leo and the rest of the diners, taking all their details and offering them a complimentary meal to make up for the 'incident' and then finishing off the rest of the service without Jean-Michel, I text my sister the same words.

Please, accept my deepest apologies.

But I get no reply.

CHAPTER TWENTY-EIGHT

Pip calls me first thing in the morning, instructing me to close for the week and avoid all press. 'If pushed, tell them we had a gas leak,' he tells me, his voice hoarse and tired.

Metaphorically, that's not so far from the truth.

'What's Jean-Michel said?' I ask him.

He draws a long breath. 'Nothing! That's the whole thing. He won't pick up. Won't speak to anyone. Won't answer his emails. So we have no choice but to wait. Everything moved so fast, possibly too fast. So the best thing we can do now is just stop and wait. Jean-Michel might never calm down, he might never come back. I mean, anything could happen. He's worse than a loose cannon, he's a freakin' chef.'

'No way, Pip,' I say, stunned at the suggestion that Jean-Michel would abandon us. After everything that's happened, after everything we've sacrificed and everything we've worked so hard to build? Jean-Michel jump ship? He wouldn't. He *couldn't*. 'Of course he'll come back, just give him some time. Trust me,' I tell him with complete confidence. 'After all, it's *his* restaurant. He's put everything into it.' A chef abandoning their restaurant is like a pilot skydiving out the emergency exit.

It's unthinkable. Absurd. It simply doesn't happen.

Pip snorts. 'It's also *my* investment. And it's located in Octavia's hotel. Just because he has his name over the door doesn't mean that he gets to decide when we open and when we shut.' I hear a grunt of frustration. 'But it's that fucking name that makes all the difference. He's got us by the balls, so just lay low for a few days, Katie, disappear, and don't make yourself available for any speculation. I'll talk to Octavia. She's got a good head, and that's what we need here. Let's meet on Friday, we'll know everything we need to move forward by then.'

'Pip, he won't let the restaurant close. Trust me, Jean-Michel would never let that happen.'

'Yeah, right.' He says as he hangs up.

Due to unforeseen circumstances, Marchand @ The Rembrandt will be closed temporarily. All reservations will be rescheduled as a priority. Details regarding reopening will be published shortly. We sincerely apologise for any inconvenience and thank you for your understanding.

Katie Kelly, Grand Chef

I type up this announcement, pinning it on the door of our restaurant and in big, bold, black lettering on our website. It didn't take me long to select the wording. Of course, I pained over every letter when making the announcement over my own restaurant. I let that sink in a moment.

What are the chances of that happening? How is it that this is the second restaurant I've closed in as many years? I'm like the black widow of success. Not exactly the most confidence-inducing accolade for a CV. I thought it was the end of the world the first time. That it was definitive. Closure meant that I was a failure and that this was going to be my permanent identity and I would be doomed to fail forever. Somewhere along the line, I had subscribed to the idea that we only get one shot. And if we blow it we're not worthy of another. But life went on. I survived. And my little restaurant, the theatre of my dreams, the realisation of my greatest ambitions, went back to being an empty room with some tables and chairs.

I google the postcode and up it pops, on the estate agent's website. *Lease agreed! Opening soon under new management!* I flick through the photos; it is just as I left it. But now it's somebody else's dream. It was lying in wait all this time, waiting for the right person with the right idea to come at the right time and give it a new lease of life. A bit like I was. Looks like we both got our second chance.

And it was Jean-Michel who gave me that chance. He was the one to get me excited again. He was the one to push me to my limits. He is the reason that I'm no longer at Parklands. There's no way I'm giving up without a fight.

I pick up my work phone and give him a call. I bet Jean-Michel feels differently this morning. I bet he woke up after a good rest and feels a lot more clear-headed. I'm his right-hand woman. I'm his grand chef. I was there when this whole misunderstanding happened. If there's anyone he can talk to, I'd like to think it's me. I want to tell him, it's okay. I know he may not know failure, but I do, and guess what, it may feel like the end of the world, but it's not. Life goes on. It leads you to your next step. For me, it led me to where I am now, which was higher than I ever thought I'd reach.

Looking back at what happened with my restaurant, what seemed like a ginormous personal catastrophe was just a blip, just a drop in the ocean. Ninety-second news for the locals, just pulling down a curtain, deactivating a website, licking my wounds and moving on.

His phone rings out again and again. *Is he ignoring me too?*

And then it stops. And goes dead.

So apparently, yes.

I lay back on my luxurious, king-size bed and try to think of what the hell I should do next. Because without my work, I have nothing. I can't call Rachel because she's furious with me for letting her down. I can't go out with Alice as she's already left the city to finish her final coaching and well-being modules. Ben's probably choosing furniture for his New York City apartment with Francesca, Mel and Zoe are run off their feet at Parklands and my lovely Martha's gone. So here I am, in one of the most beautiful, central, busiest hotel rooms in the world, and all I want is to go home.

CHAPTER TWENTY-NINE

I'm back. Skillet pan in my hand, cooking a fry-up for my dad and me.

'I just can't understand how broadband or internet connection – or what do they say, Wi-Fi? How on earth could that be a deal-breaker?' rants my father as he stands by the window, mug of tea in hand, looking out into the rolling fields. 'Who cares if there's no feckin' internet? You don't move out to the country for the fresh air and the space and walking trails and the peace and quiet to set up a multi-national company, do you?'

I flip his egg and bacon on to his plate and slide a slice of fried buttered bread on the side for good measure.

He winks at me. 'Ah, that's the girl. You know what makes the stomach sing, Katie, that's for sure.' And he digs in, thoughts of internet and estate agents left far behind as he smothers his plate in brown sauce.

I look around our old kitchen and figure that it's little wonder that he's had no serious interest in this house since he put it on the market. I know deep down that it isn't just the broadband issue. Of course, *I* adore how the dappled sunlight trickles onto the well-worn countertops, and the rows of lovingly tended herbs that sit along the length of the windowsill in their hand-painted pots. Hand-painted by us, that is, not some famous artisan but messy kids with sticky hands and a complete disregard for form or shape, just content to swirl blobs of bright colour when not flicking it at each other. I'm not sure other people would be as fond of those sentimental features, or the house's other distinctive quirks.

It is not exactly a masterpiece of contemporary interior design. Dad's DIY wooden shelving slopes at all angles by the deep ceramic sink. Bleached from the sun and laced with cobwebs, Mum's hand-sewn yellowing gingham curtains hang at the whistling windows. Squashed into the corner by the door is a small rectangular table with bench seating, resembling a greasy spoon café booth. This is where we ate snacks, threw down our homework, ironing, football boots, hairbrushes and any other manner of daily miscellany that was lost or found. It was also a place for sharing news, somewhere to leave a note or telephone message, and a space for us teenagers to gather before a night out so as not to disturb the grown-ups watching telly in the front room. Underneath that little table sits our dog's blanket-lined bed, felted with a decade of hair, pushed in against the wall, away from the Converse soles which dangled near it whenever the kitchen was buzzing with life. But I guess it's been a long time since it was buzzing with life. Me in London, my brothers travelling constantly with their jobs and Rachel married to an Australian. Now, with the baby on the way, it looks like she's made a life for herself there and has no intention of moving back. Especially as she thinks I'm not bothered about seeing her after my no-show at the airport.

I study the scuffed pale floor tiles and worn dark brown wooden cupboards with aged brass handles, and imagine what the estate agents must be thinking: *dated, complete refurb required. There's retro and then there's* this.

To me, right now, this room, filled with the scent of salty bacon, melted butter and strong, sweet tea, with its dog bowls, muddy boots, fridge magnets, shopping lists and crumb-filled toaster – it's perfect, it's all my favourite memories under one roof. Sitting here, I feel like I am my real self, no pretence, no unattainable aspiration. To be honest, this kitchen couldn't be more opposite to the one at the Marchand. There, everything has its place: every utensil, every plate, every piece of equipment, every morsel of food, even every *person* has to fight to justify their place. But here you can just be, and that's enough. Everything is just wherever it is, wherever you left it. At the Marchand, each plate is executed within an inch of its life, every mouthful studied and analysed. Here, in this family kitchen, each plate is chipped and cracked with age and use, every mouthful is a stroke of luck that someone else didn't get there first. Food is for the hungry, for comfort and for celebration. Dinners are made up of what's in season, what's local, what needs using up and what bloody tastes good. And then, to top it all off, there's always plenty of it, so by the time you leave the table, you should be feeling a hell of a lot better than when you sat down.

Can it be that I love them both? Does it even make sense that I love the natural easiness that's here but crave the challenge and the excitement of the high-class kitchen? I've only been away from it for a few days and, already, I'm missing it; I'm feeling that restlessness in my fingers.

Dad looks pensive as he mops up oozy golden yolk with his bread. 'Can you believe this, Katie? Three different viewings and not one of them showed the slightest bit of interest, walked in and then just nodded politely and walked out again. I mean, what is it they want? It's a great house. Five bedrooms, two bathrooms, garage, land. What more could you possibly want? I don't understand it.'

But I do. He's right, it is a great house, but to the prospective buyers, fresh from the city with country dreams and contemporary, urban expectations, this doesn't sell rustic charm, just cluttered old bazaar. And once they discover there's no broadband connection, they write it off straight away. So, without even going upstairs, or out the back, or looking at the views or walking the grounds, they turn on their heels straight back out the front door with a 'thanks but no thanks'.

Of course, it serves me that there's no interest. I can't hide my feelings about how much this house means to me. I run my finger over the rivets on the large wooden table and remember all the memories I have, some happy, some sad. This is where we sat to have our hair cut. *The Wonky Fringe Salon.* Usually the last night of the holidays before school restarted. So not only did we have to wake up early, but we had to wake up looking like shorn convicts or novice nuns. Mum was no hairdresser, so she just kept cutting until things evened themselves out and we ended up looking scalped. This is also where my mother sat one night when I had just turned thirteen, as everyone else settled into their beds and my dad watched TV in the front room. She asked me in for a cup of tea and handed me the scissors.

'Katie, now that you are a teenager, I know you're grown-up enough, so I'm going to need you to do me a very special favour.' And she unwrapped the scarf from her head and I saw that there were only light wiry wisps of her once wavy blonde hair. 'I hate to see it fall out. Will you cut it for me?' I did it. I swallowed every tear that streamed down my cheeks and I just let my nose run, afraid that I'd betray my upset through sniffling.

She smiled at me through her own watery eyes and told me that I did a great job. And then she kissed me on the forehead and told me that I had so much to look forward to, so much to be excited about.

'Take all your chances, baby. Don't be scared, because I'll always be cheering you on, okay?'

And then all my tears streamed down my face, sobs bubbled up from my throat, and I shuddered with every part of my body as I sat at this table and held her like I never did before.

I realise something now for the first time. How even in the most awful, dire, cruel circumstances, in her own quiet, selfless, brave way, Mum took charge. She made the next decision about what was best for her. And I think Martha did that too. And maybe that's what I should be doing. This is not the time to be vocal and selfish and fearful about uncertainly, about the unknown. It's time to be brave.

My dad puts his hand on my shoulder. 'You know, sometimes, when it's just me, I call out her name.'

My eyes sting with tears, with raw, unbidden emotion. I look up at him.

'I know it's pure madness, but I stand at the bottom of the stairs and call out, "Catherine! Catherine" and in that split second I can convince myself I'll get an answer. That there still could be an answer. For that split second before the silence floods in and dashes my crazy hope all over again, it's just like she's here. And we're the way we were. Just a normal, beautiful, ordinary moment where I call her from the bottom of the stairs and she answers me.'

I study my dad's face, his eyes closed as he explains to me in his own way how he is trying to get back and move on all at the same time. And it hits me. It hits me how unfair I've been. How I've not let him take charge. Asking him to hold on here, amongst the memories, beautiful and painful, while we've all left and gotten on with our lives. Poor Dad has stayed here, all along, until we were ready. Or rather until I was ready.

I look to the cork board by the fridge, where ripped-out magazine and newspaper travel articles about Australia – flight deals, holiday packages, stopovers, places to see, places to stay – are pinned on every surface.

I point over to it. 'You've been doing some research then, for your adventures?'

He looks at me and nods. 'Shall I show you?'

'I'd love nothing more.' It's time now. It's time for my father to move on, it's time to let go.

We spend the rest of the day gutting the downstairs and assigning all unessential items to one of three boxes: bin, charity or storage. It's hard to go through everything. To me, every corner is filled with Mum's life – her photo albums and books, her handwriting and her dishes: a place for everything and everything in its place.

There is a part of all of us, I think, that wants to leave the house the way it was, a perfect time capsule. How could we change this house where my mother raised us? How can we give a single thing away? How can we offer up this house that no one else has ever owned? This house was the only place we ever knew her. The answer to every question is that we can't, but we have to. Just like you can't imagine the world will go on without the person who died, somehow it does. You imagine that you won't be able to put one foot in front of the other, and yet somehow you do. You want to hold on to everything forever, but you can't. There it is. Holding on and letting go pulls you apart. It sucks.

Once all the clutter is out of the way, the house looks so much bigger. In my mind I thought it would look bare and soulless, but it doesn't. It looks light and spacious and airy and I can see that my dad looks a whole lot lighter too.

'Katie!' I hear my dad shout from the attic. 'Come here! Quick!'

I drop the bag I'm sorting through, run in to the corridor and start climbing the attic stairs, peering upwards into the half-light, trying to work out if the rasping crackle in his voice is excitement or despair. I reach the top and see him knelt in front of a large cream box, lined with a frilled trim. His hands are draped with a trail of white, scalloped lace and beaded satin.

'Your mother's wedding dress. We couldn't find it for Rachel's wedding. I couldn't think where it had got to and I turned the place upside down looking for it to no avail. Yet lo and behold, I come up here today and I nearly tripped over it.' My dad is shaking his head in disbelief. He holds it to his face and breathes it in. 'She was a vision in it. An absolute vision.' He looks up at me, his blue eyes pooling with tears. 'The older you get, the more like her you get, you know, Katie. Sometimes, I have to do a double take myself.'

I smile and crouch down next to him, stroking the soft, sheer fabric of a dress that was only worn once, by only one woman, so very long ago, but yet has a sense of special connection, almost a message.

My dad looks at me. 'If I was daft I'd nearly say it's her way of telling us something.' He rubs his eyes as he says this, embarrassed at sounding foolish and overly sentimental. But I agree with him.

I pull the dress its whole length from the box. It's gorgeous: vintage lace, simple, elegant and exactly the kind of dress that Rachel would have loved to have worn on her own wedding day, to feel close to Mum, to feel like she was there in some small way too.

'I'll pack this up, Dad. Why don't you go down and put on the kettle? Think we've earned ourselves a tea break.'

He nods and climbs backwards down the creaky attic stairs.

Rachel's already missed out on wearing it for her special day and marriage certainly isn't on the cards for me anytime soon. I retie the damp-stained satin bow and blow the dust off the lid, knowing without doubt that we are keeping this but still kind of unsure what for. But it's been in the family this long, it's part of us, and I can't bear the idea of being the one to sling it away.

We scrub the tiles and the walls and all the surfaces until they are gleaming and reeking of a strong lemon-scented bleach. The curtains are soaking in a basin and tomorrow I'll hand-sew any rips or tears that I find before I rehang them.

'I think you're going to have this place snapped up in no time now, Dad,' I say as we sit down with a mug of tea, our hands raw and wrinkly from our big scrubbing session.

He smiles to himself and puts his hand on mine. 'You mean I might get to visit my first grandchild before my sixtieth birthday after all?'

'Definitely! You're not sixty till next year!' I tell him. But I see an uncertainty cloud over his eyes.

'There's still no Wi-Fi connection, no matter how clean and tidy it is.'

'It's not all about Wi-Fi and connections, Dad. Some people don't want to be connected! Right, time we took charge. Tomorrow we'll tackle upstairs. I'm going to take loads of shots of the rooms in the best light in the morning, then we'll write up a brand new advert, I'll upload it onto loads of independent sites and forums when I go into town and you wait and see. We may not be able to sell immediately but we could rent in the first instance and you'll be out of the country by this time next month, now how does that sound?'

I glance at a tiny, grainy framed photo that's on the top of a stacked box. It's Mum and Dad holding me as a baby, standing outside the gate of this house. I remember my dad telling me years later that they went out as teenagers and then for a variety of stupid reasons, they broke up.

'*It took me that time apart to realise what I'd lost,*' he'd said, '*and so I put everything in to winning Catherine Kelly back. Thank goodness I had the guts to pursue it and thank goodness she had the guts to give us another chance. Otherwise, we'd have missed out on the big life adventure that awaited us. Sometimes, it's just that the time isn't right. But when it is, everything else falls together and you can find yourself in full flight.*'

My father lifts an eyebrow. 'You really think so? You think someone will want it?'

'I know so. Now drink up and get to bed, Dad, we've got a big day ahead. And god knows how many big days after that.'

The past is just that. I have to bring my head into the present. It's time to take charge and start looking to the future. Because, one way or another, tomorrow is going to come and I have to be – no, correction, I *want* to be – part of it. I want to make the very most of every moment and every chance I've got. And I want my dad to do the same.

I photograph every room of the house and type up a description as I would write a menu, understanding that we are not just putting a pile of bricks on the market, but offering the experience of living here. Once I begin to type, the words flow, as if the spirit of the house knows exactly what it wants to express.

A rare opportunity to acquire a delightful Irish farmhouse set in acres of peaceful secluded gardens and surrounded by country lanes, lakes and river streams for those leisurely walks and total relaxation.

This ultimate rural retreat offers complete freedom from the hustle and bustle of modern life and the barrage of technological distractions. Get back to nature surrounded by red deer, fox cubs, barn owls and wild salmon. The expansive views from the kitchen overlook rolling fields with plenty of rambling paths for hikers, dog-walkers or horse-riders.

Complete with a traditional log-burning fire-place, even the most wild Atlantic weather will see you snug and warm inside. There are five airy, double bedrooms, two large bathrooms with spacious free-standing bath tubs, and a large decked area for al fresco dining or to enjoy a glass of wine whilst you watch the sun go down and the stars come out in an utterly unspoilt corner of the world.

Couples, adventurers, families, big groups, and pets will love it here. Masses of open space, climbing trees, tyre swings and hedgerows of blackberries and wild mushrooms to forage. Endless fun for kids and families alongside creative inspiration for artists and writers with uninterrupted peace and tranquillity in an idyllic rural setting.

Filled with antique furniture. Easily accessible to airport with regular routes to UK and Europe. Close proximity to fresh water rivers and lakes and en route to scenic coastlines and beaches of The Wild Atlantic Way. This is a charming escape to the country which will no doubt be snapped up very quickly by discerning buyers or tenants.'

I spell-check what I've written, format it and, along with the photos I've taken, I pass it by Dad the next morning, just to make sure he's okay with it.

He squints into the small screen of my phone to read the text and swipes through each photograph. And then he looks up to me, rubbing his cheeks with both hands, as if he is literally trying to wipe the smile from his face.

'With an advert like that, I'd better start packing. Australia here I come!'

CHAPTER THIRTY

My dad drops me into the village so that I can get the internet connection to upload the advert for the house and get it online straight away. He pulls up outside our old local pub Nallen's and I smile my hellos to the pair of flat-capped old men smoking by the door. Once inside the cosy, fire-lit warmth, I order an Irish coffee (because this place makes the most delicious ones I've ever tasted) and take my seat in a quiet corner of our local pub, signing in to their Wi-Fi, password 'Ifnotnowwhen?'

As soon as my handset is reconnected, it splutters back to life, vibrating in my hand with a barrage of beeps and notifications, missed calls, voicemails and social media messages which couldn't get through the whole time I was out of range at my dad's.

I scroll through the backlog, eliminating all junk ruthlessly. So many unknown numbers, which I presume to be press looking for the scoop on Jean-Michel's outburst, wanting to know the real reason behind our sudden closure. They're certainly persistent; one of these numbers has rung me seven times!

I notice there are a couple from Ben. I can guess what they are about. Checking in how the restaurant is going. An attempt to keep in touch, now that we've got to know each other again as 'friends'. My stomach lurches. All I get is a flashback to seeing Francesca plant her big, glossy, bee-stung lips on his. Nope. Sorry. I can't do that. I delete all his messages without reading. I don't want to know about all the amazing things Ben and Francesca are enjoying together in New York. I just about managed to get over him before and that was hard enough. I'm not doing that all over again. I take a deep breath and decide that if I mean that. I've got to commit to it. So I block Ben's number too. There. It's over. Now we really are done.

I've got messages from Alice too, but nothing yet from Rachel. I know she's still travelling with work so she could be anywhere in the US right now. Is it a good time to contact her? I have no idea. But to hell with it, I can't make her much more angry with me. So I decide, if I'm ever going to set things right between us, it's now or never. I've got very little to lose and, after all, I'm the one who fecked it all up, I was the one who isolated myself and then I was the one who let her down. It's got to be me who swallows my pride and I've got to try harder to put things right before I lose her altogether.

I fetch up the advert I've written for the house. I'm going to send it to her to look over before I post it online. Hopefully, she'll like it. Hopefully, she'll see that I've changed my mind, that I've realised that all of this isn't about me; that it's about Dad and what he needs to move forward. Hopefully, she'll see that I'm sorry. And I mean it and I'm changing, that I'm trying to be better.

> *Operation get Dad to Australia is well and truly underway.*
> *What do you think? Kx*

I press send just as my Irish coffee arrives. Rachel may answer me, she may not. She might not see the message until tomorrow; she might pretend she's never seen it. She could delete it straight away. And if she does, it just means that I'm going to have to keep on trying. Because I've been such a stupid, self-absorbed, silly twat and she's my sister and I love her.

Sitting back, I take my first warm, creamy sip. This is *heavenly*. Licking the buttery, slightly bitter blend of coffee and cream from my lips while the fiery punch of the whisky hits me at the back of the throat, I decide that there are a few more people I need to contact and Nallen's password is telling me exactly what

I need to hear. 'If not now *when?*' Indeed. I've spent too much time neglecting the most important relationships in my life. I've learned my lesson and, with my second sip of Irish coffee, I vow to change. One sip at a time.

I lift the glass to my lips and take a selfie of me tongue out licking the side of the warm bell-shaped glass, sending it to Alice.

Bet you've forgotten how good these are! In Nallen's, thinking of you whilst soul-searching aka drinking alone. How're your exams?

Waiting outside exam hall right now so can't talk… Sitting my last coaching module today! Remember Ryan, HR guy?

The one you met on a course?

Exactly! He's set me up with a contract for his company. He says there is a huge niche in the market for this. Apparently, I wasn't the only stressed, fed up, over-worked and burnt-out corporate employee in the city, there's thousands. So we're setting up our own weekend residential: coaching, nutrition, meditation, time-management… not sure exactly where just yet but so EXCITED!

Alice! That is amazing! Go you!

All down to you and your crazy ass dreamin' but I soooo get it now, once you're doing something you love, you just can't imagine doing anything else, can you? All I need to do is find the perfect venue in the perfect location and 'Escape To You' holistic retreats will be ready for business!

Just as I start to reply, another text comes in.

So sorry, gotta go, need to turn off phone for exam time!
Wish me luck love ya Axxs

I wish her luck and phone still in my hand, I check the message
I sent Rachel.

Nothing.

She's travelling with work so she could be anywhere: in a
meeting, fast asleep, on a plane. I'm hoping they're the reasons
she's not responded. Might be wishful thinking though.

I glance down a final time before I go to the bar to order
another coffee, and see a blue tick appear beside the message
right before my eyes. She's online. Right now. She's seen it. *Oh
please don't ignore it Rachel! I can't bear you not speaking to me, I
can't bear the idea that you are so far away and every time you think
of me you might roll your eyes or get frustrated.*

Some little dots start to dance in grey. Rachel's typing! My
heart constricts in my chest – *please don't tell me to feck off. Please
don't make it any harder than it already is.*

And then the words pop up on screen.

Did you write this?

I can't work out the tone. Is she pleased or pissed off?

*Yes. Dad so desperate to see you, to be there for you and the
baby so just thought I'd try and gain some interest on the
house. Are you all right with it?*

Eek. I'm nervous. I hope I haven't managed to upset her again.

*Of course, it's brilliant. I'd better make up the spare bedroom!
Talk about a marketing pro! 'Discerning buyers or tenants'
will be knocking each other out over the 'uninterrupted*

peace and tranquillity in an idyllic rural setting' ffs! Bit of
spin all right! Are you good to talk? I'll be in my office in five
minutes if that suits to Skype?

Of course, can't wait.

And just as I'm settling in to the corner of this cosy little pub,
excited beyond measure to see my little sister's face for the first
time in way too long and her bump for the first time ever, an
idea hits me.

I send the advert for my dad's house to Alice. Because I think
we've got everything she's looking for.

CHAPTER THIRTY-ONE

Long after I say goodbye to a glowing, giggling Rachel, I'm still half-laughing at how she called me a silly twat before I could even get the words out myself. And I'm still dabbing my eyes and blowing my nose with the flood of tearful emotion that overcame me as soon as she told me that it was all fine, that she understood and that she just wants the best for me, for me to go easy on myself, not push myself so hard. And that she loves me no matter what. And she knows her growing little bump is going to be so proud of her 'amazing' Aunty Kate.

There was such relief in coming clean, in being open with her, in not pretending that everything is perfect when it's not. I never realised how exhausting being defensive can be, being constantly on guard and fighting unfounded, imagined judgements that only ever existed in my own head. Constantly pre-empting criticism and formulating answers to protect myself when the truth was that those who cared about me just wanted me to be happy. Not perfect, not ultra-successful, not the best: just happy. I told Rachel everything, truthfully, from how losing Martha brought back so many memories of losing Mum, to realising that I was becoming more like Jean-Michel in all the worst ways by putting the restaurant before everything else, and how even though it's taken me until now to fully grasp it, I miss Ben and I wish I'd done things differently.

But I also have happy tears in my eyes. I have uploaded my dad's house on several sales and rental sites, I've got my fourth Irish coffee ordered, and I feel like there's more to do.

There's another call I could make right now, even though Pip said he's not answering and he cut me off the last time I tried. But if there's one thing I know about Jean-Michel, it's that everything changes very quickly. Yesterday he may have wanted to be alone but today he might want to be centre-stage. I know Pip told me to wait. But this is my future at stake as much as that of the restaurant and Jean-Michel.

I raise my finger to the tiny screen and then pause. He may not answer at all or, worse still, he may absolutely throw the mother of all tantrums, a shitstorm at me down the phone. I bite down on my lip. If he does go on the attack, what am I going to say? Well, in the tiny possibility that he does answer me, that's a risk I'm willing to take. I can always hear him out and, if it gets too much, I can just hang up. My finger hovers over the call button. He can be a scary, unpredictable bastard. But I need to know where I stand one way or another. I'm going to take charge and ask what's going on, what does the future hold seeing as it's all in his hands. He's the only one who can give me the answer on this. And I want to know if he's okay, I want him to know that I'm there for him. If he wants to let me in and let me help him, I'll try to do that, I'll try my best. I've always given Jean-Michel my best and when he's in need like this, I'll not give up on him. I know from my own restaurant closure that burying my head in the sand, ignoring the problem and not asking for help is the surest way to compound failure.

I select his number.

I've got to try. Maybe, just maybe, I'll be able to help.

The phone begins to ring and I feel my stomach actually flip and fall flat. Second ring. Third. I take a deep breath.

Almost with relief, I invent a new rule of phone etiquette called '*more than four rings is rude*' so I'm ready to hang up and send a text instead.

'Hello?'

Dear God. It's him. It's Jean-Michel.

'Katie, is this you?' He sounds groggy, like I've just woke him up.

'It's me. I'm sorry the line's bad, I'm at home in Ireland. I just— I wanted to see if you were okay?'

Silence, then a heavy sigh.

'Jean-Michel, are you okay?'

'*Non*,' he says, lowering his voice to a whisper. 'Can you come?'

This is not what I was expecting. I'd never expected to hear such vulnerability from Jean-Michel. Never.

'Of course. I can come,' I tell him. My dad and the house are on their way, Rachel and I have reconciled and I'm ready to go back. And this time, find a better way forward.

He clears his throat. '*Merci*, Katie. I need… I need to speak to you – face to face. Meet me at the restaurant tomorrow.'

'I'll be on the next flight. And until then, I don't want you to worry, okay? Everything is fine.'

'It will be. Soon,' he says and the line goes dead.

CHAPTER THIRTY-TWO

As I take the corner and wait to cross the road to the Rembrandt Hotel, I can see Jean-Michel's wife waiting by the doorway. She is wearing oversized sunglasses, a black coat and black trousers. It looks like she's about to attend a funeral.

I skip up the steps and hold out my hand to greet her. She wraps her arms around me and pulls me very close.

'Thank you for coming, Katie. I don't think Jean-Michel has ever had a chef that he hasn't scared off, never mind one who actually cared about him.'

I look over her shoulder, searching. 'Where is he?' I ask. 'He said he wanted to talk to me face to face.'

She stiffens and shakes her head, taking an envelope from her pocket.

'He's not well, Katie. He wanted to come, but he couldn't face it. He's very sorry. In fact, that's all he keeps saying. How sorry he is. He needs to rest. Please accept his apologies.' I assure her I understand and that Jean-Michel has my full support and friendship and that I hope he feels better soon. She thanks me and then holds the envelope out to me. 'For you.'

I take it from her, flipping it over, trying to find some clue as to what's going on, what this is all about. Confused, I open my mouth to catch my breath and find the right words all at once. 'What do you mean he's "not well"? What does "not well" mean?'

But she just purses her lips, pulls up her collar and disappears in her kitten heels, click-clacking down the steps, across the road and around the corner. Seemingly leaving me and the restaurant and everything else that we worked so hard for far, far behind.

I feel the heavy, cream envelope between my fingers.

What the hell is going on?

On the front, my name is written in blue fountain pen by Jean-Michel's unmistakable hand.

'*Pour Katie*' is all it reads.

I can't open this here, not in broad daylight on the steps of one of the busiest hotels in London. I have a feeling I'm going to have to sit down somewhere quiet, where I can be alone and read whatever words Jean-Michel has penned to me far away from prying eyes. I take a deep breath and, looking up, spot the little Italian that Ben and I went to together. That'll do. That'll do just fine. I slip the letter in to my bag and begin the slow walk to whatever it is that I'm about to discover. It will no doubt change my life, one way or another.

I slide into the same booth I sat in with Ben. I feel a pang and a moment passes where I appreciate that not everything can be put back together so easily. But I'm here to move forward, even if that means carrying some losses I can't recover. I order a coffee, rip open the envelope and take out a handwritten letter.

Chère Katie,

Thank you most sincerely for coming. Forgive me my inability.

I am facing a crossroads in my life. I wasn't happy and I knew I had three options.

Number one was continuing as I was, working ridiculously long hours, as you well know, leaving in the morning before my wife and children and then kissing them in bed when they were already asleep. This ate me up inside. What sort of life is that, never seeing your wife or family and missing them grow up?

Number two was to cut myself some slack, but to do what a lot of chefs do these days and that's to live a lie. They continue to charge high prices even when they're not behind the stoves. That went against everything I believed in, because when I was at work, I did every single service. I came from the old world of gastronomy where the chef's place is in his kitchen. That absence, even partial, would challenge my integrity, so neither did that option lie well with me despite the fact that I had a fantastic grand chef in you. You are so capable, so very talented and so strong, but I couldn't hand over the reins as long as my name was above the door. Please know that this was my weakness, not yours.

Number three was to pluck up the courage to give back my stars and make myself unemployed, and so, as of last Friday, I cooked my final meal in the kitchen. I am tired of being judged. I had an epiphany in the middle of the dining room. I disgraced myself in the eyes of those who looked up to me and I need to change. I used to be condemned for being controversial, but I stand up for what I believe in and, at the end of the day, I wasn't going to allow myself to continue as a slave to my own insecurities.

I blame no one but myself.

There's a very big difference between obsession and passion. From the age of sixteen to forty-eight, my world was a room with white tiles and a stove in the middle. All my energies were channelled obsessively into cooking and I lost sight of my purpose, it was no longer a passion. I pushed my own boundaries too far. All the pressure, I caused myself.

I am giving myself a second chance, to do things well, but this time with balance.

*Now that I have handed back my stars, I have handed
back my status. For the future, for the first time in my life,
I am going to be kind to myself and my family and I am
going to do the things I've wanted to but suppressed, all my
life, and hadn't made the time for, like walking, painting
and just being present with my family.*

*I'm taking time to discover myself as a person, which
is what true success and true fortune is all about. The
insecurities we have today are the same as those we had
when we were mere children seeking approval, seeking love.*

*If you have the courage to turn over every stone, all the
answers to our future are in the past.*

*My message to you, Katie? Trust yourself, you do not need
me. You do not need anyone. You are more than enough.*

Adieu,

Jean-Michel

Adieu is pretty final. Not *Au revoir*. Not *À bientôt*. He's saying
goodbye. So I guess this is Jean-Michel's way of telling me that he's
not coming back. At all. Ever again. And that our big adventure
at the Marchand is over.

I flip the letter to lie flat on its front, unable to look at his
writing, unable to grasp what he's telling me all at once.

It's over.

Just like that.

I run my fingers through my hair and start to rummage in my
bag for my phone. Who should I call first? Pip? Octavia? Alice?
Dad? I can't think straight. On one hand I'm actually pleased for
Jean-Michel; I think what he's doing is really brave and probably
the biggest decision he's ever made, and he's done it to save his
family and save himself.

But that just leaves the rest of us. Abandoned, unemployed,
evicted, heart-broken.

I stop rummaging a second, as I feel a tap on my shoulder. I glance upwards and my hand flies to my chest.

'Hi, is this seat taken?' says the most beautiful man I've ever laid eyes on. A vision.

I blink and shake my head.

And watch Ben slide in to the seat beside me.

CHAPTER THIRTY-THREE

'Why are you here? Shouldn't you be in New York?' I look over his shoulder to the door, up to the counter. 'Is Francesca here too?'

Ben taps his fingers on the table and then turns towards me. 'Didn't you get my messages? I didn't want to call and put you on the spot, so I thought texting would be better, give me a chance to explain.'

Explain what? I shrug. How can I tell him that I got them but I didn't read them. That I blocked him! I shake my head. 'I'm sorry, Ben. I didn't open them,' I confess. 'Just thought it best that we left things as they were. Fresh start for me as well as you and your girlfriend.'

'But that's just it, that's what I wanted to tell you. Francesca and me… Well, we broke up. We're finished.'

I open my mouth to say something casual, trite, I should so say, 'I'm sorry'. But how can I be convincingly sorry? I run my fingers through my hair, still trying to think of something to say that will be appropriate and sound genuine… 'Sorry' is not that.

'Katie?' Ben says. But I can't, I just can't get any words out. *Ben and Francesca are finished.*

'What happened?' is all I can manage. I need to know. After all, maybe Ben's heart-broken? Maybe it wasn't his choice. Maybe he caught her cheating on him and he's angry and bitter and determined to win her back? Or maybe she was an idiot like me who walked away from the most brilliant boyfriend and best friend one could ever hope to meet in a lifetime?

'I figured it wasn't fair to lead her on,' he says with a deep sigh. 'When I was honest with myself, I didn't want to go to New York. But she did. She *really* did. And that got me thinking about you and me. How we went our different ways. *Why* we went our different ways. And the way that I found myself back here with you.'

His fingers tiptoe across the table and he places his hand right next to mine. I can't describe what it feels like to have him this close to me, speaking about us, feeling the heat of his body right by mine again without using the word electrifying. I mean terrifying. Everything about the way he makes me feel is absolutely terrifying. The way my heart wants to be held by him is terrifying. The way my knees have caved is terrifying. The way my mouth wants to be all over his skin, his face, his chest is terrifying. And electrifying.

'You see, I get it now. When I wanted to go and travel and you wanted to stay, you never made me choose. You let me go. But Francesca, she was different, everything was different and that never quite felt right, never felt the same. She gave me an ultimatum. She told me that unless we went to New York together, we were finished. But you never did that to me. You wanted me to go for what I needed to go for, even if it hurt. So I told Francesca, we were finished. That I was coming back here, back home. And that it's the right thing to do, because I'm still in love with somebody else.'

This time no words are stuck in my throat. The words slip out of my mouth before I have the forethought to check myself. 'And are you in love with somebody else?'

'Afraid so. Ever since I tasted her eggs Benedict, I knew she was the one. Tried to live without her. Not recommended.'

I feel my face flush with heat, with adrenalin, with shock... A really good kind of shock, like all my lottery numbers are flying up on screen one by one.

'Do you mean it, Ben? Are you serious? You've got to be joking.' I press my fingertips into my temples. This is all too much to take, the worst news of my life followed by the best? 'I don't know what to think any more. Please tell me straight.'

He clears his throat. 'Katie, I love you and I'm not joking. If anything, I've never been so serious. It's crystal clear to me now, that no matter what I do or where I go or who I'm with, I belong with you.'

'Kiss me,' I say, swallowing hard and slowly looking up to his face, but he's looking at my hand. He brings my palm to his mouth and kisses it, three slow, soft kisses which make the hairs on the back of my neck stand up and my heart lunge up to my throat. I can feel the heat rise across my chest, up my neck, flooding into my cheeks. Then he pulls his lips away from my hand, meeting my gaze, gauging my reaction. His eyes are dark and piercing and they're focused all over me. On my lips. On my eyes, on my neck, on my hair, on my chest. He can't seem to take me in fast enough.

Oh my god, it's too much. My head falls back against the wall when I feel his lips on the inside of my wrist, then moving up my arm, to my shoulder, to my neck. I naturally tilt my head to the side and, as soon as I do, I feel the warmth of his breath, he's that close. I can breathe in his salty, cotton-clean scent; I can just about feel his stubble, his face is that close to mine. He pauses just below my ear and I think I'm going to slide right off this seat and under the table. I squeeze my eyes shut and hope my heart doesn't explode when he leans in, because it definitely feels like it could. Ben's lips press gently against my skin, and I swear the room fades out. I swear everything else just falls away.

He works his kisses all the way along my jawline until his mouth meets my chin. I can't move. I'm literally panting for breath. I can take no more. I want to take it all. To take him all in, in to me. My hand slides up his arm and grasps the back of his head, not wanting him to pull away from me, wanting to devour him. He lifts away and looks at me directly. His eyes are smiling, knowing how crazy he's driving me. We're both breathing heavily, knowing exactly what's about to come next. What we're about to experience together all over again, remembering how it was like with us this before, impatient about how it's going to be again.

I think he's as excited and as terrified as I am right now. I brush my thumb across the back of his hand and he gasps quietly. The assent I just gave him with that tiny movement seems to break through some invisible barrier, because immediately, he slides his hand over mine and presses our palms together, intertwining our fingers. The warmth of his hand doesn't even come close to the surge of heat that shoots through my entire body. A faint smile flashes across his lips and Ben leans his beautiful face right in to mine and covers my lips with his. I slide my fingers into his hair and I am *home*.

And then I believe that it's true. Then I believe him that he knows that he belongs with me as much as I believe that I belong with him. Here, in this little dining booth, lost in a swirl of lunchtime crowds and hot trays and manic service, we are kissing like crazy. Like our lives depend on it. Our lips meet and I remember, I understand all over again, why people describe kissing as melting, because every square inch of my body dissolves into his. My fingers grip into his hair, pulling him closer. Every nerve in my body is alive, alert, craving more of him and my heart explodes. I have never wanted anyone like I want him and here he is, in my hands, on my lips, my Ben, my second chance at my only love.

He pushes me backward towards the wall, and we're laughing and kissing and stroking each other's faces, our cheeks, our lips together, making out in front of the whole restaurant and I don't care, I don't care one eensy bit. All I want is him. All I want is this moment.

I hear the clicking of a pen and a loud tutting. We stop and turn to the waitress, standing with her arms folded. 'It's lunchtime, sweethearts. I suggest you pay up and get a room.'

I turn to Ben, trying to force my lips to stay in a straight line so that I don't look like a beaming idiot. I throw a note on the table and slide my hotel key out of my wallet. 'I think she's right. What do you think?'

'What are we waiting for?' he laughs and exhales at the same time and we both give up on holding anything else back. Two beaming idiots scramble out of the booth, race out of the Italian, across the road and into the Rembrandt and straight up to my suite. Hand in hand.

CHAPTER THIRTY-FOUR

It is exactly two weeks now since what should have been an ordinary Friday night service became the last meal that Jean-Michel would ever cook. Pip requested that we meet him and Octavia at his solicitor's office by Chancery Lane. It's all very concrete and official and sombre. I expect it's about the 'severance, contractual obligations and remunerations' he mentioned he needed to run past me regarding The Marchand, which basically means ironing out the restaurant's funeral arrangements in light of Jean's effective resignation.

But I'm not facing this alone. I look down at my fingers, which are interlocked with those of the best chef, boyfriend and business partner anyone could ever dream of. Right by my side and on the same page is Ben. And we have a plan.

We climb the steps of a huge grey-brick Georgian townhouse and bang the huge brass knocker on the door. The last time I had to go through this kind of meeting, I was all alone. And it wasn't very pleasant to discover that if you don't agree with everything they offer you your only alternative is to come up with the money yourself, which means owing a shitload of money to a loan shark mobster who won't think twice about tearing out your fingernails if you can't cough up. I look down at my hands. Ouch. I'm glad I didn't go with that. But, whatever. This is where Pip has asked to meet us and he's the one we've got to get onside. And I'm smarter and stronger than I was the last time I was in a position like this.

Bring it on.

The buzzer sounds and we wait for the door to click so we can enter. Nothing is guaranteed. Of course they might reject us out of hand. But it is certainly worth a shot. And the thought of being rejected, of them throwing us and our proposal out the door doesn't fill me with as much fear as it would have done in the past. Because I've grown. I'm all right with myself. I'm not going to judge my entire worthiness as a human being on this one day, or this one judgement.

And because whatever happens today, wherever this journey leads us to next, it's already brought me back to Ben and Ben back to me. And that's probably a little bit more happiness, love and heart-bursting joy than my quota should allow. So if Pip and Octavia don't like what we've got to say, we'll survive. We'll go get some cake. We'll book a trip. We'll take each other by the hand and get ready for our next adventure.

I hear the cathedral bells ring out, twelve peals. It's time for our meeting. They'll be here any moment. It's time to find out what's next.

'You ready for this?' Ben asks as he straightens his tie and smooths his cuffs. We've left our chef whites and chequered trousers behind today. We're not here as staff. We're here as potential partners.

I nod, picking a fleck of lint from the hem of my best red dress. 'Born ready.'

A secretary opens the door and leads us up the stairs and into a very large top-floor office where Pip, Octavia and a striking black lawyer are already waiting, seated at a long walnut table, a single sheet of typed white paper placed in front of each of them. They all stand to greet us, we shake hands, and the lawyer introduces himself as Jerome. I take a seat, have a sip of water and wait for the shit to hit the fan. I'm nervous. This feels very heavy, very important. It's too quiet. Everyone's too stiff, acting too careful. We can hear each other breathe.

I pat the bright purple folder containing my business plan that I hold in my lap. Business plans being my Achilles' heel in my past life, I sought out the best help I could for this one. I think it's pretty impressive. Let's hope these guys feel the same.

The secretary closes the door and I take a quick glance behind me, but this is it, there's no one else coming. Just one empty chair by Octavia where I'd expect to see Jean-Michel. But clearly he's not coming. And neither is his wife. There's a morbid tone to these proceedings. This feels like the reading of a will.

Pip wrings his hands and licks his lips. 'Let's cut to the chase. Bottom line is that I invested in Jean-Michel and Jean-Michel has jumped ship. Therefore, I'm perfectly within my rights to do the same.'

I look to the lawyer for development, for more explanation, but he just shrugs as if to say that's all there is to it. He slides a document over to me.

'It's all in there, if any party reneges on their side, it renders the contractual obligations of the other party null and void.'

Right. Even though I was expecting this, it still comes as quite a blow. That's it. Over. Done. Finished.

Octavia clears her throat. 'I can see by the look on your face, Katie, that all of this has come as quite a surprise.'

'Yes and no,' I tell her. 'I'm not surprised the pressure got to Jean-Michel and I'm not surprised that Pip wants out. But I am surprised that we're going to let it go so easily before we look at our options. We've worked so hard. It's worth fighting for.'

Pip throws back his head and his hands fly to the air. 'Fighting! You hit the nail on the head there! There's been nothing but fighting, struggle, conflict and drama since I got involved in this freakin' place. And after all that, what have we got? I tell you what we've got. We've got no customers! We've got no service! We've got no food! And why? Because we have no freakin' chef.'

Pip reaches into his briefcase and pulls out a newspaper. He glances at the front page, sucks his teeth and throws it across the table to Ben and I.

'You think we can come back from headlines like these?'

Fall from Grace

Chef and enfant terrible Jean-Michel Marchand, 48, known as the youngest chef ever in the world to be awarded three Michelin stars by the tender age of 33, walked out of his London restaurant last week and declared that he is handing back his stars and quitting cooking forever.

I place the newspaper back down on the table and lean forward in my seat. 'Jean-Michel may be gone, but you do have two other chefs.'

'Two?' Pip does a double take. 'You two?' And then he starts laughing. 'I can't take much more, gimme a break. Let me spell it out to you guys, people don't book The Marchand because they are hungry. People can eat anywhere. So why on earth would you book three months in advance to reserve a table at one of the most expensive restaurants in London?' He turns to his lawyer. 'You ate there a few weeks back, why'd you do it?'

'Our wedding anniversary so we wanted to do something special,' he answers.

Pip's finger points in the air. 'You hear that? They wanted something *special*. Jean-Michel is what made the place special. He was the one that excited people; he was the one with all the stars and awards and accolades.' He clasps both hands on the back of his neck and shakes his head. 'There's nothing special about two unknown chefs serving food in a hotel restaurant. I'm sorry, guys. It's over.'

Octavia makes a steeple with her hands and shakes her head. 'I appreciate your efforts, but I'm afraid Pip is right on this one. You can't take this place over from Jean-Michel. Like anything, a new venture with one foot in the past will simply limp towards failure.'

Okay, it's now or never. I ball my hands into two fists to steady the quiver and I take a deep breath. There is nothing to be afraid of. We already know we can do this. We're already winning. And with that, I stand up, open my purple folder and, with a sure, steady hand, give three copies of our business plan to Pip, Octavia and their lawyer. I wink at Ben and he begins our pitch.

'We've already shown you that we can both cook, that we can run a kitchen, lead a team, put in the hours, stand the pressure.'

The lawyer scans down our stapled four-page business plan, complete with graphs and figures and everything you would expect from a world-renowned business tycoon. Trailing down the figures and projections with his pen, he suddenly stops. And then, right at the point I was hoping, he shifts in his seat, taps his pen, nudges Pip and draws a circle midway down the first page. Pip peers in, squinting to read, then as the realisation washes over him, he lifts his chin and exchanges a wide-eyed look with Octavia.

Ben continues with our pitch. 'As you can tell by the extent of our research, the originality of our concept and the detail of our business plan, we're now ready to go to the next level, to step in and take over the current premises at the Rembrandt Hotel and relaunch it. Give it a second chance with the same high-quality ingredients, the same exacting attention to detail, the same vision of excellence... but this time with an entirely different feel.'

I watch Octavia raise her eyebrows and lean in towards us. 'May I just stop you a moment, Ben?'

Ben nods graciously and Octavia focuses her attention on me, raising our business plan in the air with her right hand. 'It reads here that you've secured investment from Sir Leo Rosenblatt. Is that correct?'

'That's correct,' I tell her. 'As long as myself and Ben are the chefs. That's the condition, and we are absolutely in agreement with Leo on that.'

She regards the paper in her hand and a smile breaks her lips. 'Please continue.'

We show her our sample menus, our branding, interior design mock-ups while Pip's lawyer makes some calculations and Pip makes some phone calls.

By the time we finish, Octavia is nodding along and scribbling notes down.

'Everything you've shown me tells me that I'd be extremely foolish to throw the baby out with the bathwater. Life is a delicate balance between knowing what to keep and knowing what to throw away. Yes, in ways we've lost, but in others ways we've gained. Not everything has been in vain and we've emerged all the wiser. So...'

I can feel Ben's hand squeeze my elbow.

'Maybe this is the time to start afresh,' she continues. 'New name, new menu, new beginning. It will just be you two, laid bare. You have a lot to prove: two unknown chefs, no big name behind you. It won't be easy, of course there's still plenty of risk, but I've watched you work, watched you overcome challenges before. If there's anyone who can do this, it's you.'

Pip rubs his hands down his face, conflicted. They ask us for some time to discuss the proposal as Ben and I are ushered out of the office to the waiting room where we wait to be called back in and learn our fate.

But we've barely sat down. Barely caught our breath and loosened our collars and quenched our dry throats, when we are called back in.

And this time when we enter the room, all three are on our side of the table, smiling with their hands outstretched.

'Well, this certainly *isn't* what I was expecting to happen today,' says Pip. 'I'm feeling the love, you guys, I've got to say the energy is back. We're in. All the sums add up, Leo is as solid an investor as you can get and, well, let's do this!'

We shake his hand and then Octavia wraps her arms around Ben and I, whispering to us, 'You know, I think I'm already in love with this idea.' She pulls back and narrows one smiling eye, as if focusing on something very specific that as yet only exists in her imagination. '*Martha's Cellar* could be the greatest thing to hit this scene in a long, long time.'

ONE YEAR LATER

'Katie, come down, it's Ben on the phone! London calling!' shouts my dad from the bottom of the stairs as I carefully hand my absolutely gorgeous baby niece and god-daughter back to my sister.

I sneak one more kiss on Catherine's tiny little nose and smooth the collar of her little lace christening gown that I made from my mother's wedding dress. She smells like talcum powder and Jammy Dodgers and I adore her. My mother would have adored her too. She'd have adored every second of us all here, together, celebrating the present, excited about the future.

'Hurry up, it's long distance! It'll cost a bloody fortune,' yells Dad again.

Rachel waves me away and I run down the stairs two at a time to the landline.

'Hey you!' I say breathlessly down the line. 'How're you? I can't believe it's been a whole week. I can't talk for long, people will start arriving any minute and I've still got to ice baby Catherine's cake.'

'Sounds like Oz is treating you well. What's the weather like?'

'Sweltering, but beautiful. Alice is already brown as a berry and I wouldn't be surprised if I've got to make another cake for her and Conor at some stage in the future. There's been some serious flirting going on between those two, which is funny considering he used to make her scream and chase her down the fields with baby toads in his hands. Thankfully he's a bit smoother than that these days! The pair of them haven't taken their eyes off each other since we've arrived, so watch this space. He's even promised to rebuild the stone wall around the house, sorry, I mean "The Lodge". She's toying with the idea of expanding to camping retreats next year to keep up with all the demand and he's up for helping her! Adam is arriving in later today, so then we'll all be here, together again. Except for you, of course. Everyone says hi and sends their love. How are you? I miss you. Tell me everything!'

Ben assures me that everything is perfectly fine and under control at Martha's Cellar. And he breaks the news that we've made it into The *Time Out* Best Newcomers top five, which is a major – *another* major – achievement in our first year of opening.

'Have you time for me to read the review to you? It's a good one,' he tells me and instantly I can picture him, leaning towards the sunlight, against the back kitchen door, phone hooked in to the crook of his neck, magazine in hand, half-smile on his lips. Of course, I'm pleased about the review, but really all I want is to hear more of his voice.

'Yes, please! Do read it to me.'

He clears his throat and begins. *'Drum roll please! It's that time where we reflect – while rubbing our bellies and promising ourselves that next week will be the one where we go on a diet – on the last twelve months in eating. And this year, there's been a frankly stupid amount of brilliant restaurants. Which has made whittling the shortlist down to a manageable size one a helluva challenge. But we've done it. So here you go. The very best London restaurants of this year. We've said it before and we'll say it again: eating out in London kicks ass.*

'First place awarded to… Oh, Martha's Cellar. How do I love thee? Let me count the ways.

'Food: Gutsy platefuls of seasonal ingredients, but Chef Katie Kelly's light touch lifts the likes of cod with fresh peas, lentils and bacon, or whole Portland crab with chips and mayonnaise, to another realm. Eat the trifle. Trust me. Here is the new home of beautiful traditional cooking. From meaty croquettes to blood orange marmalade Bakewell

tart… Mmm. But this is by no means Sunday lunch, the distinction is from head chef Katie Kelly, the youngest female chef in the UK at the moment to hold a Michelin star. Teamed with seafood specialist Ben Cole, these two are a match made in heaven. Think culinary Fred and Ginger. These guys just blend, they harmonise, they excite. They just work, goddammit. And all this magic happens in a simple, elegant room, with a short blackboard selection of gorgeous regional faves. The food riffs on a range of hearty Anglo, American and French influences, but with them a British sheen. The likes of toad-in-the-hole and fish pie sit comfortably alongside chicken liver parfait and mac 'n' four cheese – and all are prepared with impressive precision.

'Atmosphere: Two long communal tables. Two settings per night. Here's where Martha's Cellar is different. You arrive for dinner at six or at nine every night, just as you would at a family gathering. Couples, solo diners, large groups, who can tell? Everyone sits and eats at the same time. It's beautiful. Somehow, it doesn't feel like this should be a new or revolutionary way of dining, but it is and it feels very, very right.

'Even if you don't live near Chelsea, you should try to visit this exceptional restaurant at least once. The decor is understated: a soothing grey-green colour scheme and unobtrusive artwork. The real artistry arrives on the plates. As "British cuisine" continues to establish its own identity, it becomes clearer how ground-breaking this new restaurant really is. It's far from faddy, and its continued commitment to well-sourced, simply cooked traditional food is attracting a lot of interest – and so it should.

'So many textures, so many colours, so many flavours. It's seriously va-va-voom. From the polished service and the serene, airy setting, this is one of the best new spots to hit our capital in an age. We are lucky, so lucky. For the best spectator seats, head to the tall stools by the bar. Because the chemistry between chefs Katie Kelly and Ben Cole is not something you want to miss.'

Omfg.

'Pretty good, eh?' Ben asks.

'More than pretty good! It's phenomenal,' I tell him, wanting so much to throw my arms around him and tell him that he is my world. That he makes my life what it is. That I'm happier than I ever dreamed I could be.

Who'd have thought this could happen? That from the moment we secured our investment, our amazing rollercoaster ride was only beginning. A few months after we opened Martha's Cellar, Ben and I were working, as normal, at the kitchen pass, side by side. Georgia's desserts had already won her a Rising Star award and this time we really were given full autonomy by our investors, so Ben and I were able to hire the team we wanted. And that made all the difference. Our team really does feel like a family. And more importantly, acts like a family. A very special family who knows exactly how much every mouthful means to us all. We look out for each other with a common purpose. Sara broke through the swing doors, looking unusually wide-eyed for an early-bird service on a Thursday evening.

'This is it!' she whispered, crossing her heart and hoping to die. 'This time for sure! I know it!'

Okay. So this time it was *real*. It was Michelin. And this time it wasn't Jean-Michel at the Marchand. This time it was me and Ben at Martha's Cellar.

Ben glanced over at me, raising his eyebrow. I smiled, place my hand over his, interlocking our fingers and giving a gentle squeeze.

'It's fine. You know, why don't we just do what we always do.'

I stayed calm. And this time I didn't have to talk myself into it. Didn't have to counsel myself to combat the shakes. Because I was excited. I was confident. I knew what we could do and I wanted to cook for this person, this diner, this inspector. Just like I want to cook for everyone. I want every meal to be the best plate I've ever served and they've ever eaten.

'Let's just do us. The way we do every time.'

And that's what we did. We didn't even tell the rest of the staff. No need. We knew they'd do a great job because they always do. Every. Single. Time.

And that's how it happened. That's how I got my first Michelin star.

But what I'm most proud of is that we did it our way. Knowing that whether we got the star or not, we'd be fine, we'd survive, we'd live to see another day.

We close two days a week and that's non-negotiable. It means we can all have a life. We can all keep our relationships. We can all get rested and recharged and come back to work renewed. That's important. And it works. I have a filing cabinet packed full with CVs of hospitality staff willing to step in and work with us anytime. So we train them, just in case, at Parklands on the last Monday night of every month. Where all the residents and their families are treated to a three-course meal on us. We spoil them. It makes them happy, but it makes us even happier. And it's all thanks to Mel and Zoe now running the place; they made this happen. Along with the herb garden, the music and quiz nights, and all the picnics and parties they've organised for the residents, Parklands is now a much, much better place. Not just a place to recall memories but also keep making new ones.

'Katie? I need you out here, love.' I can hear my dad calling me now from the veranda. Naturally, I'm in charge of the catering but he's the drinks man and boy, is he taking his role seriously. Wetting baby Catherine's head is going to be a night to remember and may well stretch long into the early hours of tomorrow based on the amount of spirits Dad has stockpiled.

'I'm so sorry, I'm going to have to go, but I'll call you tomorrow when things are a bit quieter, okay? I love you and we'll chat soon.'

'No problem, I love you too. Oh, just one last thing, okay?'
'Yep?'

'When you get back, I want to ask you something about asking you something.'

'Fire away,' I smile as I kiss my goodbyes down the line. And I hear him laugh and for a split second, everything else falls away and the hundreds of thousands of miles between us collapses and all I can hear is his voice in my ear telling me that he loves me. After everything that we've lost and everything we've found, everything we ran from and everything we rebuilt, I've come to believe that there is no 'one' way. That this journey is endless and meandering and wondrous and when you can't see where you're going in the darkness, you just have to muster enough faith to take the next step, to just keep moving, that's all it takes to stop you getting stuck and keep you pushing forward. The more I think about it, the more convinced I am that life isn't about finding your way or anyone else's way but creating new ways. So, when I get back to London and whatever it is that Ben wants to ask me, I'm ready. But he better be quick, because I just may beat him to it, I may get my question for him in first. And whichever way it takes us, I know we're all going to be just fine.

A LETTER FROM COLLEEN

I want to say a huge thank you for choosing to read *One Way or Another*. If you did enjoy it, and want to keep up to date with all my latest releases, just sign up at the following link. Your email address will never be shared and you can unsubscribe at any time.

www.bookouture.com/colleen-coleman/?title=one-way-or-another

I hope you loved *One Way or Another*; if you did, I would be very grateful if you could write a review. I'd love to hear what you think, and it makes such a difference helping new readers to discover my books for the first time.

I love hearing from my readers – you can get in touch on my Facebook page or through Twitter or my new website!

I have thoroughly enjoyed writing about Katie and discovering her journey with her.

Following your passion is so rewarding but it also involves a huge amount of sacrifice. My sacrifice in preparing for this book involved researching hundreds of foodie accounts and eating out a lot! So if you see me anytime soon in person and feel confused, yes, it is me, but now lagged with at least a couple of extra kilos thanks to all that banana bread. Creating a story about food, love, ambition, unlikely friendships and second chances has been wonderful, I really hope you enjoyed spending time with Katie as much as I did.

In this book, I wanted to explore our sense of identity, personal and professional, and how our identity is linked so closely to what we do and how successful we feel. This can be particularly challenging when we lose our jobs or homes due to circumstances out of our control, it can often feel like losing our place in the world. A donation from the sales of *One Way or Another* will be given to supporting age-concern charities across our cities. So by simply buying this book, you have helped someone, somewhere, receive a little relief, a little comfort, and a little nudge to say that their welfare matters to us, so thank you from the bottom of my heart.

Many thanks to all of you who email me, message me, chat to me on Facebook or Twitter and tell me how much you enjoy reading my books. I've been genuinely blown away by such incredible kindness and support from you all. There so many things I love about being an author; however, my favourite has got to be this immense connection with people all over the world, from so many different walks of life, making me feel that I truly have friends everywhere.

Team Bookouture, Abigail Fenton, Kim Nash, Noelle Holten and the amazing sisterhood of book bloggers and reviewers who have taken the time to read and write such beautiful words about my stories, you make my heart soar with your empathy, encouragement and relentless positivity. I am so grateful to you all and I love that we are all on this journey together.

To Betty and Sadie, you make me the most proud of all, thank you for helping me do this.

Thanks, happy reading and until next time,
Colleen Coleman xxx

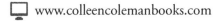 www.colleencolemanbooks.com

 CollColemanAuth/

 @CollColemanAuth